I0731033

HONOR MY DESIRES HARRIS & KAT PART III

STEELE INTERNATIONAL, INC. - JACKSON CORPORATION A BILLIONAIRES ROMANCE SERIES CROSSOVER BOOK 6

CHARMAINE LOUISE SHELTON

Honor My Desires Harris & Kat Part III
Copyright © 2022 by Charmaine Louise Shelton

All rights reserved. No part of this book may be reproduced or transmitted in any form or by any means, electronic or mechanical, including but not limited to photocopying, recording, or by any information storage and retrieval system without written permission from the author.

ISBN: 978-1-956804-12-6 (Hardcover)
ISBN: 978-1-956804-09-6 (Paperback)
ISBN: 978-1-956804-10-2 (eBook)
Published by CharmaineLouise New York, Inc.
Sexy Fantasies Fulfill Your Desires Publications

Honor My Desires Harris & Kat Part III is a work of fiction. Names, characters, businesses, places, events, and incidents are either the product of the author's imagination or used in a fictitious manner. Any resemblance to actual persons, living or dead, or actual events is purely coincidental.

CONTENTS

Free Book   v
Also By Charmaine Louise Shelton   vii
About STEELE International, Inc. - Jackson
Corporation A Billionaires Romance Series
Crossover   ix
About Honor My Desires Intrigue & Kat Part III   xi

1. Harris   1
2. Harris   11
3. Harris   21
4. Kat   29
5. Kat   38
6. Harris   46
7. Harris   57
8. Kat   67
9. Kat   77
10. Harris   86
11. Kat   100
12. Kat   110
13. Harris   121
14. Kat   131
15. Kat   141
16. Harris   152
17. Kat   165
18. Kat   176
19. Harris   187
20. Kat   196
21. Harris   207
22. Harris   221
23. Kat   234
24. Harris   246

25. Harris   257

26. Kat   267

27. Harris   278

The STEELE Family   287

The Jackson Family   289

Note From Charmaine Louise   291

Preview STEELE Series Book 1: Fulfill My Desires Sebastian & Lola Part I   293

Welcome to CharmaineLouise — The Sensual Lifestyle   307

FREE BOOK

Get the start of the STEELE International, Inc. A Billionaires Romance Series with *Discover My Desires Sebastian & Lola Prequel* FREE!

Click Cover Below or visit **bit.ly/CLBooksNewsletter** to subscribe to my newsletter for latest news and launches, books from my author friends, and sizzling reads in book promotions. Plus, start reading the steamy billionaire romance *Series Prequel* of Sebastian Steele and Lola Lewis.

Their stories. Their discovery of unknown desires…

FREE BOOK!

PREQUEL
NEVER
RELEASED!

EXCLUSIVE FOR SUBSCRIBERS!

ALSO BY CHARMAINE LOUISE SHELTON

STEELE INTERNATIONAL, INC.
A BILLIONAIRES ROMANCE SERIES

Discover My Desires Sebastian & Lola Prequel
(Available Exclusively to Subscribers)

Fulfill My Desires Sebastian & Lola Part I

Heighten My Desires Sebastian & Lola Part II

Ignite My Desires Roger & Leonie Part I

Stoke My Desires Roger & Leonie Part II

Justify My Desires Roger & Leonie Part III

Deepen My Desires Sebastian & Lola Part III

Capture My Desires Malcolm & Starr Part I

Embrace My Desires Malcolm & Starr Part II

Cherish My Desires Malcolm & Starr Part III

A Trilogy of Desires Sebastian & Lola Parts I-III

A Trilogy of Desires Roger & Leonie Parts I-III

A Trilogy of Desires Malcolm & Starr Parts I-III

Series Extras

Series Playlist

STEELE INTERNATIONAL, INC. - JACKSON CORPORATION
A BILLIONAIRES ROMANCE SERIES CROSSOVER

Tempt My Desires Lachlan & Haley Part I

Tease My Desires Lachlan & Haley Part II

Grant My Desires Lachlan & Haley Part III

Intrigue My Desires Harris & Kat Part I

Decode My Desires Harris & Kat Part II

Honor My Desires Harris & Kat Patt III

A Trilogy of Desires Lachlan & Haley Parts I-III

A Trilogy of Desires Harris & Kat Parts I-III

Series Extras

Series Playlist

ABOUT STEELE INTERNATIONAL, INC. - JACKSON CORPORATION A BILLIONAIRES ROMANCE SERIES CROSSOVER

Welcome to the titillating world of the multibillion-dollar global companies and the love affairs of the families that controls them.

STEELE International, Inc.- Jackson Corporation is a series of interconnecting Billionaire romance. Follow the Steele and Jackson families as they fly around the world chasing the women they love and their happily ever afters. Get ready for glitz, glamour, and steamy romance books. What's better than that? The Jet-set Lifestyle has never been hotter...

The Desires Series is not for the tea set; it's for the top-shelf vodka straight up in a pretty crystal glass coterie!

Don't miss any of the sizzling romance books in the STEELE International, Inc. - Jackson Corporation A Billionaires Romance Series Crossover:

Tempt My Desires Lachlan & Haley Part I

Tease My Desires Lachlan & Haley Part II

Grant My Desires Lachlan & Haley Part III

Intrigue My Desires Harris & Kat Part I

Decode My Desires Harris & Kat Part II

Honor My Desires Harris & Kat Patt III

A Trilogy of Desires Lachlan & Haley Parts I-III

A Trilogy of Desires Harris & Kat Parts I-III

Series Extras

Series Playlist

Visit CharmaineLouiseBooks.com for the complete list.

ABOUT HONOR MY DESIRES INTRIGUE & KAT PART III

Honor My Desires Harris & Kat Part III

Welcome to the titillating world of the multibillion-dollar global companies and the love affairs of the families that control them.

Harris

Well... I finally gave in to the feminine wiles of my Kitty Kat marking the end of my old playboy ways. However, fate can be funnier than me and has other plans for our new relationship...

Kat

I vow to honor Harris. But sometimes the past has bad timing. Sure they say cats have nine lives. So how many until I get my happily ever after with the man I love?

Come along for their sizzling, soul mate billionaire romance as Harris and Kat's travels take them around the globe. New York City, Glasgow, London, and the Maldives will never be the same.

Anthem: "Escapade" Janet Jackson
https://www.youtube.com/watch?v=UFX3gQHIroU

Playlist:
https://www.youtube.com/playlist?list=PLXwYvn0e218A90Sz6_dDu0IECce6Pr6GS

Visit CharmaineLouiseBooks.com

"*H*ey, Kitty Kat. Have dinner with me tonight at my penthouse. I'll get one of Lucien's restaurants to send over food. But you'll be dessert. Hmmm… Maybe some fresh whipped cream and a couple of sweet maraschino cherries on top. Licked clean, natu-rally. Sounds tantalizing enough for you?"

I smirk when Kat's gasp comes through the mobile. I can picture her alabaster cheeks flushing rosy red. Not as vibrant as her Titian hair, but just as silky to the touch. The pupils of her eyes more than likely dilate with lust, leaving only their rims a dazzling emerald green. Her little pink tongue darts out to moisten her lush lips as the air rushes past them.

My cock twitches in the trousers of my bespoke Saville Row suit at the vision of my sexy Siren aroused.

Katrina Roberts cum Katrina Jackson. Yeah… *Jackson.*

The woman who nearly toppled both the Jackson and

the Steele clans with her scheme of vengeance in alignment with Chester *Chet* Stewart. Kat—an unknown cousin of the Jacksons—partnered with Stewart Scotch, Jackson Corporation's top competitor and historical clan rival amongst the world of Scottish nobility.

And I—Harris Steele, tech wiz extraordinaire—didn't see it coming. At. All.

Too busy enthralled by that redheaded Siren to see the signs of her betrayal until it was almost too late. Three months of the closest to a committed relationship I've ever had in my thirty-two years, and it ends with her admittance of misdeeds.

Lachlan Jackson—my cousin via our mothers being best friends and my brother-in-law—as CEO and Chairman of the Board of Jackson Corporation may have chosen not to press charges. He only banned Kat from Scotland.

But I banished her from my life. For fourteen weeks, that is. Unable to resist her Siren's call, I initiated a week to fuck her out of my system. All it did was make me crave her more and realize more is just what I want from Kat Jackson. My Kitty Kat.

She redeemed herself with letters of apology to each member of my family and conducted herself in the manner of one who wants to make amends. She even donated the money she garnered from giving Stewart intel on Jackson Corporation to the Aberdeen Children's Center, where she volunteered.

I'm far from a weak man and gave her hell. But there's no point in wallowing in the fiery pits when I can luxuriate deep in her warm, welcoming core. Especially when we both acknowledge what we shared over those three months was real. Despite her initial reason to use me as a smokescreen to access the Jacksons as part of her attempt at their downfall.

Ah well…

So here we are post the Seven-day Fuckfest, a surprise trip to Maui for Valentine's Day—don't think I'm not a romantic—and a week of me in Buenos Aires for business. And I want to have My Kitty Kat cum for dinner. Yup, pun intended. And in my penthouse at The STEELE Tower on Fifty-seventh and Fifth Avenue in the midst of Billionaires' Row in New York City. My sanctuary where no women besides those of my family have crossed the threshold.

Harris Steele—Alpha male billionaire playboy—falls for The One. Hard.

The last man standing of The STEELE Quaternity—dubbed such by the media as the most sought-after of the world's eligible billionaires and heirs to STEELE International, Inc. Handsome; six plus feet; ebony hair; shades of gray eyes; powerful Alpha Doms and males. I've followed in the footsteps of my three older brothers Sebastian, Malcolm, and Roger. They succumbed and married the women who captured their hearts—Lola, Starr, and Leonie, respectively.

I once laughed and called my brothers suckers. Now, they'll laugh at me. Again. This time for good. If My Kitty Kat behaves like a good little kitten.

"Oh, Harris," she starts breathlessly. "That sounds more

than tantalizing. I'd love to have dinner with you… And be your dessert."

I growl as her response ends in a sultry purr. My cock throbs in approval.

"Excellent, Kitty Kat. I'll meet you in front of your apartment building at seven tonight," I say, ignoring the twinge in my gut from her use of the four-letter word even regarding food. I'm not all the way there yet. We end the call, and I sit back in the leather chair of my Gulfstream G650ER.

"The pilot is ready for takeoff, Mr. Steele."

I turn my gaze from the window to the flight attendant and smile as I give my consent to leave Buenos Aires behind.

As much as I enjoy being the co-head of STEELE Technology and Cyber Security with my fraternal twin Haley, I can't wait to head home. Home where My Kitty Kat will be soon.

"I APOLOGIZE, Mr. Steele. There's no getting around this accident. Shall I have a STEELE driver collect Ms. Jackson?"

A glance at my Audemars Piguet The Royal Oak Complication watch confirms we'll be late picking up My Kitty Kat. I agree with my driver, Alonso Masa's recommendation. Once the STEELE driver is outside of her apartment building, I call to let her know.

"Hi, Harris," she says breathlessly. "I'm walking towards the lobby door now."

"Hey, Kitty Kat, I'm stuck in traffic. So I won't be able to pick you up. I sent a STEELE driver with a silver Mercedes-Benz S 580 for you. He's out front. Do you see him?" I tell her.

"Yes, and I'm getting inside now," she responds, in an attempt to hide her disappointment.

Join the club. I'd rather have met her, too.

"Okay, a member of security at The STEELE Tower will give you access to my penthouse. He'll meet you at the concierge desk. I'll be there as soon as I can. Oh, wait, hold on… I have to take this call. I'll see you soon," I say, then end the call.

It's from a potential client another client referred to me while in Argentina. I can't ignore it. While I answer, I pull up the message app and shoot a text to Kat. Hopefully, it'll lessen the bluntness of my hang up.

Sorry I had to rush. Can't wait to see you. H.

By the end of the call, I've secured a new client for his company and his personal accounts. I send a quick text message to Haley as a heads-up. She sends back a grinning emoji. Then follows it with a reminder I'm behind her in our monthly new business quota by two.

We're the youngest of the Steele siblings and a surprise to our parents being three years younger than Roger. As the Dynamic Duo, Haley and I have made it our mission to make our mark on STEELE International and to contribute to our family's multigenerational, multibillion-dollar company.

Consequently, our division generates a sizable amount to STEELE's bottom line and brings in clients for the other divisions—Retail Properties, Entertainment Properties, and Residential Properties. Each of our brothers runs a division, with Baz also being the CEO and Chairman of the Board. STCS has become an indispensable part of STEELE International.

I snicker and shoot back an eye roll emoji, knowing it'll get Haley riled up.

We're hella close and love each other to death. She's as protective of me as I am of her. I'm sure she'll be okay with Kat and me getting back together since Haley instigated Kat and me talking weeks ago. Based on my conversation with my Dad Morgan and my mother Shelley's message, I'm sure they'll be open to it, even if warily. *Remain open to love. It can surprise you whence it comes.*

I keep my parents' words of wisdom in mind as I walk through the living room of my penthouse to where My Kitty Kat stands staring out the floor-to-ceiling windows.

"I'm more impressed by the view of you, Kitty Kat, than you can ever be of the Manhattan skyline at night," I say. My warm breath tickles the side of her neck as I whisper in her ear.

She shudders.

"I missed you, Kitty Kat," I rumble, nuzzling her neck. "Did you miss me?"

She places a snifter next to her mobile on a table and

turns around to face me. Her slender arms go around my neck as she stands on tiptoe to bring my face closer to hers.

"More than you can even imagine, Harris Steele," she murmurs against my lips, then nips the bottom one. The scent of Jackson Scotch wafts across my face.

I growl deep in my chest as I bend my knees and toss My Kitty Kat over my shoulder. A swat to her ass only covered by a wisp of silk from her dress makes her yelp and flail her legs. I band one arm around her thighs and stride from the living room.

"You will show me just how much, naughty lass," I rumble. "First, I feed you, then you feed me. After, we eat what Lucien has for us."

"Yes, Harris," she purrs like a good little kitten.

Off to a great start.

Once inside my bedroom suite, I carry her to the bed and place her on her feet. My hands skim the sides of her body from her shoulders to her thighs. With a flick of my wrists, I divest her of the skimpy, silky number she wore to tease me.

My Siren gasps and covers her DDs with her hands. More than her palms can cover, the luscious tits spill around them.

"Do not cover yourself from me, naughty lass," I admonish as I grasp her wrists and bring them over her head. I dip mine to envelop a puckered rosy nipple into my hungry mouth.

She groans and undulates her body.

My other hand drops to cup her round ass to still her

movements. I want her to focus on the pleasurable sensations without distraction.

I continue to lave, nip, and to suckle her delectable tits until they're heavy with her need. Another flick of my wrist and I snap the thin material of her G-string to bare her pussy to me. My fingers skim its wet seam collecting her cream.

Her pupils dilate as she watches me slip the glistening digits into my mouth and swirl my tongue around them. My groan of appreciation makes her tremble and close her eyes as she sways.

I scoop her up and toss her into the middle of my king-size bed. Her eyes pop open, then half-mast as I kick off my shoes and strip out of my suit. My muscles ripple as I stalk towards her and lower onto the bed between her spread thighs.

My Siren widens them for my broad shoulders as I bow before her dripping fount. Her cries of carnal ecstasy as I devour her sweet pussy heighten my desire to fuck her raw.

But first she must be ready to take my ten inches. My fingers join my lips and tongue to drive her over the edge again and again. Not until her cream pools beneath her ass do I plank over her sated body.

She can only move her eyes languorously as she watches me take her legs and wrap them around my hips. She gathers the strength to tighten the hold as I align the purple, swollen head of my cock to her warm, welcoming core.

A single thrust seats me deep within her pussy. She screams as her body adjusts to my girth and length. Her inner walls clench to draw me further inside.

I throw my head back and howl.

"So fucking good, Kitty Kat…" I groan. But remain still until she's ready for the ride.

"Harris… Please…" she begs as her hips squirm for much-needed friction.

Who am I to deny her?

My hips meet hers as I flex my ass and withdraw before pounding back into her quivering sheath.

Her head lolls as her mouth forms a perfect O. No sound slips past her lips. Only from her lower ones, as her wetness squelches from the driving force of my thrusts.

My grunts add harmony to the erotic symphony we create. Her high-pitched wails as she cums undone for me build to a crescendo. I erupt with an almighty roar.

My climax triggers another for My Siren. She keens as her pussy clamps down on my cock to milk it of every single drop. Her fingernails dig into my biceps to anchor her from flying into the stratosphere.

But I'm gone. Lost in the throes of passion.

I return to My Kitty Kat's soothing caresses and her whispered words. My face nestled between her pillowy mounds, my heartbeat slows. I wrap my arms around her waist and roll onto my back.

She cuddles into me as her head rests on my chest over my heart. She slides her hands around my flanks to hold me close. With a sigh, she settles.

"I missed you, too, Harris Steele," she whispers.

A satisfied smile curves across my lips.

"I missed you, too, Kat Jackson," I respond.

Her stomach growls louder than I did moments ago. She giggles and turns her face into my chest, embarrassed.

"Not very sexy, huh?" She asks as her shoulders shake with mirth.

I smack her ass and sit up.

"No. And not good for my ego," I respond wryly. "Guess it's time to feed you, Kitty Kat."

She bites the corner of her lower lip and nods. Then she lowers her gold-tinged eyelashes.

"We can always return for that dessert you promised," she purrs.

My cock twitches, ready for more.

"Abso-fucking-lutely, Siren," I swear.

Yeah, it's good to be home. With My Kitty Kat.

The early morning sun shines through the floor-to-ceiling windows to bathe My Kitty Kat's gorgeous face in an ethereal glow as she slumbers. Shadows form on the tops of her cheeks from the long fringe of eyelashes. Their golden tips catch the sun's rays. Cheeks still rosy from our fucking a couple of hours ago. Kiss-swollen lips part as soft snores slip from between them.

I wore her out. All. Night. Long.

Yet despite my morning wood, I only want to watch her sleep, not ravish her again. The last time we laid in bed, I wondered what it would be like to fall asleep with My Kitty Kat in my arms, not just for a few days. But always.

These past five days—with me waking alone—gave me time to reassess the situation. I was already partial to a second chance. Now, I want her not just in my bed, but in my home.

I feel like Baz when he moved Lola into his duplex penthouse upstairs after they met. New to the City, she didn't have a permanent residence of her own just like Kat.

Sharing an apartment—albeit a massive full-floor penthouse with her friend and colleague, Vivian Murphy—isn't like Kat having her own place. No lease to worry about, not that it would make a bit of difference. She would break the lease, and I would pay for the penalty fee.

Decision made, I continue to watch My Kitty Kat until her eyes open slowly and adjust to the sunlit bedroom.

"Good morning, sleepyhead," I say with a grin as I stare down at her.

A lazy smile spreads across her face. She lifts her hand to cup my cheek. The stubble bristles against her smooth palm as I lean into it with my eyes closed. A contented sigh escapes from my mouth.

"Good morning to you, early bird," My Kitty Kat whispers as she drags her finger across my lips.

I kiss the tip of it and smile again.

"Move in with me," I tell her, then chuckle as her eyes pop while her mouth forms a perfect O. "Is that a yes or a no?" I ask as my thumb lifts her chin to close her slack mouth.

She blinks.

Well damn, not quite the response I expected…

I duck my head at her delay and murmur, "Don't leave a guy hanging, Kitty Kat."

Then I lift questioning eyes to gaze at her from beneath my thick, ebony eyelashes.

She squeals and pushes me to my back as she straddles my hips and covers my face with kisses. Her exuberance returns a confident smile to my face.

"Yes. Yes. YES!!!" My Kitty Kat shouts with glee.

I grin like the Cheshire Cat, adding a sparkle to my dove gray eyes. I sit up and kiss the tip of her nose.

"Good Kitty Kat," I say, then smirk. "Let's do this now. Then you can thank me properly later."

She giggles and slides off my lap.

I can't resist a spank to her round ass and chuckle wickedly as it jiggles and she yelps.

During our shower, I thwart her attempts at sucking my at-attention cock—what am I nuts?—to speed things up. I shake my head at the change in priorities. But like I said, later, not never.

While I dress, I arrange for movers from STEELE International's operations department to meet us at the One Fifth Avenue penthouse. The team will pack Kat's things up and bring them to my—I mean to *our*—penthouse. Even though it's last minute and on a Saturday, the Vice President guarantees the move will take his team only a few hours to complete. Perfect.

Naturally, My Kitty Kat teases me about being spoiled rotten. I shrug. It is what it is.

Alonso drives us down to the landmark prewar co-op a block north of Washington Square Park on the Gold Coast of Greenwich Village.

My Kitty Kat rambles on about how happy she is to move in. Then she peppers me with questions about access, travel to the children's nonprofit where she works as Development Director, and what she should do with her items that won't fit.

I'll have to add her palm print to the systems when we get back. Alonso can drive her to and from her office since my five-minute commute consists of taking the family's private elevator from our residences to the floor for STCS. I also tell her we'll figure out adding her items once the movers bring everything to the penthouse. They'll organize what stays and where and what goes to storage.

She kisses my face and shimmies on the seat beside me.

Once we arrive, the doorman helps her from my Black Badge Rolls-Royce Cullinan while Alonso opens my door. My Kitty Kat and I pass through the magnificent two-story lobby headed to the elevator. She presses the button for the private tower floor on twenty-four.

The doors ping open to reveal Vivian, who throws her arms around Kat and pulls her from the elevator. Their squeals pierce the air. I chuckle and shake my head.

When they part, Vivian grins at me. She's a stunningly beautiful woman with skin that as Lucien—ever *The Sexy Chef*—says reminds him of a decadent ganache. Her toffee brown eyes gleam with excitement for her friend as she pushes a stray ebony curl behind her ear.

"Well, Harris Steele, look at you!" Vivian says as she loops her arm through mine. "Now, you and I will have a talk while Kat directs the movers. Come. We'll sit in the family room outside of Kat's bedroom."

I can't help but to grin back at Vivian and allow her to

lead me through the palatial, multimillion-dollar residence. We pass windows with incredible 360-degree views. The Freedom Tower to the south, the Empire State building to the south, New Jersey west of the Hudson River, and beyond the East River.

"Mr. Steele, we're ready to begin, sir."

I pull my gaze from the captivating panorama.

Six movers wait outside of what I presume is Kat's bedroom. Already prepared with wardrobe and regular boxes to gather her things.

"Thank you," I respond to the one in charge as I shake his hand. With a nod towards Kat, I continue. "This is Ms. Jackson. She will let you know what needs to be done."

They disappear into the bedroom while Vivian and I settle on a leather sofa. She tucks her long, toned legs encased in yoga pants beneath her. A collarless cashmere sweater falls off her shoulder to reveal a matching tank top.

Kat tells me how they do twice-weekly Pilates sessions together and how Vivian eats healthily. It's clear she takes excellent care of herself. I remind myself to introduce her to some of my buddies.

"So, this idea of Kat moving in with you just popped into your head this morning, Harris?" Vivian asks with an elegant eyebrow arched.

We've met twice only, so I still need to prove myself to My Kitty Kat's best friend.

"It's been on my mind for the last week or so. The time

we spent together made me realize we might as well take it another step," I respond honestly.

Vivian studies me a moment, then nods as though satisfied with my answer.

"Okay. But just so you know, Kat is my good friend. She made bad choices. But she's remorseful and wants to make things right between you and your family—the Steeles and the Jacksons. Especially since the latter is her family, too. So do not hurt her," Vivian states.

It's my turn to nod. I can respect their friendship and protectiveness of each other.

"Wonderful! Now, tell me about these buddies of yours Kat mentioned…" Vivian says with a wink.

I chuckle at the whiplash from the change in topic and go through my list of bachelors. Viv and I continue to talk while the movers hustle in and out with Kat's things.

"Okay, my little helpers, time to go."

I stop mid-sentence at Kat's words. Vivian raises her gaze to her friend.

"Oh, my, done so soon?" Viv asks with her hand to heart and wide-eyed, feigning surprise.

I grin and stand from the sofa.

"Well done," I say and wrap my arm around My Kitty Kat's waist.

She rolls her eyes and nudges my side with her elbow.

I pretend she inflicted a mortal wound, and the girls giggle.

We follow a mover who carries the last box from the bedroom. He heads for the penthouse's service entrance, where the movers finish on the service elevator and at the building's service entrance. The girls and I go to the residents' elevators for the ride down to the lobby.

Alonso waits at the curb and opens the SUV's door.

Vivian pauses before she gets in and turns to Kat.

"You're sure you have everything?" Viv asks.

I turn to My Kitty Kat questioningly.

She tugs on a corner of her lower lip as she considers her answer. Her emerald green eyes widen.

"Hold on, I forgot my music box. I'll be right back," she says, spinning on her heel.

"I'll come with you," I say as I follow her to the doors.

"Not to worry. It'll just take me a minute," she says as she waves me off over her shoulder and rushes inside.

I watch her go as Viv slips inside the SUV.

"Are you getting inside, Mr. Steele?"

Alonso's question draws my attention. I nod and stride to the other side of the SUV. When Kat returns, she'll sit in the middle.

Vivian's fingers fly across the screen of her mobile. I retrieve mine from the pocket of my Brunello Cucinelli cashmere down parka. Even though it's Saturday, my business email account has plenty to occupy the time it'll take for Kat to return.

Caught up in the influx of messages, I lose track of time until my mobile rings with a call from The STEELE Tower.

"Mr. Steele, the movers arrived with Ms. Jackson's items. Shall I give them access to your penthouse, sir?" The concierge asks.

I frown and glance at the clock. Twenty minutes passed. My gaze goes to the apartment building's front doors. Vivian peers at them, too.

"Yes, give the movers access with two security team members to watch over them and have my house manager oversee their activities," I respond, then end the call.

"What's taking Kat so long?" Viv asks. "I sent a text message to her, but she hasn't responded."

My frown deepens as I jump from the SUV. Viv joins me as we head towards the doors and through the lobby. The ride upstairs is tense. She unlocks the front doors to the penthouse and calls out to Kat.

No answer. Only silence.

The hairs on the back of my neck rise.

"Kat!" I yell as I race towards her former bedroom. "Where are you?!"

I round the corner. The bedroom door stands open, but no sound comes from within.

Did she fall and can't respond?

Vivian catches up to me as I burst into the bedroom.

"She's not in the rest of the penthouse," she says anxiously.

My eyes scan the empty bedroom. No sign of Kat.

Scattered pieces of what appears to be a music box litters the floor by the closest.

What the fuck???

A scream from Vivian makes me pivot. Hands fisted, ready to fight.

In front of her staggers one mover.

An unclothed mover.

An unclothed mover with dried blood plastered to the side of his head. He grips the doorframe and moans.

"What the fuck happened to you?!" I shout as I rush over and grab him by the arms before he collapses to the floor. "And where the hell is Kat?!?!?!"

His head hangs and fresh blood oozes from the gash.

In the background, Vivian speaks rapidly into her mobile. The words police and ambulance filter through the red haze that descends around me.

"Come on, man! Speak up!" I shout as I shake the mover.

He sputters incoherently.

"Harris, give him a moment," Vivian says softly as she rests her hand on my shoulder.

I nod and lead him to a chair in the family room.

"Are you sure Kat isn't anywhere else in here?" I ask Vivian.

She shakes her head solemnly as tears well in her eyes.

I turn back to the mover. I refuse to give up hope Kat is okay. Who the fuck could have gotten in here, anyway? It's a secure building and penthouse. No one knew she was moving.

"S—S—Someone hit me... while... while I was in the service hallway," the mover says. "Didn't see who—"

His sentence ends with a grunt of pain from the shake he gives to his head. He clasps it. But Vivian holds his wrist to keep him from touching the bloody wound.

Shouts ring out as thunderous footfalls approach us.

"Over here!" Vivian calls as she rushes towards them.

"Where's the service hallway?!" I yell at her retreating back.

She gestures for me to follow her along with two building security men. We run through the penthouse to the other side. As we near, the door stands ajar with a bloody palm print on it.

A small palm.

A small palm print from a woman's hand.

HARRIS

"**S**tep back! This is a crime scene. Everyone stand down. Now!"

The police officer's command stops all movement.

I face her and scowl.

"My girlfriend may still be in the building! Through that door! Someone needs to check. *Now!*" I issue my own command. We can't waste any time. Especially since she's bleeding. The asshole most likely hurt her. Or worse.

My gut flips at the thought someone harmed Kat.

What did they do? And why the hell did they do it?

The penthouse is full of expensive artwork from Picasso to Edmonia Lewis, antiques, state-of-the-art elec-tronics. Undoubtedly cash, jewelry, and designer clothes.

Why would they want to take Kat???

My fingers run through my hair and tug the strands to make me focus. No point in yelling at the cop. We need their help, after all.

"Listen, this just happened. Only twenty minutes ago, she was here. They can't be but so far," I say to the officer as another joins her.

She nods and turns to her partner. They radio in for backup and direct the security team to lock down the building. No one in and no one out, with guards stationed at each entry point. A flurry of activity ensues.

Vivian clutches my arm as the officers ask us to take a seat in the living room. I squeeze her hand as I glance down at her. She turns her face up to me. Fearful eyes stare back.

"We'll get this under control, Viv. Don't worry. Okay?" I tell her. She nods. But I worry as much—if not more—than she does.

This shit is real.

"Tell us your names and your reason for being here," the female officer demands.

Vivian straightens her spine and clears her throat.

"I am Vivian Murphy, and this is my penthouse," she responds.

The male officer scribbles on his notepad while the female flicks her analytical gaze from Vivian to me.

"Harris Steele. I accompanied my girlfriend—Kat Jackson, who's missing—here for her to move her things to my penthouse," I respond.

The male officer pauses his methodical writing at the mention of my last name. He raises his gaze to me, then arches his eyebrow at his partner. They exchange a knowing look.

"Steele. As in STEELE International, Inc.?" He asks.

"Yes," I answer.

Another look passes between his partner and him.

My patience shreds.

"Listen, we do not have time to play twenty-one questions with you. Someone clobbered one mover and abducted my girlfriend. A bloody handprint—I presume is hers—proves someone harmed her. While we're sitting here chitchatting, she could bleed to death! Get on with it, man!" My voice increases in volume as the sentence ends.

I glare at each of the police officers until they squirm in their seats. Disgusted, I whip out my mobile to place a call I never thought I'd need to make. I rise to pace the floor.

"Commissioner Flagg, it's Harris Steele," I say when the call connects me to the highest ranking police officer in New York City. I ignore the shocked gasp from the female officer and the groan from the male as I continue. "I hoped to never have to contact you for more than a social call. But someone abducted my girlfriend, and we presume injured her. We need your help."

With the commissioner on his way to the penthouse, I place the next important phone call.

"Sebastian, I need you," I say when my eldest brother answers his mobile. He knows it's serious when I use his full name and not Baz. I fill him in, and he jumps into action.

Moments later, I hang up from the second eldest, Malcolm *The Enforcer*—as we call him for his methods of handling situations for our family. He's taking his Sikorsky

S-92 Executive Helicopter in from his and Starr's residence at our family beachfront compound—Steele Southampton Village. He assures me we'll get to the bottom of the situation.

I place another call to Haley who's in Aberdeenshire, Scotland at her and Lachlan's Aboyne Castle. She puts me on speaker so he can hear too.

"Harris! Oh my God! We'll fly over now," she says, and Lachlan agrees.

"No one fucks with a Jackson! Keep us posted on all details. I'm texting our flight crew now. We'll be there in a few hours. I'll tell her mother, brother, and sister. They'll probably join us," he says, pissed as fuck.

"I'll call The STEELE Tower concierge to arrange one of the guest apartments for them," Haley adds.

An incoming call chimes. I glance at the screen—Roger.

I disconnect from Haley and Lach to answer.

"Are you okay?" Roger *The Responsible* asks. Naturally, his first concern is to his family, for which I'm grateful.

I tell him I'm trying not to lose my shit, and he counsels me to keep it together. He, Leonie, and their kids, with nannies and dogs in tow, head to the private airport outside of Paris. In the background, Leonie chimes in to tell me not to worry too much, *chéri*. I can picture the megamodel's amber eyes flash with ferocity like *The Lion* she's known as the world over.

The last call I make is to my parents. They're on their megayacht *Serendipity* cruising the Mediterranean Sea through the end of February. I hate to disturb their alone time after being with the family over the holidays. But I know they'd rather be aware than not.

"Hi, Dad, I have some bad news," I say when he answers.

As fate would have it, Uncle Connor and Aunt Lucie are aboard the luxury vessel. After he swears in Scottish Gaelic, they confirm they're on their way.

As the eldest Jackson alive and the Marquess of Huntly, Uncle Connor acknowledged Kat and her family as Jacksons, despite his great-great-grandfather's disownment of Iain. He's Kat's connection to the Jacksons since Iain is her great-great-grandfather. Like his son Lachlan, Uncle Connor is very much a clan man and protects his own.

When I hang up, I send a text message to Alonso and to Edwin Nims, my house manager. As I put my mobile in my jeans pocket, I turn to the police officers. They stare at me, unsure how to react since I went way above their heads.

As if I give a fuck. Ignoring them, I shift my gaze to Vivian. She stares back at me, then rises.

"Let's wait for everyone in the kitchen. I'll make pots of coffee and tea," she says ever the refined lady of the house.

I nod and retrieve my mobile again. This time, I place a call to one of Lucien's restaurants to cater food for everyone. Baz, Lola, Malcolm, and Starr will arrive soon.

My mobile rings just as I set it on the kitchen island—Laurent, the youngest Jackson, and my best friend.

"Har! What the everlasting bloody fuck, cuz?! I'm on my way over. Do you need anything?" He asks. When I tell him his support will do, he tells me Lydie and Lucien—the rest of the Jackson siblings—will call.

Vivian puts a mug of coffee in front of me on the marble island and sits next to me as she cradles her mug. She sighs as she blows to cool the brew down.

"I'm scared for Kat, Harris," Viv whispers.

I say a silent prayer for My Kitty Kat's safety and swift return. It still perplexes me what the hell happened. My guess is someone saw activity at the service entrance and entered the building seeking to steal from the apartment being vacated. But to take Kat when valuables remain untouched makes absolutely zero sense.

"We need to see the security footage. I need my laptop," I ramble on as my brain kicks back in from the initial shock shutdown. A text message to Edwin will have Alonso bring my laptop to me. It's a start.

Vivian places her mobile back on the island.

"The head of security will grant you access to all building cameras. He'll bring his laptop here now," she says. "At least we can see what happened."

It doesn't take him long to arrive and set up on the island. But what appears on the screen reveals nothing unusual. At least on first inspection. I ask him to re-run the feed from the alley camera.

A stray cat walks from one side to the other in front of the moving truck. Okay. Then the same cat jumps back to repeat its movement.

"Fuck. Me. It's on a loop!" I exclaim.

The head of security peers closer.

"Well, I'll be damned," he mutters.

The police officers who joined us murmur amongst themselves.

"Harris, we're here!"

Everyone falls silent at the booming baritone of Baz. A natural leader, he enters the kitchen with the air of an Alpha Dom in full control. Those gathered part to allow him and Lola to reach me.

"Baz," I say as he embraces me. Then I turn to Lola and give her a hug.

"Malcolm is twenty minutes out," he says as he turns to the laptop. "What's this?"

I fill him in, and he mutters a string of curses.

"And no word from the person who took Kat?" Lola asks as she squeezes my hand. Her hazel eyes full of concern scan my face.

I shake my head.

"Commissioner, sir."

The male officer's acknowledgment draws our attention to the kitchen's entry.

Commissioner Flagg—flanked by the First Commissioner and a Deputy Commissioner I recognize as the head of Information Technology—strides towards us with his hand outstretched. We shake, and I make the introduction of Vivian to them. Baz and Lola greet them. Eager to keep busy, Vivian and Lola pour coffee and tea for everyone.

"Tell me the latest," Commissioner Flagg commands.

We replay the camera footage, and the Deputy Commissioner pulls out her laptop. She works with the head of security to play more footage. Afterwards, she taps into the City's network of cameras to expand the coverage.

New York City is one of the busiest places in the world. It'll take time to navigate so much video.

Time, I'm afraid we do not have.

KAT

"You really think you're special now? Don't you? Well, we have unfinished business, lass."

My blood runs cold in my veins as goose-bumps break out over my entire body. My precious music box crashes to the floor. The tune dies out on impact.

Chet Stewart!

How the *bloody hell* did he find me and get in here to boot?!

I spin around to find him dressed as one of the movers, even down to the STEELE International gray coveralls and matching cap. The hat set low on his head to cover half of his face.

He snatches it off. His eyes shoot icy daggers at me, and I freeze when he pulls a handgun with a silencer from a pocket.

My heart stops as I stare open-mouthed at the jet black metal aimed straight at my chest. I realize the dark stain on the neck of the coveralls must be blood from the mover who wore them.

Oh. My. God. Chet has gone mad.

He glares at me with such animosity, the air gets sucked from my lungs.

"You ruined me, my family, our company. You will pay, Kat *Jackson!*"

My breath hitches in my throat as I close my eyes and raise my hands to ward off what must be a fatal shot. God help me. Chet plans to follow through on his death threat. Time stands still. My last thought goes to Harris and what we'll lose. A tear slips past my eyelashes and slides down my cheek.

Chet's evil laughter fills the space between us.

"Not so easy of a death for you, lass! Oh, no. I plan to play with this cat before I destroy you," he sneers.

My eyes fly open. His reddened face contorts as he glares at me. Teeth bared, nostrils flared. I suck in a breath to scream for help. But Chet lunges forward. He backhands my open mouth. My teeth cut into soft tissue.

The coppery taste of blood makes me gag. I bring my fingers to my lips, already swelling from the brutal blow. Then stare in horror at blood on my fingertips.

"Do not even think about calling for help," Chet growls, brandishing the weapon before my face. "Toss your mobile into the closet. Now, move!"

I leave my mobile as instructed. But hesitate to move further.

A small cry slips past my swollen lips when he pushes

me with enough force, I trip over the remnants of my precious music box. The shattered pieces crush under my feet as much as my heart breaks.

Oh, Harris. The plaintive wail reverberates in my mind.

Chet pushes me through the penthouse flat until we reach its service entrance on the other side. When I pause to glance over my shoulder, Chet presses the gun against my lower back. I picture a bullet severing my spine…

"Move it or else," he threatens in a menacing growl.

I stumble and reach for the doorframe to steady myself. In the hallway, stairs lead up and down to the other floors while the lift takes up a wall. Slumped next to it lies a man naked except for his undershirt and boxers. Blood pours from a nasty gash on the side of his head. He's motionless.

"Oh, my God! Is he dea—"

"I said, *shut* your trap!" Chet snarls as he knocks me upside the head with his fist.

Stars flash before the inky blackness behind my closed eyes. Pain radiates from my temple down to my neck that snaps sideways from the impact. I cry out and earn another slap and threat.

Chet grips my upper arm and bustles me down the stairs.

My head swims as I swallow back bile. But he's relentless and forces me down the entire way from the twenty-fourth floor to the basement. He drags me towards the storage units and forces me against the wall while he divests himself of the mover's coveralls. He places them with the cap inside of a duffle bag he left on the floor, then puts on an overcoat before he swings the bag onto his shoulder.

"Now, listen very carefully," Chet starts as he grabs my throat and squeezes it until I claw at his hand. "We're going to walk out of here, down the alley, and to the street. I will hail a taxi. You will remain by my side without a word. If you so much as breathe too loud, I will put a bullet in your head. If you think to make contact with anyone, I will put a bullet in them too. Do. You. Understand?"

I cringe at the sour smell of his hot breath on my face. Then gurgle when he tightens his grip at my delayed response. Instinctively, my fingers claw at his hand. Tears spill down my cheeks. But I nod as much as possible. I cannot allow anyone else to come to harm because of Chet's madness.

"Good. Let's go," he snarls. One hand binds me to his side while the other holds the handgun hidden within the sleeve of the overcoat against my side.

I flinch at pressure on my flank from the weapon and bite back a cry. My heart batters against my ribs. Sweat trickles down my spine. A silent prayer for deliverance plays on repeat in my mind as we enter the alley.

Empty. The mantra skips with no sign of the moving truck or the other movers. No one to help me. *Blast!*

Chet quickens his pace and digs his fingers into me. He growls another warning.

I nod meekly and keep my eyes down for fear of engaging with an innocent bystander. No more shed blood on my conscious. I shudder at the reminder of the dead mover. Damn Chet Stewart!

We reach the curb around the corner from the building doorman's line of sight. No one notices us as they rush along the busy New York City sidewalk. Most people keep their heads down or have their mobiles to their ears. I envy their freedom from a deranged maniac.

A cold wind whips hair across my face. I shiver, not sure if it's from the February chill or the *bloody* gun jammed into my side.

The streetlight changes. Traffic surges ahead. Yellow taxicabs dart in and out of the flow. One stops for Chet, and he hustles me inside, careful to not draw unwanted attention from the unsuspecting driver. He gives the address to a location unknown to me. But then, I've only been here for a few weeks.

He glares at me and jabs my side again. Along with a sharp shake of his head, relays his message. *Shut. Up.*

I glance from him to the back of the driver's head, only separated from us by a transparent partition. Not enough protection from a bullet. I nod, then shift to stare out the window.

The streets blur as the taxi races down the avenue. Horns blare and mingle with snatches of conversations heard from pedestrians as we wait for red lights to change to green. Then we're off again, headed south to who knows where.

The gray sky hints at the snow flurries expected later

this afternoon. It reflects the whirlwind brewing in my chaotic mind.

How will I get out of this terrifying situation?

Where the bloody hell is Chet taking me?

Can Harris find me in time? And in time to prevent what?

What will Chet do to me? When I first approached him, I thwarted his attempt at fucking me. God help me if he forces himself on me while he holds a gun in his hand. Please, God, no!

Caught up in a daymare, I don't notice the taxi stopped until Chet passes cash to the driver through the sliding screen of the partition and opens the taxi door. Chet reaches in to take my arm. I offer no resistance, especially when he cocks his head at the handgun hidden in his sleeve.

He doesn't give me time to take in my surroundings. A few long strides, and we're inside of what appears to be an abandoned warehouse. The grimy windows—some covered by wooden boards—block the little sun hidden behind thick, gray clouds. Our footsteps echo on the concrete floors in the immense space. Debris litters the floor and accumulates along the walls covered in graffiti. The stench of urine, rotten food, and decaying wood—at least I pray it's not from a dead body or bodies—fills my nostrils. Again, I fight back the urge to gag.

Chet propels us through the abysmal space quickly. The path he takes leads us to a set of rickety metal stairs. I hesitate at the first step, and he pushes me forward. Another wave of dizziness overtakes me, and I grapple for the railing. It creaks but holds firm. Not wanting to provoke another attack to my head, I do my best to climb the stairs in a hurry.

They give way to a dimly lit landing where we have to skirt around a giant hole in the floor. My heart hammers in my chest even after we pass what would surely be a fall to my death. On the other side, a heavy wooden door with a dirt-encrusted plastic window greets us.

My heart sinks at the sight of a shiny new brass lock on it. Once more, I hesitate at the threshold to my new prison. A push between my shoulder blades, and with a cry arms flail as I stumble into the room.

"Stop fucking around, Kat *Jackson*, and get your ass inside!" Chet barks.

Unable to stop the room from spinning, I land in a heap on my hands and knees. My forehead scrapes the dirty concrete floor. I close my eyes and throw up.

"*Argh*! You filthy sow!"

Chet's yell precedes the slam of the heavy door and the tumble of the lock as it clicks into place. The sound jars my already sore skull. I whimper and clutch at my head. Then it jerks back.

Chet glares down at me with a fistful of my hair. I yelp as he drags me across the floor. The rending of fabric as the knees of my jeans rip from the hard concrete surface and the scrape of my skin make me stand on wobbly legs. I scratch at his hand to stop the pain from my scalp.

"Cut. It. Out!" He snarls with a vicious shake to my head.

Another wave of nausea hits me. My hands cover my mouth. But some of the vomit seeps past my fingers. Chet grunts and pushes me towards the ground. I land face first on a lumpy surface.

A mattress!

A gasp falls from my mouth as I struggle to right myself. No way do I want to stay in this position with a crazy Chet behind me.

"Trust me, you're too filthy to touch," he sneers as he towers over me. "For now."

The last half of his statement sends a chill colder than the February chill through my body. Every cell freezes at the thought of Chet touching me. Please, God, no...

I bend my knees to my chest with my arms wrapped around them and lower my aching head. As my stomach continues to roil, I try to make myself as small as possible. With every breath of my being, I pray for a miracle.

Chet stomps around the room, grumbling to himself. Metal clangs, then water sloshes. His steps bring him to stand above me.

"Here. Clean yourself up. Can't have you stinking up the place when I have plans for you," he says as he shoves a metal bucket against my shins.

I lift my head slightly. The racking pain makes it difficult to focus my vision.

"Go on. Or do you want me to do it?" He says jeeringly.

God no!

Quicker than I believe possible, I grab the edge of the bucket and sit up straight. I tremble as Chet chuckles wickedly.

"Don't worry. You won't be able to stop me, lass," he says, then pivots and strides to the other side of the room.

I take my first actual glimpse of my confines.

Concrete floors—at least bare of garbage.

No windows except for the grimy one in the heavy door.

Two bare lightbulbs dangle from exposed wires overhead.

An interior ceiling for the room only, not the one I saw for the entire building.

A metal desk and one metal chair in the corner.

Chet lowers his frame onto the chair and watches me.

I swallow fear down and set to cleaning the vomit from my hands, then switch to my coat. Not wanting to finish soon and face what Chet has planned, I take my time.

"Forget the coat. Take it off. It's your hands and face I want clean," he commands as he leans forward with a lusty glint in his eyes.

Bloody hell…

How will you get out of this soiled mess, Kat Jackson???

KAT

"*D*on't just sit there with your mouth agape, lass. Unless you're ready for something to fill it."

My hand stops mid-stroke. A gasp falls from my mouth. Fresh tears fill my eyes as I lower my gaze hurriedly. More thoughts of escape flood my brain. I must get the hell out of here.

Chet chuckles.

"Aw, come now. Don't be bashful, lass. I guarantee you I'm a better fuck than that oaf Steele," Chet purrs in an attempt at seduction.

Yuck! My skin crawls. Bile churns in my stomach as it threatens to spew forth again. This time in pure disgust, not in fear or pain.

Between the handgun and my head wounds, I'm uncertain I can thwart Chet's sick plan of revenge. But I'll be damned if I make it easy for him.

With my eyes still downcast, I scan the room for a possible weapon. Anything.

Nothing.

As my hands wipe the front of my coat, a jingle in a pocket catches my attention. Blessed be my keys! Wedged between my fingers, they'll serve as tiny daggers. I'll slice the wanker's face and gouge out his eyes. Thoughts of victory replace doubt. I'm ready for you Chet Stewart!

"Who the bloody hell can this be?"

His question draws me from my newfound plan of attack. He whips his mobile from a pocket and stares at the screen. His lip curls as his eyes narrow.

"Great... Just what I need at this moment," Chet mumbles, then rises to turn his back to me. "Father."

Chet paces the floor as he listens to Magnus Stewart—CEO and Chairman of the Board of Stewart Scotch. Well, the former head of their family's company.

As retribution, Lydie forced the Stewarts' hands to sell 51% of Stewart Scotch to Jackson Corporation for controlling interest. Then folded Stewart Scotch within Jackson Corporation. She effectively eliminated them as competitors and tied their fate to the Jacksons forever.

No wonder Chet is reluctant to speak to his *da*. I can only imagine how livid Magnus must be with his son.

Another thought hits me square in the face. Is Magnus involved in Chet's kidnapping of me? Could he stoop as low as his wayward son?

I focus in on his side of the conversation to determine his father's knowledge. But Chet keeps his voice low and remains on the opposite side of the room. Every few steps, he throws a glare my way. I try not to shudder from the vehemence in his eyes. Despite feeling weak, I cannot allow Chet to sense how low I am.

My eyes close for a brief prayer for strength and a swift rescue.

"Fuck!"

I jolt from Chet's exclamation. Eyes wide, I stare as he slams his fist against the wall. Curses stream from his mouth. Another slap and he pivots to face me. This time, I can't help the shudder that racks my body as he stalks in my direction.

Without a word, he yanks open a desk drawer. Metal clangs against metal. A length of thick chain rises from within. Chet's narrowed glare never leaves my face.

He drags the chain behind him like a Ghost of Christmas Past as he approaches me. The metal scrapes along the concrete. The jarring sound and his malicious intent make me crab walk backwards until the wall stops my retreat. My sins return to haunt me.

Too taken aback, I forget about my keys as Chet grabs my wrist and coils an end of the chain around it. He repeats the move with my other wrist. Then moves down my body to trap my ankles. He secures the ends to metal loops attached to the floor at the four corners of the mattress. Spread-eagle on my back, I turn my head to watch him stand.

He surveys his work. A twisted gleam replaces the anger in his eyes. He nods.

"I have to step out," Chet says, then sneers. "Obviously, you will remain here. Don't bother to scream. No one will hear you."

He turns for the door where he pauses to cast another depraved look my way.

"Save your cries for later," he says with a dark chuckle.

"You. Sick. Bastard. You won't get away with this," I snarl as I yank the chains.

In a blink of an eye, he looms over me. My chin gripped between his thumb and index finger painfully. Our eyes lock.

"I already have, Kat *Jackson*," Chet sneers.

His mouth crashes onto mine. He takes advantage of my shock to shove his tongue inside. I gag as he snakes it around, lapping at my tongue. Just as abruptly, he stands.

"Sweet," he purrs, then strides from the room. The light from the bare bulbs disappears with a flick of the switch.

I turn my head to retch in complete darkness.

Nothing left in my stomach. The sound of dry heaves joins the click of the lock's tumbler as it engages.

Misery and helplessness, unlike any I've ever known before—despite years of living below the poverty line—engulf me. The pervading sense of dread heavier than the dank air of the pitch-black room. With nothing to see and belief in rescue diminishing, I close my tear-filled eyes.

* * *

MY BLADDER WINS THE BATTLE.

I cringe as a warm puddle forms beneath my ass, still fully clothed. The liquid seeps through to the lumpy mattress below. A cry of despair mixed with relief escapes my mouth. Added to the dried vomit remnants, I know I must be a sight.

The muscles in my arms and legs ache from being chained. Tingles long since dissipated. Only a dull throb remains. A reminder of my awful predicament.

Unable to differentiate time, I can only guess it's been hours since Chet left. I ignored his suggestion to save my cries and screamed for help until only hoarse whimpers passed my chapped lips. My parched throat ragged from the unsuccessful attempts.

Even my futile efforts to dislodge the chains from my wrists resulted in bracelets of fire. Time has done little to lessen the pain. Rubbed raw my flesh burns.

More accustomed to the lack of light, my eyes make out the desk and chair along with the door in the gloom. I lower my head and stare wistfully at the bucket filled with rusty water beside the mattress. Within arm's reach. If only. What I'd give to have a sip.

My stomach growls, insistent upon not being left out of some form of satisfaction. Its emptiness further exacerbated by my earlier actions. It clenches on air.

I whimper and close my eyes.

Rest. A bit of a rest to rebuild my strength.

"Oh, for fuck's sake! It smells like a barnyard in here! Have you no self-respect, Kat *Jackson*?!"

At the same time, Chet's bellow jolts me awake, light blinds me.

I whimper and turn my head aside, squeezing my eyelids together tightly. Pain shoots up my spine. My legs jerk of their own accord. It's as though a bolt of lightning zinged through my body. Another garbled cry slips past my chapped lips. My thick tongue darts out to lick cracks that form. No moisture available to soothe them.

"I've been gone for a few days and return to you lying in your own filth. What? You couldn't hold yourself? It's not as though you had any food or drink. Damn!" Chet rants.

A few days… It's been that long??? God, help me.

"You don't even deserve the dinner I brought for you, filthy sow! And certainly not the bottle of wine…" Chet continues his tirade while I try to regain consciousness.

My muddled mind refuses to process until pain rips through me. Chet releases the chains.

"I'm giving you exactly ten minutes to clean yourself. And don't think I have any clothes for you. You better make do with what you have…"

Slow by the lack of food and water—not to mention the pain as blood flows back into my extremities—my body won't obey my mind. Instead, I curl into a fetal position. The shift brings the stench to my nose. I gag. But nothing comes up.

"Nine minutes and counting," Chet sneers.

I pull on the last of my reserves to force my limbs to

cooperate. Stiff fingers fumble with the zipper of my down coat. Flakes of vomit flutter to the mattress. I shrug the coat off, peeling the lower half from my body. The bottom of my turtleneck tunic clings to my leggings. Both bear the proof of multiple accidents.

I hesitate to remove them. Only a lace bra and soiled thong would cover me from Chet's eyes. I risk a peek at him.

He watches me with a look of contempt and lust.

"Six," he sneers, then wrinkles his nose. "Hurry up. The smell turns my stomach."

Choosing the lesser of the two, I remove my tunic. Then curse myself for the demi-cup bra I wore to entice Harris. The tops of my breasts jiggle with each movement. My nipples pebble against the black lace in the chilly air.

I don't have to peek at Chet to know he's clocking my every move. His sharp intake of air gives him away.

Hurriedly, I dip the bottom of the tunic into the bucket of water and wring it out. I'll put the damn thing back on. Better to freeze than to have Chet leering at my near nakedness.

"Oh, no you won't. It's still filthy," he admonishes as I dip my head to slip the tunic back on. "Put it aside, along with those pants."

"Y—You… s—said I could make do—"

"Y—Y—You. Stop your stuttering and hurry up. Four," he cuts me off. With a wink, he continues, "After the show, I plan to eat, then have you as my dessert. So make it quick, lass. I. Am. Starved."

I bite the inside of my cheek to hold back a flippant response. No need to provoke Chet with his mind in the gutter. I shudder in revulsion.

While still seated, I remove my sneakers before I drag the leggings down. I repeat the process of dipping the top half into the bucket of water and wringing them out. With care, I avoid water on the lower half. I plan to put them on as soon as possible.

All clothing but my thong and bra spread out on the concrete floor to dry.

"Oh, so you want me to believe you didn't soil your panties, lass?" Chet's question rankles me. "I think not. Take them off. But leave the fancy bra on. I'll unwrap those juicy tits as part of my dessert. Don't you think I deserve a treat after all you did to me?"

Damn Chet Stewart!

As much as I want to defy him, I want to survive more.

Okay, Katrina Roberts, *smiogaid suas, nighean*!

I take a deep breath and sit up straight. My hips lift from the mattress for enough space to slip out of my thong. I angle my body to hide my bare mons from Chet's leer as I clean the bit of black lace. Once done, I lay them on the floor beside the other pieces of clothing. My gaze remains on them. Then my brain short circuits at Chet's next words.

"Now step aside so I can flip this sodden mattress. We'll need it later, sweet lass."

"What do you mean you didn't implant a tracker in Kat?! It's your invention, Harris!"

"Especially after all the drama we've had from The Twins' kidnapping to my motorcycle accident. If it wasn't for your gizmos and app, we would have been fucked."

Haley and Malcolm's shocked responses to my negative answer doesn't help my pissy mood.

It's been hours since Kat disappeared. Her mobile found in the closet of her former bedroom provided no clues. Not a word for ransom money. No chatter on the dark web. Eyes strained from staring at the computer, hoping to spot any sign of her in the video footage. It's bleak as all fuck.

"Listen, give Harris a break already. They just reconnected. Who would expect something to happen in such a short period of time?" Roger's sensible response soothes some of my self-imposed guilt.

I should have placed the tracker as I have for all our family members, including the Jacksons. As Malcolm stated, we can't be too careful with our history brought on by crazies. The technology saved us a lot of unnecessary headaches. What I could have avoided with a simple injection.

Fuck!

I slam my palms against the mahogany surface of my desk and rise to pace my home office.

We set it up as the central location for all activity. I gave the cops and the equipment their head of Information Technology delivered access to my den a few doors down from my office. Lucien took over the kitchen for his staff to prepare meals around the clock. The living room serves as the gathering area for everyone else. Edwin buzzes about keeping order. This is the most activity he's ever had to manage for me.

"Exactly. Besides, that's the past. We have to focus on the present," Baz adds. He turns to me. "Harris, you need to take a break. Let's get something to eat."

I open my mouth to protest. But he gives me his don't-fuck-with-me look. Ordinarily, I'd have a wry response. But I can't summon enough energy for a good quip. Besides, he's right. I nod and pivot toward the door.

A slap on my shoulder makes me glance over.

"We'll get answers soon, Harris. We equipped everyone

with the best tools we need to find Kat. You have lots of support," Lachlan says.

Once again, I nod.

My moment of respite comes to an abrupt end as we round the corner near the living room. A thick Scottish accent sounds off.

"—don't give a bloody damn! It's his fault! Why didn't he go upstairs with her? Huh?!"

Lachlan mutters Scottish Gaelic curses under his breath.

"Payton, please! That's not true. Please don't start, son—"

"Mum, you're too—"

"Enough, Payton. You will not hurl unfounded accusations around. Either help or get out," Lachlan snarls.

Of course. Payton Roberts-cum-Jackson, Kat's older brother, and the pain in the ass of their family. After hearing about him from Lach, I should have known Payton would show his ass. But guess what? I'm ready to give an ass whipping.

I pin him with a withering glare as I stalk over to him.

"You better heed your Mum and your *cousin*. I am not in the mood for your bullshit," I warn, inches from his face.

He has the sense to lower his gaze before he spins on his heels and storms for my penthouse's entry hall.

Good fucking riddance!

I turn my gaze to Allison Roberts. She decided to keep her name as it was her husband's. I hear she's a lovely woman and deserves respect.

"Mrs. Roberts, I want you to know that I will do all in my power and more to bring Kat home to us," I say.

Her mother nods as fresh tears slip down her reddened cheeks.

"Allison, come join Lucie and me."

I shift my gaze beyond Mrs. Roberts to find my mother Shelley with my Aunt Lucie. They beckon for her to join them. I nod in gratitude when she goes to our families' matriarchs. They loop their arms through hers as they usher her down the hallway to another room for privacy.

"Come on, Har. It's time for me to mother you."

I glance down at my twin's smiling face. Her dove gray eyes—so like mine—full of love. I nod and let her lead me to the kitchen.

Laurent and Lucien greet us boisterously—one with an unopened bottle of Jackson Reserve Scotch and the other with a platter of my favorite Steak Frites.

"Load up, cuz. It's gonna be a long night!" Laurent says as he pops the top and hands the bottle to me.

I can't help but to grin before I guzzle some of the peat-flavored liquid down. The warm burn settles in my belly like a favorite blanket around one's shoulders on a brisk night. It's comforting and sustaining at once.

And from the way things are slow in progressing, I'm going to need it.

* * *

"Unfortunately, we have nothing new to report at this time. We will continue to monitor the video feed. A fourth team will surveil a broader range. The First Commissioner added more detectives to canvass the area for potential witnesses and to speak with staff at the children's nonprofit. I will check in again soon."

We thank the Deputy Commissioner, and she leaves us to rejoin her teams in the den.

Two days with nothing to show for our actions. Not a damn peep.

Vivian moved into a guest apartment a few floors below my penthouse. We have two STEELE security members as her detail. For now, she'll work from home. As I promised her family, I will not allow another woman to go missing randomly on my watch.

I run my fingers through my hair and tug at the longer strands. It would be a lot messier if Haley didn't live up to her mothering role and demand I shower, shave, and change my clothes. She catches my eye as I rise from my desk.

"Har, I'm going to take the next shift of viewing the videos. Why don't you take Bella and Bonnie for a walk? I'm sure the Trips would love to go with you, too," Haley suggests.

Lachlan stands and stretches his six-foot-four-inch frame.

"I'll join you," he adds.

"Yeah. Let's make it an outing with the rest of the kids

and the dogs. A walk in Central Park will do us all good," Roger says as he calls Leonie on his mobile.

Malcolm and Baz decline. But they let Starr and Lola know the plan. They decide to go, too. A parting glance reveals my oldest brothers deep in conversation. I can only imagine what they're up to. Best to leave them to it.

We're a rowdy bunch as we spill through the front doors of The STEELE Tower onto Fifth Avenue. Six dogs; thirteen kids; four nannies; nine adults. Laurent and Vivian come along too. Michael and Charlotte—Kat's younger brother and sister—join us for a chance to see Central Park. It's their first visit to New York City, even it is under dire circumstances. Six bodyguards surround our group as we move along. Again, no chance for shenanigans.

The crisp air of February clears my head as I take a deep inhale à la Starr's pranayama breathing teachings. Peace in. Tension out. Five times and I'm ready for our stroll through the park.

"*Allez, Oncle* Harris! Too slow!"

A tiny hand tugs mine as I glance down at my nephew Rodolphe. The eldest of the Steele grandchildren and the twin of Gaspard—two of Roger and Leonie's three children —grins up at me.

I return his smile and say a prayer of thanks he and Gaspard had their trackers implanted when the nutcase who wanted Roger kidnapped them. My heart clenches at the thought of losing my nephews and the reminder of Kat missing.

But Rodolphe's delight makes me push the negative thoughts aside.

"You're right. Let's get going!" I respond and swing him up onto my shoulders.

"Hey! Me, too! Me, too!" Slade—Baz and Lola's oldest son—calls out to me.

Roger swoops him up from behind, and Slade squeals.

Everyone laughs, and we continue to cross Fifty-Seventh Street. It's the start of lunch. Throngs of people from office workers to tourists bustle along on their way to restaurants or shopping in any of the luxury shops on the avenue.

We leave them behind as we pass between the stone walls to enter Central Park. Blanketed in white from snowfall the night before, it's a sight to behold. Tree branches laced with diamonds of ice. Cobblestones peek from beneath snow-covered walkways. The Pond frozen over dazzles in the sun.

New York City activity doesn't cease, even here. Joggers run the trails bundled up with jackets, hats, and gloves over their gear. Mothers and nannies chat as they push babies in carriages. Teachers lead children on a walk. Dogs chase balls and catch frisbees thrown by their owners on the fields covered in snow.

Our dogs bark in excitement. Baz's pair of Siberian Huskies bury themselves in a snow pile as they yip. Laurent tosses a ball, and all six dogs give chase. He and Michael hustle after them while Charlotte claps spinning in a circle face to the sky.

I put Rodolphe down, and he takes off with the others to play in the snow.

"I'm glad to see you smiling, brother."

I glance down to find Lola staring up at me. Her hazel eyes dance.

"Remember, we walk by faith and not by sight. Kat will return to us," Lola adds. "That is unless she's too scared to face Leonie, Starr, and me…"

Lola ends with a smirk. Her way of letting me know she'll accept Kat back into our lives. But she will have to make up for her actions. If the girls take her within their fold again, we'll be golden.

I grin at Lola and kiss her cheek.

"Thanks, sis. I appreciate you guys a whole lot," I say.

"You better, big guy!" She retorts with a nudge to my side.

Leonie and Starr saunter over and pull me into a group hug. They offer more words of encouragement and take up Haley's mothering in her absence. I bask in their attention, grateful for their love. From one sister to four, well, five counting Lydie, who flew in last night. It couldn't get better!

We spend the next hour or so tromping through the park. Lola suggests going to an early dinner at her favorite restaurant growing up in the City—Serendipity. She makes the call and books the entire second floor for us. We head back to The STEELE Tower to drop off the dogs and to meet up with the others. STEELE Mercedes-Benz Sprinters take us to the restaurant on Sixtieth Street.

My parents, Uncle Connor, and Aunt Lucie sit with Allison and Payton—who has assumed the role of his mother's chaperone since our incident. Perhaps there's hope for him yet. The rest of us take seats along the banquette and on chairs across the long row of tables pushed together. Charlotte ohs and ahs over the eclectic mix of decorations on the walls and hanging from the ceiling. On the other side of the room, the children gather at tables with the nannies. Their laughter and antics make the atmosphere buzz with joy.

I feel like a kid myself as I sip from red and white striped straws in the giant glass of Frozen Hot Chocolate. Fresh whipped cream lands on my lip, and I lick it off happily. Haley winks at me from across the table as she sips her decadent concoction. I grin back. My heart lightens for the first time in days.

"OH, MY GOD!"

The hairs on the back of my neck rise at Haley's cry. I drop my mobile and rush to her side just as Lachlan races over. She's on her laptop reviewing video footage as she has for the past few hours of day three.

"What is it?!" Baz demands.

"What did you find, Haley?" Malcolm asks at the same time.

She turns the computer around and points at a figure in a crowd of people on a sidewalk.

I lean closer. The image tweaks a vague memory.

"Fuck. Me." Lachlan breathes.

"Tell us!!" Roger yells.

"Chet fucking Stewart. What the bloody *hell* is he doing in New York?" Lachlan responds, then continues with a sneer. "My last report placed him in Rome at some dingy pensione."

That fucker took my woman?! I'll rip his face off!

Haley snickers.

"And I'll help you, twin," she says.

I raise an eyebrow.

"Um, you spoke out loud, Har," she responds with a smirk.

"Right. Now, what's the timestamp of that video?" I ask as my fingers itch to get ahold of Stewart.

Haley gives more details. Lachlan rises to tell the cops still in the den.

"No."

We turn to Malcolm. He stands beside Baz. They shake their heads simultaneously. So much alike physically, people confuse them for twins. Their striking resemblance even more apparent now as they stand as one.

"You figure out where Stewart is without outside help. I will take care of the fucker," Malcolm *The Enforcer* says with the eerie calm of a man not to be messed with. Trained in MMA and one who thinks nothing of cave diving in some of the most remote places on Earth is fun, Malcolm fears nothing and no one.

"Right," I repeat.

Haley and I get to work on our laptops. Time to track that fucker and get my woman back where she belongs. With our family. And in my arms.

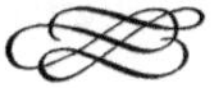

"The larger heat signatures on the second floor indicate two adults. Ignore the smaller ones as rodents or other vermin. In teams of three, we'll enter at these points. The schematic for the warehouse indicates stairs here lead to the room where the perp and Kat are here."

"Our surveillance indicates the perp returned moments ago. All signs point to him working alone."

"As far as boots on the ground. Communication with others has only been to his father. Nothing marks his involvement. However, we'll glean more info from the perp once we have him."

I listen intently to the two men who lead the rescue operation. They're a part of an elite team of former Navy SEALs and Army Green Berets Malcolm works with when necessary. That's the extent of what he tells us about them, other than he trusts them with the lives of his most cherished Starr and their children. And that's all I need to know.

A crackle over the radios, and they pause the report. While they speak to other team members, I watch the monitor. The smaller of the two heat signatures moves around on the floor. The other stays stationary. What the fuck is going on in there???

"I do not agree with you going in, Harris."

I turn from the monitor to face Baz. He sits in the van with me. Malcolm sits in another near the warehouse with more of the team. Neither will enter the warehouse. But fuck me if I don't get my woman.

"Baz, I already swore not to go beyond the two guys who will enter the room ahead of me. But there's no way in hell I will not be there for Kat. You know you would do the same for Lola. Hell, Starr fought a mountain lion for Malcolm. I appreciate your concern, but I got this, bro," I respond.

My eldest brother scans my face, then nods, satisfied.

"Let's move!"

The command snaps us to attention. Baz grips my shoulder and nods once more. I nod in return, then jump from the van.

It's after eleven at night. The streets empty in this desolate part of lower Manhattan. Dressed in all black with bulletproof vests beneath our shirts and ear comms, we make our way to a side entrance for the warehouse. The team leader clips the padlock with ease. Stewart—the dumb fuck—didn't bother to install a security system. Our win.

The streetlamps don't extend into this alley, so no light disturbs the dark interior of the warehouse to give away our entry. Night vision goggles clear the way for us to see despite the lack of light. As soon as I step over the threshold, my nose wrinkles in disgust at the foul odor of decay. I ignore it and lift my gaze towards the upper levels.

From this angle, I can't see the staircase. I glance around as I follow my team deeper into the property. I spot others as they head for various areas. Only two sets will go to the second floor. Two others guard the roof. All access points covered in case Stewart gets past us. Not happening.

Our boots make no sound as we approach the staircase. It's ramshackle but will hold. Looking up, I notice a large hole above. We skirt around it as we arrive on the landing. Across from us, a faint glow of light appears through a dirt-encrusted plastic window set in a heavy wooden door. A new lock keeps it secure. Not for long.

The leader of my team holds up his fist, and we stop on command. He points to positions we're to take on either side of the door. A finger to his lips and sharp shake of his head reminds us not to utter a word—no matter what we see beyond that door. Best Stewart won't be able to recall our voices.

My heart thuds in my chest as adrenaline pumps through my veins. So close to My Kitty Kat. I'll have you safe and sound soon, my love. And that fucker—Stewart—torn to shreds.

* * *

Kat

"Now that you're passably clean, we will eat. Come sit."

I continue to stand beside the flipped mattress with my hands covering my bare mons as I stare at Chet's smirking face. Despite my will to survive, I can't help my mouth twisting in disgust.

He sits on the metal chair with his legs spread wide as he pats his lap. His beady eyes rake over my body, pausing at my breasts and covered pussy. The tip of his tongue slips out to lick a slow circle around his lips.

My flesh crawls.

"Come sit," Chet repeats.

I shake my head as I take a step backwards. My heel bumps against the mattress. Caught between a rock and a hard place, my mind reels.

God, please let someone save me!

"Get your ass over here, Kat *Jackson*. I doubt you want me to drag you across the concrete floor. Or do you prefer it rough, lass? I hear you're a regular at those sex clubs," Chet says. Lust fills his eyes as he ogles my body again. He beckons me with one hand and palms his crotch with the other suggestively. "I've got something you'll enjoy even more… Get over here. Now!"

My terror-filled eyes flick towards the door. *Can I escape???*

In that moment, Chet lunges for me. He grabs my arm and jerks me behind him as he strides toward the table. My

60

wobbly legs threaten to collapse. Lack of food and water weakens me. With a mournful sob, I follow him.

He sits and yanks me onto his lap. The bulge in his pants pokes my hip. He laughs lasciviously as I wiggle to break free of his vise-like hold.

"Oh, that feels good, lass. It'll be even better when I fuck you. Especially here," he says as he squeezes my ass.

"Fuck you," I attempt to tell him defiantly. But my sore and parched throat makes my voice rough and low. It's more of a barely audible murmur than a menacing retort.

"Oh, but you will. Again. And again. Before *I'm* through with you. Who knows what else I have in store for you?" He sneers in my face. "But first you need to eat. I can't have you lying there like a limp rag doll. I want your active participation. Willing or not. Open wide, la—"

The two lightbulbs flicker, then go out. We're cloaked in pitch black. Unable to see, but the sound of the wooden door splintering and the rustle of movement fills our ears. Chet's shouts turn garbled as I'm ripped from his lap by powerful hands.

As though I weigh nothing, those hands lift me against a massive chest. I cry out as I struggle feebly to free myself. Fear spikes as horrific visions of being assaulted by multiple men run through my delirious mind. I doubted I could fight off Chet. Now more?

"No… Please," I whimper as the man strides at a quick pace. I sense others as we move. No one makes a sound. Even Chet remains silent.

We descend the rickety stairs. The rusted metal groans

from the combined weight. Heavy boots pound on the steps as the others follow.

I sneak a peek up at the man who carries me. Perhaps he's my hero and not a monster. Unfortunately, a dark knit cap covers his head and googles partially obstruct his face. Only glimpses of his full lips set in a stern line appear in the gloom.

He dips his head to peer at me briefly. His arms squeeze me tighter to his chest. The comforting display lessens my fear.

This man is rescuing me!

* * *

HARRIS

I'll kill that motherfucker!

My mind explodes at the sight of My Kitty Kat bared-assed on that bastard's lap. Only a bra keeps her from being naked fully.

The fucker has the nerve to hold a fork in his hand as though he was feeding my woman. The louse gapes and shouts as his head swivels in the darkness that engulfs them. His expression changes from surprise to anger, then to fear as the syringe jabs his neck. Thankfully, a black hood descends over his face, hiding his mug from me.

I need to focus on getting My Kitty Kat out of this miserable prison. With ease, I pull her into my arms and carry her bride-like through the broken door and down the stairs. My heart clenches when she begs for me not to hurt her.

What the hell did Stewart do to her during these three days???

I can't speak to her. Instead, I gaze down and hug her closer to me. I'll let her know it's me once we're in the van safely.

Stewart has the pleasure of riding in the van with Malcolm.

The side door slides open, and Baz leans out with a blanket. I pass My Kitty Kat to him. He bundles her up as I hop in and whip off the googles. Immediately, I pull her onto my lap. She slaps at my chest with a cry as she shakes her head, eyes squeezed shut. More pleas tear at my heart.

"Kat, it's me, Harris. Look at me," I say as I hold her face between my palms. "Baby, you're safe. You're safe."

She stills. Her eyes open wide and scan my face. Relief fills them as she recognizes me.

"H—Harris," she sighs. Tears spill down her cheeks. Cheeks bruised along with her swollen mouth.

I bite back a growl and press the back of her head to cradle My Kitty Kat to my chest. My eyes close as I rock her gently. Soothing words pour from my mouth against her matted hair. I ignore the smell of body waste and stale sweat that clings to her skin despite the barrier of the thick wool blanket.

We remain locked together until the van stops on another empty side street. Baz and I—with Kat in my arms —switch to a waiting nondescript sedan. Roger nods as he starts the engine. I sense he watches me from the rearview mirror. But I keep my gaze on My Kitty Kat who sleeps. Baz fills him in as we ride uptown to The STEELE Tower.

Both of my brothers watch me intently during the ride up from the underground garage. I offer them a nod. Words will wait until after our private doctor checks My Kitty Kat. Right now, I can't formulate any with the wild thoughts of what that fucker may have done to her running rampant in my mind.

The elevator stops on my floor. Baz uses his palm to unlock the front doors to my penthouse—each of us has access to the others' residences. The doctor waits for us on the other side.

Our parents invited everyone up to their duplex penthouse for dinner and movie night. We kept the rescue mission between us. Not even Kat's family knows. Best to keep the details of the situation amongst us.

I lead the way to my bedroom suite. Inside, the doctor instructs me to place a now awake Kat on the examination table he set up beside my bed. Baz and Roger wait in the sitting room. When the doctor asks me to join them, I cock my head to the side and raise an eyebrow. He nods and gets on with the exam.

Kat answers his questions while darting her gaze between him and me. She recounts the multiple blows Stewart inflicted. The more she speaks, the more it proves difficult for me to maintain control. I want to rip him to pieces with my bare hands. My hands fist at my sides.

When the doctor asks her about sexual assault, she stares at me and shakes her head vehemently.

The breath I didn't realize I held breaks free. My knees buckle in relief. It's bad enough he physically assaulted My Kitty Kat. But if he had dared to touch her—

"Harris, I'm fine."

My Kitty Kat's softly spoken words resonate in the bedroom. I take her proffered hand and wrap my arms around her. She cries against my shoulder. Her entire body shakes.

The doctor's cough reminds me to let him complete the exam. He determines she is indeed fine. She promises to heed his recommendation she takes a warm bath, pain meds as needed, and eats a good meal with plenty of water. I walk the doctor to the doors. I tell Baz and Roger, Kat is good and thank all three. They leave.

I rush to the en suite bathroom to prepare her bath. To the water, I add essential oils—eucalyptus and lavender to ease her sore muscles and to relax her mind. I return to the bedroom and carry My Kitty Kat to the sunken tub. She takes off the exam gown before I ease her into the water.

"Thank you, Harris," she whispers as she takes the bottle of water from me.

Greedily, she gulps half of it, then leans back with a sigh. Her face scrunches, and she shudders.

"You're safe, Kitty Kat. No need to worry anymore," I reassure her as I rub a sponge across her stiff shoulders. "Your mother and siblings came over with Haley and Lach-

Ian. In fact, everyone came as soon as Baz and I called them. You're not alone."

My Kitty Kat opens her eyes and stares at me. I smile, and she strokes my cheek as tears cascade down hers.

I lower my forehead to press against hers. Our breaths sync as we relax—the stress of the last few days finally subsiding. A moment later, I finish bathing My Kitty Kat. Dried and wrapped in a warm, fluffy robe, I carry her to the bedroom.

A table laden with dishes beneath cloches and bottles of water sits beside the floor-to-ceiling windows. I send a silent prayer of thanks for my brothers asking Lucien to provide food for My Kitty Kat. When I glance down at her, she eyes the table hungrily.

"Let's see what Lucien prepared, shall we?" I ask with a broad smile.

"Please!" My Kitty Kat responds eagerly.

Now, that's a plea to warm my heart.

"So, Kat, now that a week has passed since your rescue, tell me your thoughts."

I take a deep breath and shift my gaze from the psychologist to the window of her brownstone where she practices on the Upper Eastside. We've met every day. But this morning is the first time we held our session outside of Harris'—I mean *our*, as he reminds me—penthouse. I haven't had the courage to go beyond the entry hall and that's only to greet family and Vivian.

The comfort of being in the safety of the penthouse high above the streets of Manhattan and far from the gloomy warehouse helped me to get through those first days. Anytime I closed my eyes to sleep, memories of Chet hitting me and his promise to assault me woke me in fits of terror. My screams pierced the quiet of the bedroom. Sweat soaked my body, drenching my nightgown and the sheets. Only Harris' protective arms wrapped around me, cradling me to his chest, caused the nightmares to fade.

He—along with my mother and siblings, the Jacksons, and his family—provided the support I needed daily. I'll never forget the expression of sheer happiness on Payton's face when everyone walked into the living room to find me on the sofa. He raced over and pulled me into a tight embrace. His tears mingled with mine as he held me close. Never in our lives did my older brother exhibit warmth for me. Hell, for any of us. Now, he's a completely different person—loving and attentive, not mean and self-absorbed.

Michael and Charlotte told me Payton assumed the role of chaperone for our Mum and treats them a lot better, too. I had to promise I'd go with them to the Statue of Liberty and to the Empire State Building to continue their tour of New York City. It's their sweet way of keeping me from thinking about the awful kidnapping.

Instead of only my Mum hovering over me, Shelley and Lucie make it their mission to visit every afternoon for tea. Apparently, it became a ritual for them as a means to distract my Mum. At least their bonding is one positive outcome of my kidnapping. And I do enjoy spending time with The Mums as I've nicknamed the trio.

While I was gone, Starr transformed a room into a yoga studio. She insists the morning routine of mediation and breathing exercises followed by a flow class will help ease the stress. Every morning, the girls come over for our practice, followed by breakfast. It amazes me how easily they've added me back into their circle and connected with Vivian. Another plus.

Even the guys offer their support without hesitation. Malcolm spends thirty minutes a day teaching me self-defense moves. *Don't let anyone catch you off guard, Kat!* It feels good to have a bit of badass in me. Lucien makes my favorite dishes and surprises me with a different decadent dessert. *Keep your strength up, Kat!*

Just as I now have more big brothers and cousins, the Jackson and Steele Patriarchs have adopted me fully. As a member of the family, Connor insisted Harris placed a tracker beneath my skin. They explained how each family member has one, including my Mum and siblings now. The Patriarchs take on the responsibility of us all seriously. *No messing about, Kat Jackson!*

A smile lifts the corners of my mouth as I shift my gaze from the window back to the psychologist. She smiles and nods encouragingly. I take a deep breath and share my thoughts on the abundance of love and support everyone has for me. But just as important, the need for Harris to not treat me like a fragile flower.

Although he holds me, he has yet to make love to me. I've initiated intimacy, but he stops my advances and spoons me. Every. Single. Time. I need more. I want to banish the horrific memories of Chet's filthy touches and crass words. Forever.

And only Harris can do it. But he won't. *You need your rest, Kitty Kat.*

AARGH!

The psychologist tries to cover her giggle with a cough. But I cock my head and smirk.

"Go ahead. You can skip the professionalism. I'd laugh if I wasn't desperate for Harris," I say.

She grins and gives me the absolute best advice.

After our session ends, I walk into the waiting area and smile at the sight of my man. He insisted on accompanying me since it was my first foray outside of our penthouse. I don't mind his hovering either. I just wish he would hover *over* me as he pounds me into the mattress…

As though sensing my presence—or need—he glances up from his mobile. He searches my face, then sighs in relief when my smile broadens.

"Good session?" He asks as he strides over to me and kisses my forehead chastely.

I slip my arms around his neck to pull him down to me. My mouth crushes his. My tongue demands entry. It sweeps into his mouth as it hangs agape, stunned by my forthrightness. I tease his tongue with mine until they tangle. My pelvis grinds against him, hungry for friction. As his cock grows, I undulate my hips and moan in the back of my throat.

My teeth nip his lips, along his jaw, and up to the shell of his ear. I tug the lobe. It slips from my teeth, and I lap the erotic pain away.

"Fuck me, Harris Steele. Take me home now and Fuck. Me."

He groans and places his hands on my waist. His eager fingers dig into my skin even as he pushes me away gently.

"Oh, no you will not. What you *will* do is rid me of the horrible images of Chet plaguing my mind. With each brutal thrust, you will erase that scoundrel from my memory. Now, Harris Steele, let's go home," I demand.

He blinks down at me. Dove gray eyes blown obsidian by lust. His swallow audible. He bites a corner of his full mouth as he considers my words.

I pivot on my heel and head for the front doors. An exaggerated sway to my hips. Over my shoulder, I call to him.

"Now, Harris Steele."

His deep, seductive chuckle makes me shiver.

"As you wish, Ms. Jackson."

I yelp as pain blossoms on my ass.

Harris presses close behind me as we stand in the vestibule between the inner glass and outer wooden doors of the brownstone. The air thickens with our mutual desire. The hand that didn't spank me slides around my side to my lower belly and presses me closer to his hard body. Feeling his impressive bulge, I'm thankful we didn't wear coats. The soft silk of my shift dress proves a limited barrier from his wool trousers.

"Are you being a naughty lass, Kitty Kat?" he murmurs. His warm breath skitters across my cheek. Open-mouthed kisses trail along my jaw. "Or a recommendation from the psychologist?"

I wiggle my ass as my fingers dive into his hair to pull him to my mouth. I let a toe-curling kiss answer for me.

Harris groans and tightens his grip while bending his

knees to align his hard cock with the crack of my ass. He grinds up against me, and I just about spread my legs for him to take me right here. Right. Now.

He chuckles wickedly and pushes the wooden door open.

"After you, Ms. Jackson," he purrs.

I almost skip down the stairs, delighted to have Harris on the same mind frame as me.

We're going to fuck! At last!

I thank Edwin as he holds the door open of the Cullinan, then silently urge him to drive faster. Harris laughs at me bouncing on the seat. With a shake of his head, he pulls me onto his lap and kisses me breathless.

"Patience, Ms. Jackson. I've got you, babe," he murmurs against my swollen lips.

I sigh contentedly and lean against him.

On the ride up in the private lift, I blow kisses and wink at Harris' reflection in the doors. He smirks at my flirtatious antics and squeezes my hand. When he opens the entry doors, he leans in and whispers in my ear.

"Straight to the bedroom. Stand in front of the window with your back to the doors. Do not move," he commands.

A shiver races down my spine as my breath hitches. A smack to my ass drives me forward with a squeal.

I make haste to do as Harris commanded. Time passes. I try not to fidget or glance over my shoulder. Instead, my mind drifts. The memory of seeing Harris for the first time in the lobby of Jackson Town House replaces the images of the Manhattan skyline. A tremor runs through me as I recall every sensual touch and each electrifying kiss from him. I smile at his insistence I lay claim to this posh penthouse.

In those moments, my desire to build a life with the man I love increases exponentially. No one and most of all not Chet will take the happiness Harris and I have together away from us. We will move past this more than a bump in the road stronger than before. His family and my Jackson family accept me once again. Nothing can stop us.

"You're right, Ms. Jackson. *Nothing can stop us.*"

I gasp and spin around to find Harris mere feet away from me. His smoldering eyes rake over me from head to toe. He sucks his plump lower lip into his mouth with his teeth as he advances. I shiver in anticipation as waves of his carnal lust roll over me.

"I did not expect you to talk to yourself when I left you to think through what you want from me. However, I agree with you completely," Harris says.

He slips his hands onto my hips and leans down. His lips centimeters from mine. I rise to my toes. But he tsks.

"And I did not tell you to turn around. I said, *do not move*, naughty girl," he adds as he spins me to face the window again.

His fingers glide along the outside of my thighs to the hem of my dress. They bunch the soft material and slide it up slowly, sensuously. It skims along the stretchy, buttery leather of my mid-thigh boots to tease my skin. His knuckles leave goosebumps in their wake. Up and over my head, the dress goes. Harris drops it to the floor and cups my breasts.

They grow heavy in his hands as he kneads them and tugs on my nipples through the lace. They pucker from his touch. I moan wantonly as my head lolls back against his chest.

Harris takes advantage of the space to drag his lips along the column of my throat. Little nips send thrills rocketing through me. He sucks the sensitive skin at the juncture of my neck and shoulder into his mouth. His teeth worry my flesh, sure to leave a mark.

"Mine," he growls.

"Yours," I purr.

He chuckles wickedly.

The front closure of my bra pops open. He moves the cups aside to massage my aching breasts. I arch my back, pushing them further into his magic touch. My fingers dig into his muscular thighs. I need something, anything, to ground me. Or I'll float away in sheer bliss.

The musky scent of my arousal wafts in the surrounding air. It mixes with the compelling Dionysiac aroma of his cologne—floral, earthy, and vanilla—heightened by the heat of his body temperature. We're on fire for one another.

I shrug out of the bra as Harris hooks his thumbs in the sides of my G-string.

He crouches and lifts one of my feet, then the other, before he drops the lace on top of my dress.

"These boots weren't made for walking. They're made

for fucking," he growls as he slides his hands up the backs of my legs.

His left hand clutches my thigh to encourage me to bend my knee up against the window. Fully open to him, he burrows his nose into my pussy, past the slick lips. He nudges my engorged clit with the tip of his nose as he hums in appreciation.

"So wet for me already, Kitty Kat," he murmurs between bites of my lower lips and clit. "I want you to cum for me again. And. Again. Until you beg for me to fuck you."

A stream of Scottish Gaelic curses pours from my mouth as I sag against the glass. My palms and forehead press against its coolness. Condensation from my pants forms on it, receding and extending with each breath.

True to his word, Harris eats me like a starved man. Lapping at my cream as it gushes after each mind-blowing orgasm. I lose count. His guttural groans of pleasure drive me over the edge repeatedly. My body quivers. But for his grip on my hips, I would crumble to the floor completely boneless.

"P—P—Please fuck me..." I wail as my pussy clenches around his dangerous tongue.

He growls and rises so quickly, I wobble. His arm bands around me, locking me against his firm body. The sound of his zipper and his sigh of relief draws a moan from deep in my throat. He kicks my feet apart, bends his knees, and rocks forward onto his toes as he impales me on his massive cock.

My pussy struggles to accept his girth and length. But

Harris has none of it. He grips me tighter and thrusts deeper until he's fully seated deep within me.

"Fffuuuck…" he groans. "So tight. So wet. So warm."

My palms slap the window, then slide up the slippery surface as Harris pounds into me. The stretch burns oh so good. In ecstasy, I rise onto the balls of my feet still encased in the sexy boots. I throw my head back and keen.

"Still with me, My Kitty Kat?" Concern gives Harris pause.

In response, I drop hard onto my heels and grind onto his throbbing cock.

He growls.

A slow drag out to his tip precedes a sharp snap of his hips to impale me once again. He continues the deliberate pace until I beg for it faster and harder. With a fierce chuckle, he obliges me.

I explode anew.

Stars on a white shimmery backdrop dance before my eyes. My mouth hangs slack. The muscles of my core clench so intensely, my stomach cramps. Cream gushes like a fountain to coat his cock. The natural lubricant eases his passage.

He hisses in satisfaction.

Carnally connected as one, we avow *nothing can stop us.*

"You slept well last night. Feel better, babe?"

I snicker at Harris' words as I roll over in our bed to face him. A glint of mischief dances in his dove gray eyes as he stares down at me. Leaning on an elbow with tousled hair and stubble around his luscious mouth, he smirks.

"Oh, do you mean the few moments you allowed me to close my eyes? And not in ecstasy?" I respond with a wry grin of my own.

He chuffs and planks on both elbows to hover over me. His warm breath mingles with mine as I gasp at the pressure of his heavy balls and ramrod cock on my lower belly. A knowing grin spreads across his handsome face.

"As I recall, you begged for it *faster and harder,* more and more. Not to mention the fact you screamed my name as you broke for me over and over," Harris says. His hips swivel with each word to further remind me of my pleas.

I groan and lift my hips to meet his teasing thrusts. My hands fling over my head to brace against the headboard.

"Take me again, lover!" I demand.

Harris bows his head to my breasts. His lips and teeth add to his teasing hips as he tugs at my puckered nipples. Not quite enough to make me cum. But the right combination to increase my carnal desire.

I buck beneath him. My head tosses from one side to the other as I bow my back. My movements force him to grip my hip to still me. I growl in frustration as he continues to taunt me. He merely chuckles.

"Harris, don't tease me. Please!" I beseech him.

He rewards me with two thick fingers breaching my sopping seam. They scissor within me, then flip to stroke the sensitive tissue of my G-spot. One. Two. Three times. I gush into the palm of his hand.

Toes curled, back arched on a soundless wail, my body convulses. His fingers never stop their carnal caress until I sink into the bed, mouth parted, eyelids drooped.

A musky scent fills my nostrils. My eyelids flutter open as Harris slips his fingers coated with my cream between my lips. Automatically, the tip of my tongue darts out to lap at them greedily.

He presses the digits further inside my mouth, then groans as I suck them clean. He drags them from my mouth, down my chin, and to my nipple. A pinch and I writhe.

"Good girl," he croons.

I preen.

"Come. Let's get you showered before your yoga session," Harris says. He rolls from the bed and extends his hand to me. "Up and at 'em, Kitty Kat."

I take it and rise to my knees. My other hand cups his heavy sac. I lick my lips seductively as I massage his balls between my fingers.

His eyes close as he draws in a sharp breath. The bobbing of his veiny, velvet-covered shaft encourages my ministrations. A tortured groan slips past his lips.

"Fuck my mouth, Mr. Steele," I purr in his ear with a decisive squeeze to his sac.

I lie down on the bed with my head hanging over the edge. His thick thighs bracket me as I stare up into his face. The feral desire in his wolfish eyes makes me mewl. My mouth opens wide. The flat of my tongue reaching past my lower lip beckons to him.

With a growl, he fists the base of his engorged dick. He pumps his fist along its length and squeezes the angry purple tip. A large bead of pre-cum dangles from it.

I tip my head back further to catch it, then hum as I swallow it down. It undoes him.

"Open!" Harris commands as he grips my chin between his thumb and index finger.

Happily, I oblige.

He groans and I moan as his ample girth widens my mouth. The tip of his cock bumps the back of my throat.

Tears fill my eyes as my gag reflex kicks in. Wanting to pleasure him, I breathe through my nose and relax my throat.

Harris' eyes narrow at the outline of his cock as it stretches my throat. All ten inches.

The tears spill from the corners of my eyes to pool in my ears. Again, I ignore my body's natural reaction to dispel his erotic invasion. It's a conquering I'll gladly take. His dominance sets me off as much as my willingness does him.

My hands cup my achy breasts while my fingers tweak my nipples. I squeeze my thighs together and buck my hips. I want to cum.

Harris reaches out. His fingertips trail along my throat. The sensation of him stroking his cock through the thin layer of my skin makes me hum. He groans as his fingers continue between my breasts, over my belly, and between my folds. He pinches my swollen clit.

The moan as I climax triggers his need to release.

His hands grip the sides of my head. He pistons his hips, dragging his dick in and out of my mouth from root to tip. The controlled, measured thrusts turn uneven and feral. Now he wants to cum.

I hallow out my cheeks and suckle.

With a primal roar, Harris crushes my face to his crotch and spews ropes of hot semen down my throat, straight to my hungry belly. My fingernails dig into his quivering thighs as he pulses on my tongue.

His dick pops from my mouth as he drops to his knees. He hunkers down with his back against the bed and his head on the mattress beside mine. Our pants match as we struggle to catch our breath.

"You'll be the death of me yet, Siren," Harris rasps.

"You look radiant, Kat. That man of yours come through? No pun intended…"

I join in Vivian's giggles.

Another recommendation the psychologist gave was to get back into my routine. So after yoga and breakfast, Vivian and I ride to the office. She waggles her eyebrows as she grins.

"Nothing like some good loving to make you happy!" Viv adds with a wink of a toffee brown eye, then pouts. "Now if I could just get some."

I shift on the backseat of the Cullinan to face her.

"What happened during your date with one of Harris' buddies?" I ask.

She shrugs and shakes her head.

"I postponed it. I couldn't go out with my girl gone, you know," she responds as she peeks at me from beneath her thick eyelashes.

Yeah, that…

Viv nudges me, and I glance back at her.

"But you're back!! You can help me pick out a fabulous outfit to wear. He invited me to a Chelsea art gallery opening with dinner afterwards next week," she enthuses. "Maybe we could make it a double date?"

I laugh out loud and shake my head vigorously. The last time I went to an art gallery with Harris, my entire world flipped.

Viv's frown changes to a wide-eyed stare as she recollects my story. She sputters to respond. Words of blunders and rotten friend pour from her mouth. But I grab her hand between mine.

"Not to worry, Viv! You're by far the best friend I've ever had. Truly! And don't you go walking on eggshells around me too," I say with a laugh. "But I'll pass on the double date. Not because it's at an art gallery, per se. Rather, you need to have your first date with this guy alone. If you like him, Harris and I will join you for dinner or something. Okay?"

She bites her lower lip as she studies my face.

I tug her hand and grin wider until she nods and wraps her arms around me.

"Kat, you do not know how scared I was for you. I blamed myself. I should've gone upstairs with you or noticed sooner—"

"No, Vivian! No one is to blame except for that crazy prat. Let's forget about him anyway," I say adamantly.

She nods, then peeks at me again. Her mouth opens, then snaps shut as she glances away.

"Out with it," I tell her.

"Whatever happened to him? Has Harris said anything?" Viv asks quietly.

Good question. In all of this time, it never occurred to me. I guess my mind is more determined to forget that prat than I realized. I glance back at Viv and shrug.

She nods, then brightens and claps her hands.

"Okay, so back to my outfit. I was thinking we could go to Versace…"

"I know it's not the most suitable after-dinner talk, but I forgot to ask before. Whatever happened to Chet? Do I need to give a statement or something to the authorities? Have a trial? I'd like to finish with all of it. Move forward from the whole mess completely."

The jovial chatter in the living room stops by the end of my request.

I shift my gaze from Harris. I glance around to Roger with Leonie in his lap beside us, Sebastian and Lola next to Lachlan and Haley on the sofa opposite, then to Malcolm and Starr on chairs. All heads turn to the second oldest Steele.

"Oh, that fucker? Well, he's on a slow boat to Antarctica with some eager playmates. I assure you the boys will keep him company," *The Enforcer* responds, then sits back and sips his Jackson Scotch. "But whether he makes landfall will prove impossible."

Sebastian chuckles darkly and murmurs in Russian, to which a predatory smile spreads across Malcolm's face.

"No need for you to speak to anyone, Kat. Just forget he ever existed," Sebastian adds.

Well, fuck.

Now I sit back and gulp half the contents of my snifter. The rich amber liquid rolls down my throat and settles in my stomach. With closed eyes, I cradle the crystal to my chest.

Holy crap. I picture the prat begging *the boys* as I did him to not sexually assault me. Now it's his turn to fear, except there's no rescue for him. Does it bother me? Do I care?

A sinister smile spreads across my face. I open my eyes and pin a steady stare on *The Enforcer*.

"Tell me more. I want to hear everything. From the moment you left here to the moment Harris carried me through the front doors to that prat setting sail. Leave no sordid detail out," I say.

The tension in the room vanishes.

Malcolm throws his head back and roars with laughter. Sebastian leans forward and high fives his brother. Lachlan blows out a round of curses in Scottish Gaelic before he lifts his snifter to his lips, curled in a smirk. Roger slaps Harris on the back, then grins at me.

"So, you're not upset, babe? You won't tell anyone?" Harris asks as his eyes scan my face for any sign of distress or disloyalty.

I snort and raise my snifter in the air as I stand.

"*Ah pinnae, ken,*" I respond.

Lachlan laughs and rises with his snifter held high. He glances around the room and winks as he translates: "*I'm dreadfully sorry, sir. But I have no idea what you might be talking about.*"

The others jump to their feet and join our toast. We cheer and wish the prat a much-deserved journey.

"Well, now that's cleared the air, I say it's time for a Couples' Getaway! I have a special fitness retreat scheduled for next month at LEVELS Laucala Island. I'll hear no excuse not to attend," Starr says once everyone returns to their seats. She flicks her gaze at each of us, then continues. "I'll email the itinerary to you and the others tomorrow. A week in Fiji will do us all some good."

We toast to her announcement and pledge our attendance.

The rest of the evening passes comfortably. Our guys talk about sports. The girls fill me in on the fun retreats they've had in the past. My excitement grows when they share what I can expect at the first exclusive members-only BDSM resort, or BDSM on the Beach as Starr dubbed it. We'll have the fitness session at her Starr Light Fitness & Wellness Laucala Island. She opened it to keep LEVELS LI members limber. And I cannot wait!

"**K**at adjusted well over the past month. A lightness replaced that haunted look in her eyes."

"Or could it be the good lovin' my boy's *adjusted* her to?"

I nod at Baz and throw a smug smirk at Laurent, who chuckles. Then I glance over my shoulder towards the middle of the STEELE Gulfstream G700.

We're headed to Laucala Island for Starr's Couples' Getaway as promised. The $75-million-dollar private jet can accommodate up to eighteen passengers with sleeping space for nine. Its powerful Rolls-Royce engines and technological advancements allow it to fly internationally with ease. The spacious, luxurious interior affords five living areas with a forward galley for the flight crew.

Malcolm and his thrill-seeking buddies—cousins Anton Alexeyev and Borya Alexeyev—shift in their oversized white leather chairs to get in on the conversation. To rib me more specifically.

"Ah, the youngest of The STEELE Quaternity has fallen for The One, has he?" Anton asks as he bats his glacial blue eyes and clutches his hands to his chest.

Borya guffaws and responds in Russian, to which Baz, Malcolm, and Anton throw their heads back and laugh heartily. The former MMA world champion known as *The War Defender* continues to smirk at his own joke as he nods at me.

I turn back and roll my eyes, clueless as to what he said, but know it's at my expense.

"Whatever, Borya. I notice Márcia occupies your time. Or perhaps not enough of it since my business ranks high for you?" I retort. Sure, it's a death wish to fuck with Borya. But I am the jokester of the family.

His glacial blues pin me as a rumble brews in his massive chest.

Bad idea, Harris? Ya think?

Then Borya guffaws and slaps me on the shoulder.

"Good one, *umnik!*" He responds.

"Yeah, Harris is a *smart ass!*" Malcolm translates. "The best we have."

Patrick Rockett—once a bitter rival of STEELE International with his family's multibillion-dollar construction firm—roars with laughter. The Scotsman adds his commentary gleefully.

My gaze returns to Kat.

She sits on the white leather sofa between Vivian and

Márcia Souza. The Brazilian spitfire and Starr's assistant has the giant Russian wrapped around her pinky finger. Just as much as Kat has me.

Sure, I've given her my *good lovin'*. But it's also the release of the burden she has to worry about Stewart, compounded with making up to everyone for her erroneous actions. He's gone for good, and we've forgiven her.

Watching her laugh easily with Lola makes me smile. I feared Kat's lies about her parents' death in a car accident would ruin any chance she had to regain Lola's affection. My sister-in-law truly lost her parents to a drunk driver. This past month my sister and my girlfriend grew closer than before.

The kidnapping changed a lot for all of us. Life is too short to hold on to the past. Time for the future. And a beautiful one, I muse as I grin at gorgeous My Kitty Kat.

Even from this distance, her emerald green eyes shine with joy. Warmth floods her alabaster cheeks with a rosy hue. The sunlight sparks on her Titian hair as it swirls around her face with each bob of her head. Her tinkling laughter at something Vivian said makes my heart swell.

My Kitty Kat high fives Yessenia Rodriguez—who captured Laurent's heart. The Southern Belle twang of Billie Chandler—Lola's Coterie's Chief Operating Officer and Patrick's love—rings out. Adrienne Anthony—Anton's girl and SLFW's Co-CEO—reaches over and nudges Starr, who giggles as she flicks her sorrel brown eyes towards Malcolm. She catches my stare and whispers to My Kitty Kat.

She glances at me and blows a kiss, at which the girls fall out in laughter. With a wink, she returns her attention to her friends.

Yup. Life is definitely moving forward in the best possible way.

"I THOUGHT MAUI PHENOMENAL... But, Harris, this... Oh my... Absolutely breathtaking!"

Kat whispers in awe, eyes glued to the scene outside the window as we prepare to land on Laucala Island.

The luxury private island surrounded by varied depths of turquoise waters Malcolm purchased for Starr still makes me ogle like a newcomer. The tropical paradise's pristine white sand beaches and lush landscape in an explosion of vibrant colors dazzle the eyes and temper any stressed mind.

Not only does Laucala Island serve as the location for a LEVELS resort and SLFW center, but our family also has twelve villas secluded on the other side. Each residence sits directly on the pristine beach or perched on the cliffside with jaw-dropping views of the expansive Pacific Ocean.

"Wait until we go on a hike through the interior. There's a spectacular waterfall under which we swim in the refreshing water. You'll love it!" Starr says, delighted by My Kitty Kat's reaction.

I watch their interaction with a smile. A movement by Malcolm draws my gaze to him.

He flutters his eyelashes à la Anton then smirks when I

roll my eyes skyward. Like he did not lose himself in his *Angel* from the moment they met...

The jet lands, and we disembark to a row of silver Range Rover SVAutobiographys. The drivers take our luggage as we wait around the SUVs. We watch as the jet carrying those based in Europe lands moments later.

My Kitty Kat waves as Haley and Leonie walk down the steps. Blair Thomas—Lola's Coterie's Chief Marketing Officer—walks out next. They wave back as Lachlan, Roger, and Luc Montaigne—the French multibillionaire bank scion and Blair's love—follow them off Luc's Gulfstream G700.

Squeals erupt as the girls run to each other. Heads bob, arms clutch, feet dance as they greet one another. Their excited chatter fills the air.

I laugh along with the guys at their excitement for our Couples' Getaway. We exchange bro hugs and claps on the shoulder. Then wait for our women to glance our way before we round them up into the SUVs. With a promise to meet at Malcolm and Starr's beachfront villa for breakfast, we head to the residences.

On the ride to the other side of the island, I point out the roads leading to LEVELS Laucala Island and to Starr Light Fitness and Wellness Laucala Island. Signs handcrafted by local artisans announce what's ahead for guests. Palm trees and flowery bushes line the roads to welcome them to a sinful paradise. The buildings surrounded by the foliage sit tucked back from the primary thoroughfare.

My Kitty Kat cranes her neck for a better view as we drive by, then turns in her seat to face me.

"I can't wait to see this LEVELS! Haley told me how incredible it is. Perhaps we can go tonight?" The redheaded Siren asks with a seductive smile on her gorgeous face. Emerald green eyes glow full of carnal lust.

I lean over and grip the back of her neck. Drawing her to me, I lower my mouth within centimeters from her full lips. Our breath mingles as I stare deep into her eyes. The pupils dilate as her breath comes out in puffs. The sweet scent entices me closer.

My mouth captures hers in a searing kiss. Teeth nip until her lips part. The tip of my tongue rims just inside her wet warmth. On a needy moan, the Siren opens wider and laps at my tongue like a naughty kitten. I angle her head to retake control of the kiss and plunder her mouth. My tongue replicates the thrusts of my cock in her lower, wet warmth.

Breathy moans make my cock twitch. Delicate fingers skim along the outline of my burgeoning erection as it lengthens between my joggers and thigh. A naughty pinch to the tip makes me groan in need.

Hell yeah, we can go to LEVELS tonight!

We arrive at my villa. My Kitty Kat's jaw drops at the sight of four sprawling bures—traditional Fijian men's houses nestled against the cliff amongst tropical flowers and trees. Between the two main bures, the glistening turquoise waters of the Pacific Ocean spreads out as far as the eye can see.

"This must be what an eagle's aerie feels like high above the ground with the gentle breeze of the wind," My Kitty Kat says when we step out of the SUV. She spins in a circle, arms spread wide like an eagle's wings. "Incredible, Harris. It's only yours?"

I grin and pull her into my arms, nuzzling her neck as I nod.

"Welcome to my love nest in the clouds, Kitty Kat," I murmur against her soft skin. Her fragrance proves more alluring than the seductive scent of the surrounding frangipani. "Ready to play hide and seek?"

She melds her body against mine as she palms my ass, my erection thick between us.

"You promised breakfast," she breathes.

I chuckle wickedly and nip the sensitive juncture at her neck and shoulder. She whimpers.

"Oh, I promise you a full meal," I respond as I grind my cock against her lower belly.

She squeals as I toss her over my shoulder and carry her to the bure for my bedroom suite. Her squeals turn into cries of passion as I fill her belly, then her pussy, with my seed.

"Well, well, well, look who decided to join us."

"Um, you almost missed breakfast, slowpokes."

I help My Kitty Kat into a chair at the table and smirk at Laurent and Haley.

"Oh, I guarantee you I ate, and Kat had more than her fill," I say.

Haley scowls and covers her ears.

"Harris, please! Spare me the details of your sex life. Ugh!" She says as she rolls her eyes.

Laurent snickers and Yessenia nudges him.

"Don't encourage him, *Mi Amor*," the Latina beauty chides, then turns her tawny brown eyes to My Kitty Kat. "What are we going to do with these two cavemen?"

Laurent slides the curtain of waist-length curly black hair aside and leans over to kiss her slim neck. He murmurs indecipherable words in Spanish to his love. Her golden brown cheeks blush crimson. She takes a sip of water. He sits back and drapes his arm over her shoulders, then throws a smug look at me.

I chuckle and shake my head. The rascal. That's my boy!

"And so anyway… I believe Starr was in the middle of sharing plans for today," Haley says to Laurent and to me pointedly. Then she shifts her gaze and smiles saccharine sweetly. "Starr, kindly continue despite the nature of that unnecessary interruption."

Starr hides her smile behind a sip of pomegranate juice before she tells us we have a free day with a sunset dinner at Lucien's villa. After which those who wish to play can head to LEVELS LI for Masquerade Night, as she and Malcolm plan to enjoy, Starr adds with a wanton grin. He pulls her in for a possessive kiss.

"Not you, too!" Haley groans. She throws her white

linen napkin onto the table and plops back against her chair, arms folded over her chest.

Lachlan holds her chin between his thumb and index finger and kisses her silly. When they part, she swoons.

"Now you were saying, Haley, dear twin?" I ask.

Her cheeks flush a darker shade of red before she tucks her face into Lachlan's neck.

"Exactly!" Laurent and I say at the same time.

Everyone laughs.

Once we finish breakfast, Laurent and I take Yessenia and My Kitty Kat for a tour. We stop by our villas to add bathing suits under our clothes and to grab towels and bottled waters, then take the scenic route around the perimeter of the island.

As we ride along in a Range Rover, we point out different spots. The girls can't get enough of the island's natural beauty. Even Yessenia—who was born and raised on Puerto Rico—appreciates this island's allure.

Laurent and I lead the girls blindfolded along a narrow sandy path cut through palm trees. They giggle and cling to our arms to keep their balance. When the path ends, we pause to remove the red silk from around their heads. The girls gasp at the sight of the empty white sand beach set in a secluded cove.

"*Mi Amor!* This is unbelievable," Yessenia exclaims.

My Kitty Kat claps her hands and darts ahead. She pulls her cotton dress over her head and tosses it to the sand. She spins around, kicking her sandals off and beckons to us.

"Last one in is a rotten egg!" She yells, then pivots back towards the waves.

"Not me!" Yessenia shouts as she dashes after My Kitty Kat.

Laurent and I exchange glances. I shove him aside and race after the girls.

"Guess it'll be Laurent!" I laugh as I grab the back of my t-shirt and yank it off. Then grunt when something hits me between the shoulder blades. Laurent's flip flop falls to the sand. My hesitation gives him the advantage, and he charges ahead with a war cry.

Our Alpha male competition surges through us.

Not to be outdone, I catch up to him before he reaches the water's edge. A well-aimed foot makes him stumble. I dive into the first wave and reemerge next to My Kitty Kat triumphantly.

"Take that, take that, take that!" I chortle at Laurent as he lopes into the water.

"Fucker," he mutters.

Yessenia glides over to him and wraps her arms around his neck. She kisses his lips, then jumps back. Water splashes around them.

"Peeyoo! You stink, Rotten Egg!" She giggles as she fans a delicate hand across her face.

Laurent growls and lunges towards her. With ease, he grabs Yessenia's waist and tosses her backwards through the air.

She yowls as her arms and legs windmill far above the

water's surface. She drops below, then pops back up, spluttering a string of curses in Spanish.

Laurent sloshes over and swoops her into his arms. He covers her face with kisses until giggling, she pushes him away. He doesn't let go. Instead, he floats her onto her back with her head against his shoulder.

"I hear you can put even the mighty Great White Shark into a catatonic state if you flip one upside-down. Perhaps it'll work on my fiery Yessenia," Laurent says with a laugh.

She huffs but lets him float her around.

I stand with a goofy grin on my face as I watch my partner in playadom so in love. We've come a long way from our nights—and days—of fucking around. He and Yessenia make a great couple whose love is unbreakable. But that's for another story…

"This is truly spectacular, Harris."

My Kitty Kat draws me from my lovestruck musings.

I turn to her and cup her cheeks. The pad of my thumb brushes across her mouth. She parts her lips and sucks the digit into her warm wetness. She hums. I groan.

The zing shoots from my thumb to my cock like a lightning bolt.

"The way you tempt me, Siren," I murmur in her ear. "If we were alone, I'd put your mouth to good use…"

She laughs huskily and pulls harder on my thumb. My cock throbs. It wants in on the action.

With a shake of my head, I pop the moist digit from her mouth. She pouts.

"Later at LEVELS," I promise.

. . .

"Fuck, Siren… Take me deeper… Uunnhhh, yes…"

Less than an hour passed since the redheaded Siren and I arrived at the club for LEVELS Laucala Island—the five-star beachfront resort spans across several buildings around the club. After an eye-opening tour of the seven levels for her, we settled in a private alcove.

Instead of being like the other clubs in one building, each level exists in different Fijian bures. Or rather Malcolm and Lucien's luxurious versions of the traditional Fijian men's houses. As always, they play on the local area when they design a club. Beverly Hills is within a famous Hollywood costume designer's atelier and storefront with a view of the iconic Hollywood Sign.

Here, the Sky Lounge in the 7th bure sits on the beach with stunning views of the sunset over the Pacific Ocean and a bar, restaurant by day, dance club by night, with a coverable pool to extend the dance floor. The bure for the 6th and 5th levels that comprise the multilevel dance club with two bars and a lounge for food and drinks sits to one side of the Sky Lounge. On the other side, the 4th level bure has the Level 4 Restaurant and bar open for breakfast, lunch, and dinner. Rising above the dance club and built into the cliffside is the 3rd level with a two-story bure for twelve private bedrooms where members can continue their pleasure apart from the BDSM levels. Next to it above the Sky Lounge is the bure for the 2nd Level Peepshow for BDSM with seating alcoves, main stage, performance rooms, and a bar that serves non-alcoholic mocktails. A bure serves as the entrance where the 1st level Cellar BDSM dungeon with mocktails bar built directly into the cliff as a giant cave as opposed to being below ground. Covered paths lead from one bure to the other for an interconnecting city of consensual sin.

Overall, my boys did an amazing job recreating LEVELS to match the tropical island vibe while maintaining its core purpose. As Starr says, it's BDSM on the Beach at its finest.

And the way my sexy Siren deep throats my cock is on par with our surroundings.

My head hangs back as the cords in my neck tighten. The first tingling of my climax swirls in my belly. My ass tightens as my hands lock her head in place. The anticipation builds. An epic release promised.

Her enthusiastic hum vibrates over my engorged shaft. She swallows, and the motion ripples along my length.

My hips pump as I rise to the balls of my feet. The angle changes. My heavy balls draw up, ready for the release rolling down my spine.

With a feral roar, my seed spews down her throat straight into her hungry belly. Shockwaves roll through me. I sway on my feet. White light flashes before my eyes squeezed shut in pure ecstasy.

"Fuuuck…"

My grip of her hair lessens. The silky tresses slip from my fingers as she leans back on her heels. My cock pops from her mouth, leaving a trail of saliva from the tip.

The sexy Siren winks up at me as the tip of her little pink tongue darts out. She licks my cock clean from root to tip. She watches with a smug expression on her beautiful face as I stuff my junk back into my leather pants.

I hoist her up from a cushion on the floor into my arms and carry her to the oversized vamp red leather bench. She curls up on my lap like a good little Kitty Kat. My head rests against the wall as I stroke her back, breaths evening out. She purrs contentedly.

My mind drifts to earlier. We may be at a LEVELS club. But I'm with *my* woman. The only one I want. Forever.

Yeah, the players have come a long way from fucking around. No doubt.

"It's just a little further to go. Come on. You got this!"

My body groans in protest, despite Starr's encouragement. We were up late last night with dinner and a bonfire on the beach in front of Lachlan and Haley's villa. When Harris and I returned to ours, he worshipped my body like I was the goddess of love. For hours.

Now, he squeezes my hand and smiles down at me as we trudge behind the others. We're headed to the waterfall as the grand finale for our Couples' Getaway. Besides the amazing sight, Starr promises a refreshing swim in the cool waters and a delicious lunch courtesy of Lucien. Once we return to the villas, everyone will have the rest of the day and evening to themselves. The perfect ending for an incredible trip.

So, sure I can go along with this hike.

I grin up at Harris and return the squeeze.

We continue for another twenty minutes. The beauty of the island's interior makes the time less of a hassle and more of a walk through paradise. Harris points out colorful birds and butterflies as they flit amongst the lush vegetation surrounding us. He plucks a white flower from a bush and places it behind my ear.

"Add to your beauty, Kitty Kat," Harris murmurs.

My heart swells. This man has me good. And I couldn't be happier!

"All right! Here we are!"

Starr's words make me glance in her direction. She stands with her arms outstretched. Behind her, the path widens to reveal the dazzling waters of the waterfall. The sun sparkles on them as they rush from the cliff down to the lake. The burble of the water fills the air as it splashes. A mist hovers above the surface.

It's a majestic sight to behold.

Starr beckons us forward.

It only gets better.

The area opens up to include a carpet of green grass around the lake circled by palm trees and flowering bushes. To one side stands a white gauzy canopy with its four posts covered in ropes of frangipani. It floats above tables with floral bouquets at their center. Chairs have more gauzy material draped over them with bows in the back and wreaths of flowers. The billowy topper blows in the gentle breeze. Another canopy floats above a table laden with platters covered by silver domes and buckets of Champagne. Servers stand at the ready.

"Time for the swim I promised you!" Starr calls out.

I grin at Harris.

He nods and leads me to the area where blankets spread out over the grass. He stops beside one and kneels. His hand takes mine.

"Oh, I can get my boots off, Harris!" I giggle as I tug my hand. "No need for you to do it, silly."

He bites his lower lip and shakes his head. His mouth opens, then closes. He gives his head another shake before he peeks up at me. A cough clears his throat.

"Kat… You make me feel what no one ever has. Or ever will. I never want to spend a day of my life without you by my side. Each day I awake, it's your face I want to see first. And every night the last. I love you more than you can ever know."

He pulls a little navy blue box from his shirt pocket.

My mouth gapes.

His eyes return to mine.

"Kat Jackson, will you become Kat Steele? Will you marry me?"

The top of the box opens at the press of the sapphire cabochon. Nestled in navy silk rests the biggest diamond I've ever seen in my life. The massive stone shoots sparks of fire as it glitters in the sunlight.

Tears fill my eyes as my mouth opens and closes. Words prove impossible to form.

I fall to my knees before Harris and throw my arms around his neck as I nod fervently. My entire body shakes.

He bands his arms around me, holding me close to his

powerful chest. The beat of his heart as fast in tempo as mine pounding against my ribs. He presses his lips to the shell of my ear.

"Words. I will have your words," Harris commands.

"Yes! Absolutely, positively, yes!" I respond.

Harris leans back and places the engagement ring on my finger. My hand trembles slightly, and he brings it to his lips. As he kisses the diamond, his eyes bore into mine.

In that moment, I know just how much Harris loves me.

Clapping and whoops rise around us.

I startle, having forgotten everything and everyone but Harris. He grins bigger than the Cheshire Cat as he stands and pulls me off my feet. He swings me around as his shout joins the others' hollers. I throw my head back and scream yes for all the world to hear.

Harris' mouth finds mine. He kisses me breathless. I cling to him to remain anchored to this world while my heart soars to the heavens. The words I love you run on repeat in my mind.

Once he settles me on my feet, hands grab me. My girls pull me in for hugs and kisses. They admire my ring—as big as the diamonds on their left hands. Vivian most of all, even though she's yet to find her Prince Charming. Their words of best wishes and welcome to the Steele family fill me with immense joy. My face aches from the huge smile.

I catch glimpses of Harris being bro hugged and getting slaps on the back by his boys. The happiness on his face adds to my joy. He catches my eye and winks.

Servers walk amongst us with trays of Champagne in

crystal flutes. Harris grabs two and saunters over to me. I bite the corner of my mouth as I watch him approach. He holds out a flute, then wraps his arm around my waist. Melded to his side, I raise my flute with his.

"To my gorgeous fiancée. May her love for me never end!" Harris exclaims.

"Hear! Hear!"

"Salud!"

"Salutations!"

Boisterous cheers ring out louder than the waterfall cascading behind us.

I rise onto my toes and offer my mouth to my fiancé.

Harris captures it for another toe-curling kiss. He bends me over his arm as our tongues tangle. Wolf whistles and calls for get a room make us laugh. He sets me right and bows for the crowd.

I cover my kiss-swollen mouth with my hand and giggle.

The glint of my princess-cut diamond catches my eye—twenty-three carats, Lola assures me. I give a shriek and wiggle my hand in the air. My girls stomp their feet and clap.

"Ah, yes, our Laucala Island brings out the most romance in everyone—including Harris, the last man standing of The STEELE Quaternity!" Malcolm announces with a tilt of his head. "Right, My Angel?" He pulls Starr into his side and nuzzles her neck.

Harris agrees and tugs me closer, then plants a kiss on my temple.

"Let's take a dip in the lake to cleanse the old and prepare for the new," Starr—ever the yogi—suggests.

Everyone agrees, and we strip down to our swimsuits.

Harris swoops me from my feet and carries bride-like into the sparkling azure water. He keeps me close as he dips below the surface. I squeal and cling to his neck, then gasp as he rises. He slings his wet hair and chuckles as I duck from the deluge.

"Are you happy, Kitty Kat?" Harris asks with a grin wider than the Cheshire Cat's.

I cup his face between my palms. My lips slant over his. I let the passion of my kiss answer for me. Words can never be enough to express my absolute happiness. The man I love asked me to be his wife, to live our lives together forever. How can joy not fill me?

Loud catcalls and wolf whistles break out around my fiancé and me. Laurent tells us to get a bure; Haley groans.

I press my forehead to Harris' and smile.

"I love you, Harris Steele," I whisper.

His dove gray eyes gleam.

"I love you, Kat Jackson, soon-to-be Kat Steele," he murmurs.

After our swim, we gather at the buffet table to select our lunch. The servers fill fresh glasses of Champagne.

I stand at my seat. My gaze goes from one to the other before it settles on Harris. I raise my flute.

"Harris, I promise to love you for all time and to give you all the joy you give to me and more," I say, then glance around the table again. "To my family, I thank you for allowing me back into your lives—permanently!"

More boisterous cheers fill the air.

Once we're settled, Leonie turns to me.

"So, *chérie*, I'm sure I speak for all the girls. We'd love to help you plan your wedding!" She says as her feline amber eyes glitter.

Lola claps.

"Most definitely, Kat! Not to mention the Sergeant and Lieutenant," she says gleefully.

Starr snorts and shakes her head. Her long, dark brown curls bounce around her face. Dimples deepen as she giggles.

"I'd love for you to help me. But I'm sort of in the dark. Who are the sergeant and lieutenant?" I ask.

"Oh, Sergeant Shelley and Lieutenant Lucie. Being you're a Jackson marrying a Steele, they're bound to handle your wedding planning as they did with me. Lola, Leonie, and Starr had the Sergeant for their nuptials," Haley responds with a grin. "But of course, your Mum will have as much say as they have—well, and you, too!"

"Maybe!" Starr says with a hearty laugh. "At least you can hope. But they know their stuff, and my mom helped, too."

I agree to their help wholeheartedly.

I do not know how to handle a society wedding to a multibillionaire. The closest I've come to one are the photographs in magazines and newspapers of socialites smiling up into the faces of their equally handsome husbands at their posh weddings. Their gowns master-pieces in couture. Engagement rings and wedding bands glitter. Incredible backdrops for their nuptials: cathedrals, castles, ballrooms. Incredible. Or rather incredibly intim-idating…

"So, Harris, how much time will you give your soon-to-be wife time to plan?"

Roger's question draws me from my thoughts.

I shift my gaze to Harris.

"None," He smirks.

The girls and I gasp. The guys chuckle.

"That sounds about right to me," Sebastian adds.

Harris uses his index finger beneath my chin to close my mouth. He leans over and kisses me softly.

"Only kidding, Kitty Kat," he says. "If it were up to me, we'd get married right now, right here. But I want you to have the wedding of your dreams. Well, as long as it's within this year. I won't wait but so long to make you my wife, Kat Jackson, soon-to-be Kat Steele."

Tears fill my eyes, and I nod. I say a silent prayer of thanks for this man who's so good to me. I close my eyes as he swipes the tears with the pad of his thumb. He murmurs words of love, and I bury my face in his chest. Strong arms hold me close. The rhythmic beat of his heart soothes me.

"Aaawwww… It's too much! My little girl grows up." Vivian exclaims.

Everyone laughs, including me through my tears of happiness.

The rest of lunch goes by with more talk of wedding

ideas. I'll need time to think of where to have it. New York City makes sense with Harris having a bigger family and most based there. But I wouldn't mind a destination wedding. So many choices. For now, I want to revel in our engagement.

My gaze slides to my left hand. The princess-cut diamond winks at me as the sunlight sparks on its massive surface. Who would have thought a girl like me would have such an opulent ring?

"It's a family heirloom. Do you like it, Kitty Kat?"

Harris' softly spoken words filter through my admiration of my engagement ring.

I wrap my arms around his neck and hug him close as I tell him just how much I love it. Nothing could be better or make me happier. It's simply stunning. Just as incredible as the rings my future sisters-in-law have on their left hands.

We take another swim in the lake and pose for photos beneath the waterfall. I float on the hike back to the main road where SUVs await us. If Harris weren't holding my hand, I'd float up above the fronds of the tallest palm trees.

We pile into the vehicles and head back to our villas. Once inside Harris', he leads me onto the terrace overlooking the Pacific Ocean. We sit on a sunbed, and he pulls his mobile from his pocket.

"When it's later in the day in Scotland, we can call your Mum. I'm sure she'll want to know you said yes—"

"She knows?" I cut in.

He lowers his gaze as his cheeks flush.

"I asked Allison for your hand in marriage, Kitty Kat," he responds sheepishly.

My heart leaps. My fiancé—the undisputed playboy—went traditional and asked my Mum if he could marry me? Holy mackerel! This man loves me truly.

I crawl onto his lap and kiss him silly.

"Well, I wanted to call my parents and let them know. But I guess that can wait until later, too," Harris says huskily as he squeezes my ass with his sizable hands.

"Mmmhhhmm..." I purr as I nip his full lower lip.

Hours later, Sergeant Shelley and Lieutenant Lucie eagerly agree to report for wedding duty as soon as I return to New York City. After dinner, my Mum recalls how Harris called her. She wishes us the best and reminds us how love conquers all.

Later that night, as I rest my head on Harris' chest in bed, I say another silent prayer of thanks. We have the support and love of our family. I cannot wait to become Mrs. Harris Steele!

KAT

"Sydney? As in Sydney in Australia? Well, that's different. Are you sure? Not here or Glasgow?" Harris' befuddled face makes me giggle.

I finally decided where I'd like us to have our wedding. Sure, people would expect New York City or Glasgow as the location. But it was in Sydney—Australia!—I started fresh and on my quest to get my man back. It's the perfect place for us to start our new life together as husband and wife.

"Yes, Sydney in Australia," I respond, suppressing another giggle. I continue when Harris cocks an eyebrow questioningly. "Last New Year's Eve, I wanted to start the New Year in the first big city to celebrate. So I flew to Sydney, Australia. It represented a fresh start before I started my new job in New York City. And where I vowed to get my man back—you!"

A smile spreads across Harris' handsome face as he absorbs my words.

"So, you began your Siren's mission in Sydney, Kitty Kat?" He asks.

I bite the corner of my lower lip and nod.

"Okay, sounds good. I'll go along with it," he says. "Now, when?"

"New Year's Eve?" I say cautiously since he wanted to get married before the year ends and that's the last day of the year.

As I guessed, Harris groans and falls back against the sofa.

"Kat, you are killing me, babe! That's eight months away! I know I said before the year ends. But did you really have to choose the absolute last minute?!" He bemoans, eyes squeezed shut and brows knit.

I cup his cheek and rub it as I purr.

He pulls away with a huff.

"Seriously?" He asks.

I nod, "Seriously. But look on the bright side. I won't make you wait to have sex until after we're married, like Haley did Lachlan."

Harris pales.

"No… way…" he asks in astonishment.

If his eyes weren't open, I'd assume he would need smelling salts to revive him. The thought of having no sex for eight months finishes him off.

"Yup. So it's not so bad after all, huh?" I respond with a

giggle, then yelp when I land on my back with Harris looming above me.

His dove gray eyes flash.

"Not so bad after all, huh? Not *so* bad?! I'll show you bad, Siren,"* he growls.

The tank top I wear gets yanked above my head and wind around my wrists. Harris stretches my arms and presses them against the armrest. My boobs bounce as he wrenches my yoga pants and G-string down my legs. He tosses the garments over his shoulder.

His eyes narrow as they sear a path from my face to my heaving breasts, pausing at my pulsing pussy, then down to my parted thighs. He mutters *bad* under his breath as he grabs the back of his t-shirt and rips it over his head.

Biceps bulge. Pecs and eight-pack abs flex.

I dare a peek at his crotch. The outline of his burgeoning erection clear beneath his gray joggers makes my mouth water. I wiggle my hips to entice him. Then yowl when he spanks my exposed pussy.

"Do. Not. Move. Naughty lass," he commands.

I can't help but to shudder at his dominance. Another spank gets me to focus. *Stay still, Kat Jackson!*

Harris grips the backs of my thighs and lifts them to his shoulders as he lowers his torso to the sofa cushion. My gaze travels down the planes of my body to watch him. His flattened tongue darts out to lave my seam from start to clit.

A low moan escapes my mouth as I try my best to hold

position. My fists clench above my head. Arms press deeper into the armrest to ground me.

Harris repeats the erotic taste of my pussy. The juices of my arousal coat his tongue. I lie there, mesmerized by the sight of him feasting on my cream.

One thick finger joins his tongue. It curls inside my pussy to stroke my G-spot.

My pussy clenches. My back bows. The sensation in my lower belly intensifies. I cry out.

WHAP. WHAP. WHAP.

The orgasm that barreled towards me dissipates with each spank of my pussy. I yowl in pain instead of scream in pleasure. My eyes snap open to glare at Harris.

"Hey! What the *bloody hell* was that for?" I snarl.

He wipes my cream from his mouth and chin onto my inner thighs, then gives me a smug look.

"You will not cum until I say you can, naughty lass," he answers.

Now it's my turn to throw my head back against the sofa. Eyes squeezed shut and brows knit in frustration. I growl.

Harris returns to his torture.

Each time an orgasm is within reach, he stops and smirks at me. My body shakes. No coherent thought possible. I'm wound tight with no relief in sight.

"Eight!" Harris pronounces.

I can't even begin to ask what the bloody hell eight means. But I don't have long to wonder.

"One lost orgasm for each month I lose having you as

my wife, naughty lass," he continues triumphantly. He sits back on his haunches and smirks at me. "Now, should I allow you the pleasure to cum?"

Unable to formulate words, I nod.

Harris takes pity on me and lets my non-verbal response slide. He stands and strips out of his joggers. Once again, my thighs go over his shoulders. He aligns the mushroom head of his cock to my swollen pussy lips. One hand bands around my waist while the fingers of the other entwine with my fingers above my head.

With one thrust, he seats himself within my core fully. Hip bones grind into mine. His heavy balls slap my ass. I scream his name.

Harris jackhammers into me. My pussy walls clamp on his thick, ten-inch dick, never wanting it to leave. I writhe beneath him and beg to cum.

"Cum for me, naughty lass. Cum all over my cock. Coat it with your cream," he growls between grunts.

White light blinds me. Stars dance behind my closed eyes. My body stiffens. Toes curl. Tears of carnal bliss stick on my eyelashes. A wail from the depths of my soul pours from my slack mouth. I convulse from the strength of my climax.

Harris grunts as my pussy holds his cock in a vise-like grip. His fingers dig into my hip as he fuses our groins together. His cock swells deep inside of my core.

"MINE!!!" He roars as he bathes my pussy with his hot seed.

The world ceases to exist as I float free. A moment

later, the weight of Harris as he collapses on top of me brings me back to Earth. I wrap my arms around him and stroke his back to soothe him as tremors run through his body.

"Sydney as in Australia in eight months, huh?" He murmurs against my sweat-slicked neck.

A smile blooms on my face as I respond, "Sydney—as in Australia—in eight months."

* * *

"Oh Harris, sweetheart, you won't have to sit through all our planning. But you do need to pay attention for this first one!"

"Exactly, Harris, honey!"

I giggle at Sergeant Shelley and Lieutenant Lucie's attempts to keep Harris from his mobile.

We're in Shelley's home office in her STEELE Tower duplex penthouse on the fifty-seventh and fifty-sixth floors where she and Morgan live on the top two floors. If one considers three generously sized rooms an office. An anteroom for two assistants' desks, a sitting area, and a bathroom, a conference room, and her inner sanctum with an en suite bathroom comprise Shelley's version of a home office. She runs her private activities from here and her foundation work from that office on the executive floor of the corporate office.

Vivian, Lola, Starr, and two wedding planners sit with us at the table. Along with Lucie, my Mum, Charlotte,

Haley, and Leonie join us via video conference. The girls giggle at Harris' disinterest, too.

"Mom, Aunt Lucie, I love you with all my heart. But this is just not my thing. I will honor whatever Kat wants; Kat can have. Okay?" He tells them.

They glance at one another, then shrug.

"Fine. Go along and make some other techie gadget then," Shelley says.

"Leave the actual work to us!" Lucie chimes in.

Harris leaps from the chair, kisses me, then his Mum and aunt and blows a kiss to my Mum. He waves at the girls as he rushes from the office without a backwards glance.

We laugh, then get back to business.

"So first things first. Location and date," Sergeant Shelley says. Her Montblanc champagne gold rollerball pen hovers over her Smythson of Bond Street leather-bond notebook. She gave each of us a matching pen and note-book to track our responsibilities for the wedding planning.

I take a breath and hope she doesn't have the same reaction her son did to Sydney. Just the thought of him edging me eight times makes my pussy moisten and soften. I feel my cheeks heat. Prayerfully, no one can guess my thoughts…

"Sydney and December 31," I respond.

Lucie coughs. I shift my gaze to her on the television monitor. She arches an elegant brow.

"As in Australia?" She asks.

My shoulders shake as I laugh out loud. Everyone stares at me, but I can't stop. They give me a moment to get it together.

"So sorry! It's funny because Harris said the exact same thing!" I say as I fan my reddened face.

I go on to explain my choices, and they agree it's a good idea. Besides, as they tell me, they've had their fair share of exotic destination weddings. So why not Sydney as in Australia!

"We have the STEELE Sydney we can use for the ceremony and the reception. It has a superior view to the Park Hyatt Sydney," Haley says with the same smug expression as her twin.

Shelly and Lucie nod. We update our notebooks.

"Well, other than Starr, Monsieur Valentino created couture gowns for us. Even though it's become a tradition, do you have another designer in mind, *chérie*?" Leonie asks. "I can get any of them to make your gown and other dresses. Just say the word."

"And of course, Lola's Coterie will create your signature lingerie trousseau! We know Harris' favorites for you," Lola says with a wink.

My mind races at the thought of a Valentino original wedding gown. Few have the opportunity to wear his custom creations. It goes beyond my wildest fantasies. I nod vigorously.

"I would love for Monsieur Valentino to design my dresses," I respond as I clap gleefully. "*C'est incroyable, merci beaucoup!*"

Shelley agrees she and I will call his atelier after the meeting.

Lucie speaks up next.

"Now, Allison and Kat, you have to come up with your list of guests. We'll need names and addresses. I will handle the nobility and royalty, along with Scottish and European society. Shelley will handle the Western Hemisphere. But we need to know what size wedding you prefer—intimate or all out."

Butterflies swirl in my belly. Not nobility and royalty! I hadn't considered the Jackson side of my family and them being nobles and all that comes along with it.

I glance at my Mum, and she's just as awestruck. But she smiles at me and nods encouragingly.

"Other than Kat's siblings and a few friends, I'll leave the list to you ladies. You'll know best," she says. "And Kat, love, you shine as bright as any noble, royal, or society lady."

"That's right!" Charlotte pipes up with a grin.

Their remarks ease the butterflies. I grin back at my Mum and my sister.

"Yes!" I whoop. "As far as my list, Vivian and Isla. I'll leave the rest to you and Mum Shelley, including the wedding size. You'll know best."

They nod and tell me I have no reason to feel less than anyone. They assure me I'm noble since I'm a descendant of the Marquess of Huntly and I can use the title Lady. Combined with me as Jackson becoming a Steele, I rank higher than the majority. Their words dispel the remaining butterflies.

I sit back and beam at everyone.

"Well, we settled the most important items on our agenda. Kat and I will call Mr. Valentino. Then we'll have lunch at La Goulue," Shelley says with a smile.

"Oh, I'm so jealous! I love La Goulue! You must get the *Moules sauce "Poulette!" Non, non, le Pavé de saumon aux lentils!*" Leonie exclaims.

Lola laughs.

"We know you and your favorite restaurant, Leonie! I'll savor each bite just for you!" She tells her best friend, who sticks her tongue out at her teasing.

Sergeant Shelley and I go to her interior office to make the call. Monsieur Valentino himself comes to the phone and tells us how very pleased he is to continue the Steele tradition. I share my thoughts on the wedding dress, and he promises to have sketches ready in a few days. We plan to meet in Paris for me to select one and my first fitting.

While we eat delicious dishes at La Goulue, Shelley turns to me.

"Kat, sweetheart, Harris tells me you're the Development Director for a children's nonprofit and your university background," she says, then continues when I nod. "Well, we believe in keeping things within the family. I'd like to show STEELE Foundation to you. You would be a great addition to us."

I'm surprised by her request. But the idea of working at the family's foundation intrigues me. I would still do what

I love and it would go towards our family's endeavors. Children would still benefit from the affordable housing the foundation builds. So, it's a win-win situation.

I smile broadly at Shelley.

"I would love to see STEELE Foundation. Your work is incredible, and it would thrill me to be a part of it," I respond.

Shelley's smile matches mine.

"Excellent, Kat. You'll be a part of our family through and through!" She says, then arches an elegant eyebrow while the smile plays on her lips. "And speaking of children, when can I expect another grandchild?"

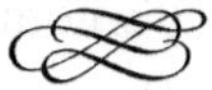

"How's the wedding planning going, bro? Leonie tells me Kat's been pretty busy."

Roger's question with a smirk makes me chuckle.

We're having lunch at one of Lucien's restaurants in Paris while My Kitty Kat has a fitting for her wedding dress. My Mom, Aunt Lucie, and Mum Allison are the privileged few who can see Kat's dresses. She wanted to keep her attire a surprise for everyone. Obviously, I want to see her in them during the parties and at our ceremony.

Over the past few weeks, she's blossomed under the attention my mother and my aunt have given her. Every day, My Kitty Kat tells me more of what she's learned about proper decorum for a *Lady* of her standing engaged to a man of mine. Her emerald eyes shine with happiness as she recalls guidance from Aunt Lucie.

I try not to laugh since I know My Kitty Kat takes it seriously. I understand her desire to make the right impression on people since her Mum raised her in a not so fortunate household. However, I couldn't care less about her upbringing. She's what matters. And I adore her. Tremendously.

She's also made herself at home in our penthouse. A great place before. Now, it's comfortable with her touch. She's blended her style with mine for a home we call our own. We added paintings of Iain's to the walls—after I told Little Lord Fauntleroy Kat can have some of her great great grandfather's artwork. If not for her, the Jacksons wouldn't have known anything about him or his creations.

The expression of pure joy on her face when she opened the crates made my heart swell. Giddily, she pointed out which walls she wanted to hang the four paintings—including the one of Iain's muse and her great great grandmother in repose. I want nothing but happiness for My Kitty Kat.

When we parted in front of STEELE Place Vendôme, she hugged me fiercely and whispered, *I love you* before she slid into the back of the Rolls-Royce Phantom.

So, yeah, wedding planning is going well. Very well indeed.

"Pretty good, bro. No complaints from me," I respond with a cocky grin.

Roger chuckles.

Our father clears his throat. We shift our gazes to him.

"Harris, you make your mother and I proud of you, son. You followed your heart and made a tough decision. Seeing you and Kat together proves you belong with each other. No matter what. Well done," he says.

His words fill me with contentedness. He and my mother encouraged me to follow my heart, and it paid off. Kat will be my wife—in seven months, that is. We'll have the rest of our lives together as a couple. What could be better?

"Thank you, Dad. That means a lot to me," I reply.

"Yeah, Harris, we're all happy for you," Roger adds.

I nod. It's good to have my family's support. That's what makes us Steeles. We always have each other's backs. Loyalty and love reign supreme.

"And I understand she accepted your mother's offer to work at STEELE Foundation. Another good move," my Dad says. "We can benefit from Kat's experience with development. Especially with the Annual Gala in a few months. Your mother says Kat is a natural."

I grin from ear to ear, proud of my fiancée. She'll definitely make a positive impact on our family's foundation. It makes sense for her to move into the role.

The rest of lunch we discuss business, my recent tech program, and summer plans. Since Kat and I will be married, we'll have to find a property near the family's beachfront compound in Southampton Village. I'm sure I can convince a neighbor to part with their home...

"HEY, babe. I didn't know you were back already. Why didn't you call me?"

I enter the Presidential Suite to find My Kitty Kat stretched out on one of the silk-upholstered sofas in the main salon. Her Titian hair piled atop her head in a sexy bun makes me want to fist it as I pin her beneath me. I shake my head to clear it of the lascivious thoughts.

She opens her arms to me with a big smile.

"Hey, yourself, fiancé," she responds. "I didn't want to interrupt your time with your father and Roger. You know, bro time and all."

I drop onto the sofa and pull her onto my lap. My mouth finds hers for a passionate kiss. I swallow her moans, hungry for more. My cock presses against the zipper of my trousers as it responds to her luscious curves.

I let her come up for air, and she cuddles against my chest.

"Wow. You really missed me, huh?" She says breathlessly.

I pat her hip and nod.

"Always, Kitty Kat," I murmur as I inhale her alluring perfume.

"Ditto, Harris Steele," she says with a contented sigh as she burrows further into me.

We recall our time apart. Her enthusiasm for her dresses makes me eager to see her walk down the aisle to me—in seven months...

"Oh, have you decided on our honeymoon yet?" She asks coyly.

I chuckle at yet another attempt to wrangle that info from me. My Kitty Kat is like a kitten with a ball of string

—she won't let it go for a minute. But as I told her the first dozen times she's asked me, it's a surprise.

"I think a stay at the hotel should suffice. What do you think?" I ask to mess with her.

She recoils as she gasps. Wide emerald green eyes stare at me. Her mouth opens and closes like a fish gaping.

I try my best not to laugh. But I fail.

She slaps my shoulder as I throw my head back and guffaw. She mutters how terrible I am under her breath and makes to rise from my lap.

I bind my arms around her while I continue to laugh.

"Harris! You're so mean!" My Kitty Kat wails. "You can't possibly mean that? Can you?"

Catching my breath, I decide not to keep her in suspense.

"No, I don't mean it," I respond, then go on when she sags in relief. "But if you don't stop asking me, I may change my mind, naughty lass."

She bows her head and sighs.

"Fine. Be a meanie, Harris Steele," she says glumly.

I cup her chin and turn her to face me. I kiss her lips softly.

"Do you trust me?" I ask. She nods, and I continue, "Well, leave it to me. I won't disappoint you, Kat Jackson, soon-to-be Kat Steele."

She settles back against me. I hold her for a bit more before we have to get ready for dinner with the fam downstairs in the restaurant run by Lucien.

While she's slipping black strappy sandals on her feet in

the dressing room, I come up behind her. My hands rest on her hips. She startles, but I hold her in place.

My red-headed Siren enthralls me in a white mini dress that hits mid-thigh. Capped sleeves and a scoop neckline make it sweet. But the laser cut-outs at the upper thigh and the hem make it sexy. Her Titian hair cascades down her back to brush the top curve of her ass like an arrow. And my bow is ready for its mark.

"Hey there, babe," I murmur against the side of her neck. "You look good enough to eat. We can skip dinner, you know."

She gives a throaty laugh as her head falls back against my shoulder.

"Now, who's naughty, Harris Steele? I think not. But we always have later…"

I chuckle and turn her to face me.

"I have something for you. Check my pockets," I instruct.

She bites her lower lip as her eyes gleam. Her hands reach into my trouser pockets, and I tell her to keep going when she pulls out one jewelry box. Diligently she dips into each pocket of my trousers and suit jacket. Six boxes sit atop the console when she's finished.

"Okay, open them," I tell her with a grin.

Her gasps grow as each box unveils platinum bangles encrusted with pavé diamonds. I place three on each of her wrists. Her smile widens with the click of the closures. She crosses her forearms in front of her breasts.

"Wonder Woman has nothing on these babies! Thank

you, my love!" She exclaims, then wraps her arms around my neck and kisses me.

"Am I still naughty?" I quip.

She purrs and rubs against me like a content kitten.

"No. But off to dinner we go!"

✱ ✱ ✱

"THANK you for letting us inside the Tower even though it's now your private space. It means a lot to my family to see where Iain painted."

My Kitty Kat has tears in her eyes as we stand in the lower level of the Tower at Jackson Castle. Once Iain's studio, then demolished by his father, and now lovingly restored by Lachlan for his and Haley's retreat, the Tower holds much history.

When we left Paris, we made a stop to Banff in Aberdeenshire, Scotland to visit them, Uncle Connor, and Aunt Lucie. Lachlan's offer to show My Kitty Kat and her family the Tower was as unexpected as it was kind.

Payton, Michael, and Charlotte flew in on Lachlan's helicopter from Glasgow to join us. Along with My Kitty Kat and Mum Allison, they stand in awe.

"Yes, thank you, Lachlan. This is special for us," Payton says. Again, surprising us with his maturity.

Lachlan acknowledges their words with a nod.

"You should see where it all began for you. My father will take you on a tour of Jackson Castle. It's his favorite pastime," Lachlan says, then takes Haley's hand. "Let's head back."

We climb into the Range Rovers for the ride back to the baroque mansion built in the early eighteenth century. I tell Allison and Kat's siblings how it replaced the original fortified castle the Jackson family erected two hundred years earlier. The giant status symbol has a four-story center structure with two grand curved east and west wings of three stories each. Six staircases, elaborate fireplaces, and elegant formal entertainment salons along with an extensive art collection make for a splendid interior.

I point out areas of the landscaped grounds that are just as spectacular as the castle with carriage drives and horse trails, walking paths, and a few ornamental buildings, including a chapel. Over five hundred acres along the coast of northeast Scotland comprise the Jackson family seat.

"The architecture is incredible. I can't wait to hear Connor's history on it all," Michael says from the third row.

I ask him about his studies, and his zeal makes me smile. He's most excited about his summer internship at STEELE Paris directly with Roger. Michael's updates carry us to the front door of the castle. He's so into it, he doesn't notice we stopped until Kat opens her door and hops out.

We laugh and head inside. Uncle Connor greets us exuberantly.

"There you are! Well, let's get started! Gather around here in the Great Hall," he booms. His love for Jackson Castle as strong as Michael's zest for architecture.

Although I've heard it countless times, I follow along holding My Kitty Kat's hand. As we pass through the myriad rooms, I whisper how I'll take her behind a tapestry and have my way with her. She tries to hide her giggles but fails.

Uncle Connor raises an eyebrow mid-sentence but doesn't stop his recounting of a battle as depicted in a large painting in the arms room.

I bow my head, and My Kitty Kat pokes me in the side. Her emerald eyes dance with mirth.

"Busted," she mouths.

We finish our tour on the stone terrace off the back of the castle. My niece and nephews nearly topple me as they jump into my arms.

"Whoa there, Leith!" I call out as I catch the second oldest of Haley's triplets. Lilias—the eldest and only girl—wraps her arms around my leg while Lewis jumps on my back. "You trying to knock your uncle out or what, Wildlings?"

Haley tells them to leave me be while she plays with the younger twins Stirling and Struan on a blanket in the grass. I remind her I'm the uncle and can tell them if they're bothering me, and they are not. She throws out how it's time I get my own.

My gut clenches.

"Aye, Harris, lad. Even though they'll bear the Steele name, they'll have strong Jackson blood in their veins!" Uncle Connor chimes in.

My heart skips a beat.

I chance a sideways glance at Kat.

She stares at some point in the distance, detached from the surrounding conversation.

My gaze flicks back to Uncle Connor.

"Er, at this time, let's get through the wedding before we have talk of babies," I respond and add a chuckle to lighten the mood. I reach for Kat's hand. "Right, babe?"

She blinks and turns her head towards me. I can't read the emotions in the depths of her eyes. But she smiles, and I breathe again.

"Right, babe," she repeats.

I know I'm not ready for kids yet. I have enough nieces and nephews to last a lifetime! Thankfully, My Kitty Kat feels the same. At least I hope that's the case.

"Fine," Uncle Connor says, then walks to Kat. "My dear, I know I can never replace your *Da*, and I do not know if your brothers would mind. But it would be my honor as the head of the Jackson clan to walk you down the aisle."

Kat sucks in a breath. A crimson hue blooms on her porcelain cheeks as tears shimmer in her emerald green eyes so like Uncle Connor's eyes. She nods her head vigorously.

"Excellent! Let's have some Jackson Scotch to celebrate," he says as he embraces her.

Later that night, I make slow, passionate love to My Kitty Kat. I try to use all my skills combined with my love to show her she means everything to me, even if I'm not ready for her to have my baby. Some day. Just not soon.

KAT

"Kat, sweetheart, that's amazing news! The Wright Corporation has been elusive for a while now. Kudos for your procurement of their pledge for one million dollars in the short time you've been here. Well done!"

Shelley's high praise during our weekly executive team meeting at STEELE Foundation fills me with pride. To make such a major contribution proves I didn't just get the position because I'm Harris Steele's fiancée. Rather, my skills and experience make me a valuable asset to the team.

Not that everyone treats me differently. No. All but one member of the staff has welcomed me.

Beatrice Montgomery.

A Park Avenue socialite from an old New York family. Twenty-five; gorgeous; long, raven hair; ice blue eyes; tall, lithe figure. The type found in the society pages at functions throughout the season or vacationing during holidays.

Beatrice made it clear from the moment of our introduction she was far superior to me and was none too pleased to learn Harris was my fiancé. Oh, not so obvious. Rather subtle comments.

Scotland? My family traces its lineage to England. But my ancestors established us in New York centuries ago. What town are you from?

Interesting, Harris went all the way to Scotland to find his future wife. You must be special, Kat!

I chance a glance at Beatrice where she sits to Shelley's right across from me at her left. Despite the slight smile on Beatrice's face, her icy blue eyes hold no warmth. They pierce me like a shard of glass.

Instead of cowering, I roll my shoulders back and straighten my spine. *Smiogaid suas, nighean!*

My girls prepped me for the haters since they experienced similar outcomes once the world learned of their engagements to the Steele men. Suddenly pushed into the spotlight the minute the press releases reached the media. Instagrammers created profiles to follow their activities and clothing choices. Bloggers dedicated entire posts to their supposed beauty routines, exercise habits, meals. Hashtags and the couples' combined names became the norm.

The very same happened for Harris and me. #HarKat anyone? Bah!

As Independent Women, my girls and I don't take

kindly to people assuming we're gold diggers. We weren't out to score a billionaire or lay claim to a Steele bachelor. No. We fell in love, and they claimed us. Like the cavemen they are, as Lola calls them.

The thought makes me giggle. But I hold it back as now is not the appropriate time. Especially with Ms. PAS—Park Avenue Socialite—shooting ice daggers at me.

"Thank you, Shelley. I want to contribute to the team in every possible way," I say with a gracious bow of my head.

"And how did you accomplish such a huge ask, Kat? I've known Ash Wright since we were babes, and he's definitely a charmer."

Another one of Beatrice's subtle hater comments. As if I fucked the man to get the million dollars! When will she let it go already???

I take a deep breath and shift my gaze to Ms. PAS.

"Is he? I wouldn't know since I met with his father. The senior Mr. Wright—as you probably know—still has ties to Aberdeen and contributes to the children's center there. I met him when I was a volunteer. Last week I reached out to him, and we had lunch. He understands the importance of a solid home for children to reach their fullest potential. STEELE Foundation provides such. Mr. Wright agreed to donate."

"Ah, I see..." Beatrice says with a smirk, icy blue eyes glint.

"Let's move on to the next item on the agenda," Shelley says, to change the subject deftly.

The other executives murmur their agreement and

hasten to proceed as though sensing the underlying current of tension in the room. I choose to rise above it. I don't need to prove my superiority.

As the conference room clears out after the meeting, Shelley asks me to stay. I settle back in my chair and wait for the others to leave. Beatrice casts a quizzical glance over her shoulder at us as she walks towards the door.

"Beatrice, sweetheart, kindly close the doors behind you. Thank you," Shelley calls out, then waits to speak until the click of the doors sound in the room. She turns to me. "You do realize I know what's happening with Beatrice, right?"

I blink since Shelley has mentioned nothing before now. And I certainly don't mention Beatrice's behavior to her or to Harris. Why bother? But it's interesting, Shelley noticed. It makes me wonder if others are aware too.

"Shelley, I don't want to cause any trouble. Beatrice is of no consequence. Truly," I add when my future mother-in-law arches an elegant eyebrow.

"Yes, but her attitude over the past few weeks has not gone unnoticed by the Associate Director and COO. The receptionist told me she overheard Beatrice in the bathroom making disparaging remarks about you. Fortunately, the other woman did not engage with her," Shelley says.

She gives me a moment to absorb the news. Before she continues.

"Your friend Vivian would make an excellent addition to STEELE Foundation. You mentioned you're having lunch with her today. Why don't you invite her back here and meet in my office? I'd love to speak with her."

I grin and agree wholeheartedly. It would be great to work with my best friend again!

Finally, lunch rolls around, and I head to a restaurant near The STEELE Tower. Viv and I decided to eat closer to my office since we'll stop by afterwards. I enter the bustling eatery and thank the hostess for a table by the window.

People-watching entertains me while I wait for Viv. It amazes me the variety of people and their attire who walk along Manhattan streets in the summer. One man rollerblades by with the skimpiest shorts and a tank top, avoiding pedestrians effortlessly. Two teenaged girls stroll arm in arm in colorful printed maxis dresses that flow above their gladiator sandals, free hands clutch multiple shopping bags. A tourist pauses for a selfie in front of the sign for Fifth Avenue. I smile and take a sip of water. My eyes never leave the view.

"Hey, you!"

I shift in my seat just in time to catch Viv's hug. The familiar, soft floral scent of her Jo Malone perfume wafts around me. I grin. It's good to see my bestie.

"Hey, yourself! And look at you in your glamour girl shades!" I respond when she settles in the seat across from me.

She shimmies her shoulders and grins.

"Oh, I just bought these the other day. You like?" She

asks as she takes them off and angles them back and forth. "Bulgari Flora, darling!"

That's what I love about Viv. She's as much, if not more of, a wealthy socialite as Ms. PAS, but my friend doesn't make me feel like dirt trampled beneath her Manolo Blahniks. In fact, she's taught me so much about the most luxurious clothing and accessories, the It places to go, and where—and not to mention who—to avoid. My very own Fairy God Sister!

"Fabu, daahling!" I say with a wink.

The server appears to pour iced tea and takes our order. When she leaves, I lean forward to share my news with Viv.

"I didn't bother to tell you about this woman at the foundation who treats me like a less-than. But now—"

"Hold on, Kat," Vivian interrupts with her hand raised to stop me. Her toffee brown eyes darken. "Who?"

I grin at my bestie's protective growl. I've been the same for her. When I tell her Beatrice Montgomery, Viv tells me she knows all about the snooty socialite. Of course, they travel in the same circles.

"Oh, please. And so anyway… Pass me the pepper mill, girl," Viv says with a toss of her curly ebony hair over her shoulder.

I giggle and hand it over.

"Well, Mum Shelley is eager to speak with you. I hope you'll consider her offer seriously. It would be great to work together again," I say.

Vivian nods as she finishes her bite of Maine Lobster

Roll. After she takes a sip of iced tea, she responds, "I will absolutely! The offices are not the same without you, Kat. You and I came up with some great and beneficial ideas together."

The rest of lunch we catch up on her dating life and my wedding planning. I asked Viv to be my maid of honor. Monsieur Valentino will create her gown too, with her first fitting next week. We made it a Girls' Getaway for the weekend, with Leonie and Haley joining us. Harris grumbled about me going to the City of Love without him but gave in after I showed him just how much I love his cock!

Now Vivian and I stroll arm in arm to The STEELE Tower. A member of the security team behind their station greets me by name and buzzes us through the turnstile. Viv nudges me and giggles. She gives a low whistle as we ride up on the private lift to the floor for the Foundation. I guide her to Shelley's offices, and her administrative assistant waves us towards the inner office.

I knock on one of the open double doors and wave when Shelley lifts her gaze.

"Kat, Vivian, sweethearts! Come in," she says as she rises from behind her Lucite desk gracefully. "Have a seat over here. Would you care for tea or coffee?"

We opt for tea as we sit on the white silk sofa. After she asks her assistant for tea and biscuits, Shelley joins us. She double kisses us before she sits on a chair.

"Did you have a pleasant lunch?" She asks. Following our responses, she continues. "Vivian, how are your parents? I haven't seen your mother since they moved to their villa in Tuscany when her father retired. Perhaps they'll join Morgan and me on *Serendipity* this summer."

Vivian's eyes widen in surprise.

"I didn't know you and my mother knew each other," she replies.

Shelley smiles and adds, "Oh, yes! Years ago, Crystal would frequent the boutique I worked in—a STEELE property no less and how I met Morgan. Ever fashionable, your mother would select the best pieces. I used to think how a young woman like myself could have such an innate style. The difference being she was wealthy, and I was middle-class. However, we became friendly. Then, after I married Morgan, Crystal and I would see each other at social functions. She loved how I went from shopgirl to a billionaire's wife!"

My mouth drops and I exchange glances with Viv, who's equally stunned. I knew Shelley's story, but not the part about Vivian's Mum. Aunt Lucie—a bartender in a Jackson pub—and Mum Shelley's love stories make me swoon each time I think about them.

Her laughter tinkles in the air. Eyes full of merriment, she goes on.

"Darlings, don't look so surprised! I was a hard-working girl, nowhere near a socialite, before I met Morgan. I was a personal shopper for Crystal. And enjoyed it, might I add!"

"My Mom never told me! I guess she hasn't put it together with Kat being a Jackson when I speak with her about our fun. Next time I talk to my Mom, I'll tell her!

And I'm sure they'd love to spend time with you aboard your megayacht," Viv says between giggles.

Shelley smiles and leans forward.

"Now, I say all of that to let you know our connection in hopes it will entice you to join Kat and me here at STEELE Foundation. We would benefit greatly from your experience as the Marketing Director. I've admired your work for some time, Vivian," Shelley says.

I sit back, surprised since Ms. PAS holds the role currently. No wonder Mum Shelley prefaced her conversation with me about Viv with Beatrice's poor behavior. She's axing the sow!

My gaze shifts to Vivian.

"Wow, the surprises keep rolling in, huh?" She asks with a smile. "I'm flattered you think well of me, Shelley. However, I've been with the nonprofit for several years and need time to consider your offer. I do hope you understand."

Shelley's dark brown eyes scan Viv's face, then nods appreciatively.

"Absolutely, Vivian. I know money holds no concern for you. But know we offer a considerable package for a Chief Marketing Officer," she says.

Viv's eyes pop.

"Chief Marketing Officer?" She asks.

Shelley's smile broadens.

"Naturally, we would not expect you to make a lateral move with your level of expertise," she says with a triumphant gleam in her eyes.

"Wow. Well, in that case, I accept and will tender my resignation with two-week notice today. Thank you!" Vivian says as she extends her hand.

Shelley takes it and seals their deal with a handshake.

We finish our tea with more talk about Vivian's dress and our upcoming Girls' Getaway. As Vivian and I walk to the private lift for her return to the nonprofit, we bump into Ms. PAS.

She makes a show of double kissing Vivian's cheeks. Ever the proper lady, Viv greets Beatrice. However, my bestie uses her subtle comment about not seeing Beatrice at some to-do function as a way to prove she's not included in all of their circle's gatherings. We part from a stupefied Ms. PAS with our heads held high. Once on the lift, we burst into laughter.

And so anyway...

KAT

"**Y**ou love to carry me off. Don't you, Harris Steele?"

"You know I do, Kat Jackson, soon-to-be Kat Steele. And you love it more. Especially this wee trick I have up my sleeve…"

My grin widens as Harris' dove gray eyes gleam with mischief. We're flying to who knows where on his Gulfstream private jet. The unknown-to-me destination will have to top all the phenomenal others he's taken me to since he first carried me off to the Channel Island of Jersey.

I still can't believe that trip was a year ago. Thirteen months since we first met in the lobby of Jackson Town House. Together, apart, together. Now, engaged with only five months until our wedding. Incredible.

With a contented sigh, I climb onto his lap from my seat on the sofa. Forehead pressed to his and arms wrapped

141

around his broad shoulders, I close my eyes and just breathe. The warm and sensual scent of his Tom Ford *Noir de Noir* cologne fills my nostrils. A deep inhalation sends me into the compelling world of Harris Steele. I will never get enough of my man.

His strong fingers knead my thighs. The thumbs massage the tops of each leg in circles. Closer and closer they sweep to the juncture of my core. His warm breath mingles with mine as his excitement mounts.

Oh, how I ache for him to mount me.

"Do you tempt me with more miles added to our Mile High Club, Siren?"

I mewl in response as I grind my ass atop his muscular thighs. They flex beneath me. But it's the reaction of his gigantic cock that earns a moan. It twitches. I whimper for more.

"I take that as a positive response," Harris murmurs before he blazes a trail of nips and kisses from my jaw down the column of my throat. He presses his lips against the indentation between my clavicles, then noses his way beneath the thin strap of my maxi dress.

The material gives way to slide down my arm. A wet warmth engulfs my bare nipple. It pebbles further as Harris suckles. Hard.

My head lolls back with eyes closed in carnal bliss. A hum in the back of my throat slips through my slack mouth. Heat rises from my belly over my heaving breasts, covered by Harris' pleasurable mouth. I shudder when he clamps a tender bud between his teeth and growls. My pussy softens as it weeps for him.

"Oh, Harris… I need you…"

He rewards my plea with his hand skating beneath my maxi dress. It bunches up around my waist. Clear to plunder my aching core, Harris thrusts a thick finger past my soaked pussy lips. He groans when he finds me wet and ready for him. And only him.

"Yessss!" I cry when he pulls back to add another skilled finger. My hips buck as I hiss from the stretch. "Unnhhh!"

"Always so tight for my cock, Siren. So. Fucking. Tight."

Harris punctuates each word with a thrust of his finger. They fuck me as I beg for his dick. Once again, he obliges me. The sound of the zipper on his jeans makes me shiver with anticipation.

Too eager to wait, I reach between us and free his massive cock. It lands heavily in the palm of my hand. He groans and shifts his hips upward, seeking more of my attention. It's my turn to answer his silent plea.

Too large for my fingers to wrap around his girth, I do my best to circle his shaft in my fist. From root to tip, I stroke. A bead of pre-cum serves as a natural lubricant to swirl over the bulbous head.

I pinch, and he bites.

We sound our carnal delight.

I extricate my breast from his mouth and slide down to kneel between his thighs. The plush platinum gray carpet cushions my knees. I grip the sides of his jeans with the black silk boxer briefs and tug.

With a smirk, Harris lifts his hips to allow me to yank the offensive garments from his delectable body.

"Eager much, Siren?" He quips with a wicked chuckle.

I growl and reach for the hem of his v-neck sweater. Then rip it off when he bends at the waist and raises his arms. I chuff at his laughter.

Completely bared to me, I sit back on my haunches to revel in the splendor of Harris Steele's magnificent body. Corded calves lead to sculpted thighs. His cock stands proud, like a thing of beauty Michelangelo could never capture in marble. Behind it, an Adonis belt and eight-pack abs define his midsection while pecs finished with flat male nipples flex. Sizable hands begin to stroke his fat cock. Forearms and biceps bunch to handle its girth and length. Tendons line his neck as he swallows thickly.

When my hungry gaze finally reaches his lips, he curls them.

"Do you plan on finishing what you started, Siren? Or must I find my own release?" He asks with hooded eyes beneath a cocked eyebrow. I shake my head, and he nods as though silently telling me to proceed.

I do.

I grasp his veiny cock from his grip with one hand while the other cups his heavy sac. The balls roll between my fingers as my mouth engulfs his purple head. A hum of satisfaction at his delicious, musky taste vibrates from me to him.

"Fuuuck, yes," Harris groans as I watch him watch me

swallow his dick between my lips. "Take every fucking inch. I want your throat stretched by my cock."

I bob my head, eager to fulfill his desire even as my gag reflex kicks in. Tears fill my eyes. He's so *bloody* big. I pull back to collect myself, then return with gusto. Tongue swirls. Cheeks suction. Teeth drag.

Before long, Harris' hands dive into my hair. He grips the sides of my head to lock me at just the angle he wants. Long and even thrusts last but so long before his cock swells impossibly larger, and he juts his hips.

My fingernails dig into his thighs as my body wants to fight the invasion.

"Breathe! Dammit! Breathe for me."

Harris' demand snaps my focus back.

I inhale on his outward thrust, then relax my throat for his plundering return. We find our rhythm.

"Make me cum, Siren! Swallow! Every! Drop!" Harris bellows as jets of his hot cum slide down my throat, straight to my hungry belly.

I moan around his girth as I struggle to not spill a single drop.

Harris falls back against the sofa replete. His cock pops from between my lips. A satisfied smile plays at the corners of his mouth as he leans forward to swipe a trace of cum from my swollen lip.

"Good, lass," he croons, then lifts me to swap places. His broad shoulders spread my thighs as he dives between them to lap at my slick seam. He groans rapturously. "Oh, so good, lass. You've earned your miles."

My body responds to his praise like a preening kitten. I purr and arch my back as my hands stretch up behind me. My palms slap the private jet's walls as Harris eats me like a ravenous wolf. His feral grunts and growls send shivers down my spine. My pussy creams. He laps it up in wild abandon.

By the time we land, we rack up *thousands* of points. Cha-ching!

My head may still linger in the clouds, but my eyes widen at the sight before me when Harris removes the red silk blindfold that covers them.

"Wh—what is this place?" I stutter in awe.

From the backseat of the Chevy Suburban, I glimpse Spanish moss hanging from mature trees. They form a canopy with their interwoven branches above what I can only describe as an elaborate treehouse. Not just one. Rather, several buildings nestled amongst a copse of trees. The hidden jewels float above a ground strewn with leaves. Manicured lawns surround the copse like a green lake. On one side, an oversized bed swings from ropes strung from rafters beneath one treehouse. It invites a night a decadence for two.

My gaze moves between the fantasy treehouses and their surroundings. Through the window Harris opens, humid air carries the sound of birds chirping. It fills the SUV. I lean out to take a closer look.

"Amazing…" I whisper as we near what has to be the most unusual, yet wonderful destination Harris has whisked me away to visit.

"Told ya," he says smugly. "Come on, let's go."

He opens the door and helps me from the SUV. The driver handles our luggage in the boot.

Hand in hand, Harris leads me towards the treehouses. We circle around the exterior, back to the set of stairs. I glimpse a painted replica of houses above the hanging bed. I make a note to return later.

Up the stairs on the white railing-lined landing outside of the larger treehouse, we find two ornate bathtubs. Perfectly situated to take in the incredible view of the Spanish moss-covered trees and water beyond. I thought the hanging bed would be my favorite spot. But these bathtubs? Wow!

From there we climb a short wrought-iron ladder to a deck with a cafe table and two chairs. The higher elevation is great for coffee in the morning or wine in the evening. Before we enter the primary treehouse, Harris guides me to the wrought-iron spiral staircase. Two basket chairs hang beside a dual-head outdoor shower. Can this get any better?

"Oh, but it does."

I blush when I realize I spoke aloud and giggle. Harris nods towards the primary treehouse.

We head down the spiral staircase, then round the corner of the salmon-colored wooden structure. Two walls of windows flank a set of black French doors. Wrought-iron and glass sconces hang on either side. Two of the walls have windows of varying sizes interspersed from the roofline to the slate-colored wooden deck.

I try to peek inside, but the sun reflects off the glass. The image of Harris and me greets my curiosity.

He pulls an antique iron key from a box beside the planter and opens the French doors. As he steps aside, he gestures for me to enter. His smug grin still lights his handsome face.

"*Entrez s'il vous pla"t, mademoiselle,*" he says with a bow.

My breath catches when I step inside.

To our left, a pale blue velvet tufted settee with platinum leaf on the wood sits before the windows. A clawfoot tub with the same luxurious gilt stands on an elevated platform with an antique mirror as its backboard. Between the two, a wood-burning oven offers warmth from the corner on a chilly day.

Not only because it's July, but the lustful heat rising in my body is more than enough to dispel the cold when my gaze lands on the king-size antique French bed. It's a cloud of sumptuous white linens. The centerpiece of the spacious interior offers more than a welcome respite. It begs for couples to enact a sensual scene from Versailles. *Vive la France!*

Above it, a loft accessible by a set of stairs beckons for more seductive surprises. A glimpse of crystal chandeliers and the curved lines of furniture hint at what's more to come.

The last piece lies in the right wall staged as a kitchenette. The dark brown vintage wood of the lower cabinetry blends seamlessly with the decor. Only the three rows of shelves belie it's not another luxurious sitting area.

"You like?"

Harris' question draws me from my fantasy as a French queen playing hide and seek with her naughty king. Her long gown billowing behind her as she runs through the Hall of Mirrors. His randy reflection flicks from one to the other as he chases her with his wig askew.

I jump into his arms. He catches me effortlessly.

"I love it! But not as much as I. Love. *You!*" Each word punctuated with a kiss to his smiling lips. Then my mouth slants over his for a French kiss *extraordinaire*.

"Well, that's a rousing start to our six-months-back-together anniversary, Kitty Kat!" Harris says with a chuckle. "I can't wait to see what you'll do for our one-year wedding anniversary. That is, once we're married in *five* months…"

I giggle and kiss the tip of his nose.

"Good things come to those who wait, you know," I say as I make to stand.

But he tightens his grip and walks us to the claw-foot tub. He moves me to his hip and turns on the faucets. A scoop of lavender-scented bath salts, and he sets me on my feet. He makes quick work of my maxi dress and his clothes before he carries me into the tub with him.

We settle with me between his legs as he rests against a side. The panorama beyond the wall of windows serves as a splendid vista to unwind after our active flight. I let my head fall back against his shoulder. A contented sigh escapes both of us.

As the water loses its warmth, Harris takes a sea sponge

and pours patchouli-scented body wash onto it. The spicy musky fragrance pairs well with the lavender to relax my sore muscles. I all but moan as he soothes the sponge over my skin. *Divine.*

"Your turn," I say, turning to face my man. He smiles and leans back with his arms draped over the edge of the bathtub. "You always make me feel so special. Thank you, my love."

I lean forward and kiss the space over his heart. Its rhythmic beat pulses beneath my lips. I lavish his body with the tender loving care he afforded mine.

When I'm done, Harris lifts us from the tub, and we dry one another. Body lotion with the same scent softens our skin. We don fluffy white robes.

While I climb amongst the pillows on the massive bed, Harris fills crystal flutes from the Champagne bottle left in an ice bath on the nightstand. He passes the plate of chocolate-covered strawberries to me and knees his way onto the bed. I accept the flute from him with a smile.

"Here's to many, many more anniversaries filled with love, Kat Jackson, soon-to-be Kat Steele," he says as he touches his flute to mine.

We take a sip, then I feed a strawberry to him.

He bites it and pins me with a smoldering stare as his lips slowly slip over my fingertips.

Heat flares immediately from the erotic point of contact. It zings up my arm to my heart and lights my core on fire. I inhale sharply, then my eyes half-mast filled with carnal lust.

Yes, there will be many, many more anniversaries filled with love… and passion.

Five months can't come fast enough.

HARRIS

"Are you certain you want the property on the other side of Roger and Leonie's? Or would you rather a new build on some of the land between Haley's and ours? No, it will not sit oceanfront, but your timeline will not hinge upon the existing neighbors' whims."

I consider my Dad's questions as we sit on the deck of my the Steele Southampton Village megamansion overlooking the Atlantic Ocean. Sure, Kat and I could combine a few of the acres from this residence I share with my parents and some from Haley's. But every time we're near the water, My Kitty Kat loves watching the sunrise over the ocean. I want to give it to her. We need that footage.

"Listen, let me call my go-to residential realtor—Robin Sanchez-Waghorn. Her reach extends to the Hamptons. We'll get her take on the holdup," Baz offers.

My ears prick up at his suggestion.

"Oh, yes! She helped me find my Sutton Place penthouse and did the closing for Starr's parents' penthouse in my building," Lola adds, then claps. "Robin to the rescue!"

Tension melts as I laugh along with everyone.

"But as I told Harris, I'm happy with whichever property he selects," My Kitty Kat says. She turns her face up to mine and smiles. "Home is here for me."

I melt when she touches her dainty hand to the spot over my heart.

Ohs and ahs fill the air. But I only have eyes for My Kitty Kat. I take her hand and bring it to my lips for a kiss.

"Thank you, babe. But it's *our* choice. And I want to watch your face as the sun rises with the early morning rays glowing on your beautiful face—"

"Holy shit! Listen to the *playa* now!" Laurent guffaws.

Okay, so I stepped in that one. I shake my head as I chuckle. Me, waxing poetic... Damn, but this woman changed my life. For real.

I catch more ribbing from my brothers and cousins. What can I say? Not a damn thing. So, I take it like a man, then stand for a bow.

Everyone claps jovially. Laurent gives me a standing ovation. The fucker.

"But seriously, I know you don't mind. However, settling is not an option," I say. "Plus, we can build guest houses. One for Mum Allison and Charlotte to share, and another for your brothers. You know, dudes have to have their space. Maybe Michael would like to work on the design."

He whoops and agrees. Leonie offers to create the interior design scheme.

"Son, I concur now I have the knowledge of Kat's joy of an ocean sunrise. We provide for our women, no matter the situation. I will contact some people. Between them and Robin, you will have the property," my Dad says firmly. All the guys voice their agreement.

Some may say we're a bit over-the-top. But that's because they don't have men in their lives who love the way we do—deep and hard in and out of the bedroom.

We move on to talk about the plans for the weekend.

Everyone converges on the family compounds in Southampton Village for the month of August through the second week of September. Malcolm and Starr use their home as their primary residence. He commutes to the City for work via helicopter, and Starr is based out of SLFW Southampton Village. So, they're always here.

Aside from me, the others have personal residences. Haley and Lachlan's property bridges the gap between the Steele compound and the Jackson's to the west. They persuaded a neighbor to part with the beachfront mansion successfully, then made it their own.

Both compounds span a vast stretch of ocean frontage and land right behind. The property I have my eye on sits to the east, past Roger and Leonie's. Starr's parents—Sun and Peace—bought the oceanfront property on the farther side.

So getting that last parcel makes not only sunrise sense, but it's a solid investment. We would own all land on this much sought-after peninsula. A private enclave with a value to increase for generations of Steeles and Jacksons.

The thought of those who come behind my siblings and me reminds me of the big children's question. It dances in my mother's eyes. I overheard Mum Allison asking Kat if I want wee ones. I skipped past the living room before she could respond. Too close!

I shake my head and clear it of the unwanted-for-now thoughts. Focus on the present, as Starr says.

"I have a foursome with potential clients at the club," Roger says.

Haley sputters her orange juice. Leonie giggles as she pats her back.

"Oh, *chérie*! The golf club, not *that* club! Besides, I do *not* share!" She says between laughter.

My twin's cheeks flush crimson. She sneaks a peek at our parents. Then sags in relief when she finds them engrossed in a conversation with Uncle Connor and Aunt Lucie.

"Nice going, Hal!" I say loud enough to draw their attention to our end of the table. She glares at me, and I continue. "Where's *your* mind, missy?"

I catch the grape she throws at me and pop it into my mouth with a smirk. She mouths, *fuck you*, and I throw my head back, laughing.

Some girls decide to go to SLFW for a class with a guest teacher. The rest opt for the village.

I give My Kitty Kat a kiss and remind her to use the AMEX Centurion Card I gave her. She frowns, then yelps and glances around when I spank her ass. No one notices since they're busy getting ready to head out for the day.

"*Ours*, naughty lass," I growl in her ear, then nip it. A lick has her mewling. All thoughts of not using her Black Card dissipate. "Good, lass. Now, have fun, and I'll see you later."

I watch as she sashays away. She throws a wink over her shoulder as she follows Charlotte and Yessenia.

"She'll be back, soppy boy."

I chuckle as I shift my gaze to Lachlan. He makes goo-goo eyes and kissy noises. I throw a pillow from my chair at him. He catches it deftly and hugs it to his body, batting his eyelashes.

"Wanker," I mutter. "If you can get past fucking with me, we can decide what to do today."

He tosses the pillow back, and I put it behind me.

"My vote's on kitesurfing," Malcolm says.

"I say deep-sea fishing. We can catch tonight's dinner," Lucien says.

"Do both," Patrick says as he rises from the table.

We part to get ready, then head to the marina. The crew helps us get the kitesurfing gear aboard. Those who prefer to catch our dinner check the fishing tackle. No interest of mine, I go with Malcolm, Anton, Baz, and Laurent to the toy area at the stern.

"Get something good!" I shout over my shoulder at the fishermen. They give me the thumbs up.

We reach open water and anchor. Surface waves break as wind hits the deep blue water of the Atlantic Ocean.

Consistent enough for kitesurfing yet won't disturb the fishing lines. A glance towards the shoreline revels fairy towns with buildings that resemble dollhouses.

"Let's get at it!" Anton exclaims as he suits up.

Soon, we're racing amongst the surface waves and flying into the air. Baz skims past me with a battle cry. Sunlight glints off his mirrored goggles. I change the angle of my kite and surge ahead. In my periphery, I glimpse Anton taking air at least seven feet above the surface. He somersaults. His victorious cries ring through the air. Wind under my kite lifts me, and I take advantage to grab the side of my board. We outdo one another as we challenge nature. Adrenaline from the stunts beats through my veins.

We catch wind-driven acrobatics while the others catch Mahi Mahi. A win-win for all.

On the trip back to the marina, we trade tales as we eat a hearty lunch. Borya has the best story with catching and releasing a marlin. The MMA champ had his hands full with the powerful fish. He chuckles as he reenacts the fight.

Once ashore, Lucien takes the Mahi Mahi to one of his restaurants to prepare for our feast. The rest of us climb into the Chevy Suburbans.

I check my mobile and grin when I open the message app. My Kitty Kat beams at me from a selfie she took with Charlotte. Shopping bags rest at their feet while they sip Champagne in a boutique. My fingers fly over the keyboard.

Well done, Kitty Kat!

The three circles appear as she types a response.

Even a surprise for you! ;)

I grin stupidly at the screen. Visions of My Kitty Kat in sexy lingerie spread-eagle on our bed play out before my eyes. My cock twitches, intrigued by the sexy fantasy.

"Hey, Har, Robin responded."

I glance over at Baz scanning his mobile screen. He summarizes her message.

"The parents still own the property. So the son can't decide to sell or hold up an offer. Robin can get it to them in Provence. Seems they retired there and don't plan to use the property anymore. They left it as a getaway for the son."

We fist pump.

Sunrises and smiles, here we come!

"THIS WEEK WAS BEYOND CRAZY! I can't wait to unwind with a glass of wine and sit on the deck for a lovely sunset. Maybe even the entire bottle!"

I chuckle at My Kitty Kat as she makes a loony face and twirls her fingers on either side of her head.

She's adjusted well to her new role at STEELE Foundation. But the weeks leading up to the annual STEELE White Party over Labor Day weekend prove hectic. It's the culmination of the year's work and the highlight of the

Hamptons season. Not to mention wanting to impress my mother since it's her baby.

I pat My Kitty Kat's thigh.

"We'll land soon enough, and you can get that bottle," I assure her.

"Starr and I can join you. She just texted me about opening a bottle before dinner," Malcolm adds across the row from us in his Sikorsky S-92 Executive Helicopter.

We're commuting with him, Roger, Leonie, Haley, and Lachlan. Blair and Billie fly with Baz and Lola on their helicopter since their schedules align.

"Sounds wonderful!" My Kitty Kat says.

"Well, count us in, too!" Haley pipes up from the rear of the helicopter. "I say we order delivery for dinner instead of going to the restaurant. I'm sure Lucien wouldn't mind having free tables for a busy Friday night."

Lachlan pulls out his mobile.

"I'll send a text message to him. He can open up the reservations since we booked the last tables," Lachlan says. As he types, he adds, "I'll tell Baz, too. He'll let the others know the change in plans."

By the time the helicopter lands, everyone confirmed, the food order set to arrive in ninety minutes, and the house staff arranged the deck for the impromptu cocktail hour followed by dinner. Our parents have plans and won't return home until late. The nannies will mind the children and dogs while the adults hang out. It comes together smoothly.

Suddenly energized, Kat bounces in the second row as I drive to the compound. The tiredness in her eyes replaced by glee. She chats with Leonie and Haley about their outfits for the gala. Then it's should Haley get a new hairstyle to debut at the event. Next, they switch to the designs Leonie has for the new beach house. The way they jump topics makes me dizzy.

I nod in response to the look Roger gives me from the passenger seat. Yeah, better to leave them uninterrupted. Happy wife, happy life and all. It's a lesson Baz taught my brothers, and now I use.

We drive past the stone wall that surrounds the compound and reach the impressive gates where the security guard waves from the gatehouse. As my Dad says, *leave it at the gate*, all tension drains from me the moment we drive through. I take a deep, cleansing breath.

The briny scent of the ocean fills my lungs from the open windows of the SUV. The calls of seagulls ring out. It's peaceful on the peninsula with over twenty acres. Its incredible surroundings include native trees, grassy areas, and closer to the ocean's sandy dunes.

On either side of the primary driveway, secondary ones appear as we drive along. I turn off to one on the left. A shorter driveway ends in a circle before a classic Hamptons-style three-story mansion. Robin egg blue shutters lean against gray weathered shingles. Beneath, the windowsill flower boxes filled with white blossoms add to the beauty of the home.

Roger hops out and helps Leonie from the SUV. They'll

ride a golf cart to our parents' residence—as will Haley and Lachlan—after I drop them off at their house.

My Kitty Kat and I decide to take a shower to wash off the week. I would prefer my nightly bath soak ritual, but we don't have enough time. But I do make time to fuck her against the marble wall of the Roman shower. Always time for some good lovin'!

I set her on wobbly legs and use a fluffy towel to dry her skin. I use the excuse of applying body oil to play with her clit and nipples until she shatters for me. Combined with its scent of lavender and the toe-curling orgasms I gave her in the shower, My Kitty Kat has recovered fully from a stressful week. I carry her to the dressing room where I slip a floral maxi dress over her head.

Knowing she's bare for me beneath her dress will keep me horny until we go to bed. But the erotic torture is well worth it. Her DDs jiggle with pebbled nipples pressed against layers of silk chiffon. I imagine her curves hidden by the loose fit as the dress flows down her body to the ankles. Sexy as fuck.

I leave her putting on lip gloss to enter my dressing room. I don an untucked white linen shirt, natural linen pants, and brown leather slides. My Kitty Kat stands in the doorway as I roll the sleeves up my forearms.

"Hey, sexy," she says as her eyes blaze emerald fire from my head to my toes. "I hope your fiancée isn't home. I have plans for you this weekend."

I slip my arms around her waist and lean down to murmur in her ear.

"My fiancée is a fierce kitty who doesn't share her balls. So I'd be careful if I were you."

She gives a throaty laugh that makes my balls tingle.

"Oh, I can handle her. Don't you worry, big boy," she says as she squeezes my ass.

I chuckle and place my hand on the small of her back to guide her out of the room. Otherwise, we'll miss our impromptu evening plans.

Out on the deck, the butler and a maid stand at the ready. Even though I told them it would be a casual cocktail hour and dinner, they wait to see if we need their help. They bid us a good evening when I thank them.

Haley and Lachlan arrive first. They grab glasses of Jackson Cabernet Sauvignon and Chardonnay from the drinks table and join us at a seating area.

"Isn't that the maxi dress you bought from the new boutique the other week?" Haley asks My Kitty Kat who confirms. "I told you it would look good with your skin tone. The pinks and greens complement your alabaster skin and emerald eyes. Thanks, Haley!"

Kat stands and twirls, then kisses my twin on the cheek.

"You were right! I love it," she says as she smooths the silk chiffon along her thighs. "And the fit is comfy yet chic."

"Excellent choice!" I add with a smirk, knowing my intentions vary greatly from those of my twin.

"Hey, hey, hey!"

We turn to find Laurent bopping in with Yessenia on his arm. Behind them, Roger, Leonie, Baz, and Lola walk through the open wall of glass doors.

"*The Sexy Chef* does it again! He always remembers my favorite Prosciutto Wrapped Shrimp with Smoked Paprika." Lola exclaims as she pops one in her mouth. "Mmm mmm!"

Luc, Blair, Patrick, and Billie come around the corner of the lane that leads to the driveway. Norman Green and his wife Anita walk with them.

The former Heavyweight Champion of the World and owner of Norman Green's Elite Training Facility pretends to square off with Borya when he bumps him from behind. The two athletes and friends greet each other heartily. Márcia and Anita hug.

Malcolm, Starr, Anton, and Adrienne stop to chat with them before they converge on the drinks table. Glasses in hand, they join us at the seating area.

"Viv!" My Kitty Kat squeals when she spies her best friend.

My Mom raves how fantastic Vivian is since she accepted the position of CMO. Already she's implemented a prize-worthy marketing plan. On the personal side, Vivian has spent quite some time at the penthouse Kat and I share. We've had double dates with her and some of my buddies.

It appears as though one of my Harvard Business School friends—Perry Franck—has snagged her heart. He has a possessive hand on her lower back as he guides her towards us.

"Kat!" She squeals as they hug.

I rise and shake hands with Perry.

"Hey, man, good to see you," I say as I pull him in for a bro hug, then continue so only he hears. "You treating my girl right?"

He slaps me on the back and nods.

"Naturally. My mother raised a gentleman," he responds.

I know since she's friends with my mother. His family is one of the oldest book publishers in the world based in Paris with offices around the globe. He heads up the marketing department for their multibillion-dollar empire.

"Keep it that way," I tell him, then turn to Vivian for a hug. "Hey, Viv! A pleasure, as always. What can I get you to drink?"

"Hey, Harris!" She says, then glances around at the others' drinks. "The Chardonnay, thanks!"

I quirk an eyebrow at Perry, and he requests the Cabernet Sauvignon.

Everyone laughs and talks while we enjoy the sunset drinking good wine. We eat more of Lucien's delectable dishes, including a variety of desserts. Anton turns into the deejay and pipes his playlists through the surround sound system. The night turns into a dance party beneath an inky sky full of glittering stars.

When everyone leaves, I carry a tipsy Kat up to the balcony on our wing of the house. More than the stars glisten as I ravage the redheaded Siren. All. Night. Long.

"Yes, we have the gala this evening. But we must take time for self-care. Lucie, Josy, Sun, and Allison will rejuvenate with me at my favorite spa in the village. I booked it out for the day. We have the morning shift, and you, sweethearts, have the afternoon. The glam squads will arrive at your residences two hours prior to the gala. Ladies, this is our time to shine!"

We give Mum Shelley a rousing cheer for her pep talk. She beams. Then claps her hands.

"Let's go!" The Sergeant says.

We leave the breakfast room and head to the entry hall. Leonie loops arms with her Mum Joséphine Beaulieu. Although Leonie has her Parisian father Guy's height and mahogany hair, it's her Tunisian, petite mother she resembles. Her ebony hair cut in a stylish curly bob frames her fawn-colored, oval-shaped face. Pouty lips turn up in a joyful smile as she smiles at her daughter. In her early sixties, Josy could model as much as *The Lion*.

I take my Mum's hand as I reach her side. She squeezes it with a smile.

"I'm so very proud of you, honey. Shelley tells me you've done marvelous things at the Foundation. Tonight, you will definitely shine," she says. She peeks up at me and goes on. "And I'm glad you like Henry."

Ah, yes, her new man friend—Henry McGowan. He's a distinguished gentleman she met at an event Aunt Lucie hosted in Aberdeen a few months ago. His family owns a chain of popular grocery stores throughout the United Kingdom. I say, go, Mum!

And of course, Harris did a complete background check. All good.

"As long as he makes you happy, I'm happy. You deserve a special someone in your life, Mum," I respond with a squeeze to her hand.

We reach the front doors and step out onto the drive-way. Rolls-Royce SUVs await us. I give my Mum a hug and wave to the other mothers, then hop into one headed to Starr Light Fitness & Wellness Southampton Village.

"What a lineup! Meditation, pranayama, ending with a flow session and yoga *nidra*. I cannot wait!" Billie says in her Southern Belle drawl. Her Granny Smith apple green eyes glow with excitement.

"Yoga *nidra*?" Charlotte asks with a frown. "I've heard of pranayama—the breathwork."

Leonie giggles and shifts in her seat to face my sister.

"It's yogic sleep. It can relieve stress by placing you in a sleep state during which the teacher guides you in meditation. The first time I tried yoga *nidra*, I didn't only 'reach a deep level of relaxation.' But fell asleep, then woke myself with my loud snoring!"

We laugh and talk about more the benefits of the eight limbs of yoga. Perfect for the day of self-care Mum Shelley encourages.

Starr, Adrienne, and Márcia greet us when we arrive at SLFW SV. Standing in their Carbon38 Sweaty Betty, and Free People sports bras and matching leggings, they are every bit fashionable fitness enthusiasts.

"Good morning, girls! We have a fantastic day planned. Ready to get started?" Starr asks after everyone hugs, then leads the way inside.

Clients mill about the tranquil interior, sitting at tables near the café, browsing in the boutique, and on line for check in at the front desk. Everywhere women and men with amazing bodies from yoga, Pilates, Barre, and strength training sessions fill the space. The sound of piped-in music, excited chatter, and the whir of blenders for smoothies circulates in the air.

We pass studios on our way to Starr's private one. The further in we go, the more serene the environment. Cream walls with elaborate Indian woodwork surround us. Stone floors transform to warm red wood beneath our bare feet. Clients speak softly as they move to their classes. Open doors reveal some lying on mats or lined up at barres stretching before their sessions begin.

Starr's large studio accommodates us easily. We settle on mats already placed on the floor. Gracefully, Adrienne lowers to a cross-legged position on the mat beside Tibetan singing bowls. She leads us in mediation and pranayama, implementing the sounds.

Márcia takes us through a powerful dharma talk focused on self-love. She explains the asana sequence will allow us to follow our hearts, opening us up to recognize what brings us happiness. The flow expands our chests and includes heart opening poses fish, crescent moon lunge, camel, and bridge. We smile with joy when she ends with standing star pose.

The sense of jubilation continues with Starr's yoga *nidra*. Her guidance includes our recollections of joyful moments at varying stages of our lives. A sense of ease settles over me as my mind floats free to the soothing tones of her voice. At the end of the hour-long session, the calming influence of yoga *nidra* makes us feel as though we slept for hours.

"Starr, Adrienne, Márcia, thank you for wonderful sessions, as always!" Haley says once we rouse.

"*Sí*, I love the love you spread, *chicas*!" Yessenia exclaims as she re-tightens her long ponytail.

Anita—also a fitness instructor and meal prep connoisseur based in Paris—nods in agreement.

"Ladies, I always enjoy taking part in your sessions. You rank as my gurus!" She says with a bow.

We make our way to the locker room. Inside, we relax in the steam room where the scent of eucalyptus eases our sore muscles as it soothes our minds. After we shower, Adrienne reminds us about lunch at the café.

Perfect timing leads to our spa day. We walk through Southampton Village to Mum Shelley's favorite house of beauty. The manager welcomes us with frosty glasses of refreshing citrus water. Hours pass while the aestheticians buff, wax, and massage us, ending with glossy mani/pedis.

"Oh, I am *so* ready for the gala!" Vivian says as she wiggles her fingers with white nail polish. "Do you think I should blow my curls out or pile them atop my head in a sexy updo?"

I consider the Grecian gown she showed me last night, then suggest the updo like a gorgeous goddess. Viv shimmies and nods enthusiastically.

Everyone asks for similar input as we ride back to the compound. The glam squads await us.

"Well, well, well, look at this beautiful Siren before me."

My team just left, and I stand in front of the full-length mirror outside of my dressing room. As I turn to face Harris, my palms glide down the scores of white glimmering sequins covering the Italian satin column. The strapless gown would be demure except for cutouts from my flanks to midsection with a band of more sequins around the waist. A high slit in the back allows me to move sensuously as I pivot.

A seductive smile plays on my lips.

"Why thank you, my love," I purr. My gaze trails over his tuxedo-covered body. "And don't you look appetizing?"

He smirks. His eyes glitter like the diamonds in my ears and around my neck I borrowed from Bulgari—the event's jewelry sponsor. I paired the pieces with the diamond bangles Harris gave to me.

"We'll be sure to indulge in one another after the fireworks. Or make some of our own," he responds. "Come, let's go."

I take his proffered elbow.

Outside the side door of his parents' megamansion, my administrative assistant—Foster Alcott, who came with me from the children's nonprofit—approaches us.

"Hi, Kat. You look fabulous!" He exclaims with an approving nod.

Foster has become my other source for fashion advice. He and his partner rank amongst the best-dressed men I've ever seen. Including the perfectly tailored classic tuxedo he wears.

"You're a handsome devil, Foster!" I say with a wink.

He grins, then gives me an update on the gala as we walk towards the platinum gray carpet with step and repeat. It highlights the event sponsors, including STEELE International, Inc., Jackson Corporation, Lola's Coterie, Starr Light Fitness & Wellness Center, Banque Montaigne, Bulgari, and other notable companies.

As we near, the calls of photographers from local to international media outlets and the paparazzi ring out. Guests pose for the flashing cameras or speak into microphones. Stunning evening wear and incredible jewels sparkle. The area hums with activity.

Beyond, I spy our gang at various spots on the carpet. After Foster finishes, Harris and I make our way to them.

"Showtime. Smile for the cameras," Harris tells me with a wink. He places his hand on the small of my back possessively.

We pose with his siblings and answer questions from the media. Most of it centers on our upcoming wedding. But the professional Development Director in me guides the narrative back to STEELE Foundation and our multi-million-dollar goal for the evening.

Foster catches my attention and tells me Mum Shelley and Vivian need me for an interview. I follow him, leaving Harris with Laurent and Yessenia.

When the interview ends, Viv introduces me to her parents and brothers. Mum Shelley invited them to the gala. She's determined to have everyone in the fold. Viv's parents greet me like a daughter with hugs and promises of lunch or dinner before they return to Tuscany. Her handsome brothers shake my hand warmly.

Another hand on my waist makes me turn.

Harris smiles down at me, then lifts his gaze to Vivian's brothers. Even though they introduced me to their dates, my caveman still finds the need to flex. He extends his hand to each brother and welcomes them to Steele Southampton Village.

When Perry tells Harris he and one of Vivian's brothers

took classes together at Harvard, Harris smiles. They catch up while Viv and I listen on.

Aunt Lucie appears with Uncle Connor to introduce me to a princess and her husband. They RSVP'd for the wedding. Harris and I excuse ourselves and turn to them. After speaking with the couple, Aunt Lucie takes us around to other notables who confirmed their attendance.

It's been wonderful how they've taken me under their wings. Aunt Lucie even shared a notebook with details on key people for me to familiarize myself with. Each week we have a video conference not only for the wedding planning but for quizzes. I love it!

Harris and I mingle with other guests before the announcement for dinner. We join the throng of guests as they head towards the giant side lawn. Aglow by thousands of fairy lights and lanterns, it has two sumptuous pavilions, one for dinner and the other for dessert and dancing. We converge on the dinner pavilion where the scent of dishes crafted by Lucien and his team tantalizes us.

Mum Shelley rises to make her speech. Once she reaches the podium, she calls for Vivian and me to join her. We smile broadly when she introduces us and praises our efforts with the Foundation and the gala. We return to our tables to vigorous applause.

Harris stands and kisses me on the cheek. I lean into him before I take my seat.

The rest of the evening passes with the silent auction, dancing, and fireworks.

As promised, Harris and I slip away and make our own dazzling display. All. Night. Long.

* * *

"THAT'S SUCH a sweet photo of you and Harris, Kat!"

Charlotte beams as she holds her iPad up for me to see the website. We're on the deck having brunch the morning after the gala. It's recap and refuel time.

Charlotte, Vivian, and I—along with our administrative assistants—scroll through the media coverage to date. We have a press clippings agency. But I like to see what I can find, too. It also gives me a thrill to see my image on the society pages firsthand!

Viv—who's used to such exposure—does it from a business standpoint. But she nods in agreement with Charlotte's pronouncement.

"Aaaw! You guys are adorbs. The way you're leaning into him as he smiles down at you. His eyes full of pride and love," Viv says as she smiles at the photo.

Admittedly, my heart swells at the sight of it. I make a note to contact the photographer for the digital file. I'll print two and put them in matching sterling silver frames and give one to Harris. Then, I'll put mine on my desk at the office.

If the Foundation still employed Ms. PAS, she would puke her eyes out.

I giggle at the cartoonish vision and swipe to another website.

Overall, the coverage aligns with the goal—get more donations—since the initial numbers show an increase over the time of the event compared to the prior. We send our findings in a report to Mum Shelley, the CFO, and the rest of the executive team.

Work done, Foster and Viv's admin leave to enjoy the rest of the day.

We head down to the beach for a walk to the edge of the peninsula and back. Since Charlotte returns to Scotland tomorrow, I want to spend the rest of the day with her.

Tonight, we'll have dinner with Harris, our Mum, Henry, Payton, and Michael. They're staying through the end of the week. Michael will remain longer since he'll work at STEELE International for the fall semester. Roger says it will give him hands-on experience and count towards his university work. It'll be great to have my brother in the City.

As we stroll through the surf, I notice a shimmer of kelly green amidst the foam from a wave as it slides back to the ocean. Bending down, I collect it before it washes back into the Atlantic Ocean. I smile as I rinse the sand from the piece of sea glass. Shaped like an oval, its surface made smooth and frosted from the years it spent in tumbling in the saltwater.

"Here, Charlotte. I found a piece of sea glass. You admired the collection of colorful bits of glass in the entry foyer Mum Shelley collects," I say as I hand it to my sister. "Keep this as a reminder of our weekend."

She takes the piece and holds it up to the sun.

"It's beautiful, thanks Kat!" She says as she hugs me. "I'll treasure it forever."

Harris stands on the deck and raises his hand in greeting as we near the megamansion.

"There's your future hubby, Kat. Picture perfect. I'm so happy for you," Charlotte says with a smile.

I grin and nod. My heart swells the closer we get to the home. Can it get any better?

KAT

"OMG, Lola! This corset is unbelievable! However do you come up with your designs?"

Vivian asks as she admires an antique gold lace corset in the New York City flagship of Lola's Coterie in The STEELE Tower mall. She grins as she holds the matching garter belt and barely there G-string.

Lola smiles like the Cheshire Cat. Her hazel eyes twinkle with mischief.

"Well, I envision all the ways I can make Baz lose his mind with kinky lingerie. The colors and materials just speak to me," she says. "Then I wave my magic wand and the sketches appear."

We laugh at her shenanigans and continue to look through the luxury lingerie.

The boutique is breathtaking and resembles Lola's other locations—not cookie-cutter replicas, each distinct. This one gives a nod to New York City with the Manhattan skyline featured in the hand-painted wallpaper instead of Parisian street vignettes, as in her original boutique on the Champs-Élysées. It's the largest of her boutiques with three floors and includes office space, a section for custom design requests, and private rooms like the one we're in.

"Here, I think this set would look fantastic on you, Kat," Lola says as she pulls a silk hanger from a rack.

It's a sensual and provocative vision. A corset of emerald green lace with a center panel beneath the demi-cups and a busk of silk satin. Eyelash lace and pleated tulle trim the tops of the demi-cups to make them wink. The laced gold grommet portion above the hips flare out to reveal tulle panels. Lacings trail through more gold grommets along the solid black back leading to an open and lace-trimmed backed panty. Simply stunning.

I grin and practically skip to the dressing room. An assistant helps me put on the corset. I emerge to wolf whistles from Lola and claps from Billie, Blair, and Viv—who wears the antique gold ensemble. It's as perfect against her ebony skin as my set is with my emerald green eyes.

We strut our stuff and strike poses à la *The Lion*.

"Fabulous, ladies!" Billie says. "It's going to be a Lola's Coterie night!"

"A *Lavish* Lola's Coterie night!" Blair adds. "All the girls have their lingerie selected from here and the London and Paris boutiques."

Viv hip bumps me and says, "I can*not* wait!"

I grin.

Harris came up with the idea to host an Annual

Halloween Masquerade Party at LEVELS New York. He explained his parents and each of his siblings have family events: Dad Morgan and Mom Shelley Labor Day; Malcolm and Starr Memorial Day; Haley and Lachlan July 4 (even if in Aberdeen); Sebastian and Lola Thanksgiving; Roger and Leonie Christmas and New Year's. Since Harris is the trickster of the family, Halloween is the best holiday for us.

We decided to open the night up to friends, too. Each one could invite two people. Harris thought it a good way to vet prospective members. We'll close LEVELS Peepshow and the Cellar to members for the night. They can still access the upper levels for dining and dancing. And we'll still have plenty of room.

Earlier, I met Harris at the Meatpacking District flagship location. We checked the decorations on both levels matched our Rogues & Sirens theme. Oversized flat screens display movies including *9 1/2 Weeks*, *The Lover*, *Body Heat*, and *Bound*. Platters of carnal edible delights will rest on strategically placed tables, some with naked men and women covered with them.

A deejay will play sensual music on Peepshow. Male and female dancers in cages set around the room. The Rogues and Sirens can grind on the new dance floor cordoned off near the deejay.

Signature mocktails crafted by Billie—our mixologist— will flow from ice fountains sculpted in the naked form of men and women. Those not willing to imbibe the essence from a frosty penis and nipples can opt for service from the bartenders dressed only in black leather ties and black leather penis sheaths.

The Cellar—LEVELS' BDSM dungeon, an expansive, grand hall, austere in design—will have platforms where willing subs of both sexes offer themselves to Rogue Doms and Siren Dommes. Fascinating new toys available for all to play with during their scenes.

Those who don't have masks can choose from a selection of unique handmade ones commissioned from an artisan in Venice. Harris chose an ornate platinum and cream Joker's mask. I wanted to play on my name with a gold metal filigree and Swarovski Crystal cat mask.

As I carry my Lola's Coterie shopping bags to our penthouse, I envision my mask with my emerald green lingerie. It's going to look awesome. And like Viv, I can*not* wait!

"WELCOME to the inaugural evening of decadence in honor of Halloween Erotic Eve and all Rogues and Sirens who thrive on the carnal delights of this night. No rules? Oh surely, you *jest*. Rule One: only consensual play. Rule Two: all must remain shrouded in mystery behind your masks. Let the tricks and treats begin!"

Harris' proclamation earns cries of passion from our guests gathered around the primary stage of Peepshow. He raises our clasped hands in the air, then to his lips. The heat from his penetrative stare nearly melts the gold metal mask from my face.

I shudder as my nipples pebble against the molded

demi-cups of my corset. A flush rises from the tops of the mounds up my neck to color my alabaster cheeks.

He hops down from the stage. His eyes follow the curvy shape of my body, cinched by the corset. My pussy softens and moistens as he stares at my core blatantly. His nostrils flare as though my arousal teases his senses. The tip of his tongue slips out to lick his full bottom lip. He tastes me on the air.

My Rogue continues to devour me with his molten platinum eyes as they skim down my long, toned legs ending in fuck-me gold marabou mules. He grasps me by the waist and lifts me off the stage to stand before him.

"I'll say it again. You win the Sexiest Siren Award," he murmurs in my ear. His warm breath teases the delicate shell. His hand dips from my waist to squeeze the bare cheek of my ass in emphasis. "So many curves for me to make my personal playground. Where shall I start?"

A moan escapes my slack mouth.

He growls low in his throat. The feral sound vibrates through my body.

I shudder in response.

"Wherever you wish, My Sexy Rogue," I purr. My fingers grip the front of his colorful silk shirt. Acting on instinct, my hips gyrate to grind my pelvis against the tops of his muscular thighs beneath black leather pants. I groan at the pressure against my lower belly from his thick erection. "I. Am. All. Yours."

He fists my ponytail and yanks my head back. I hiss from the unexpected sting.

"Mine!" He growls through clenched teeth before he slams his mouth over my parted lips.

The possessive kiss leaves my lips swollen and me breathless.

My Sexy Rogue pivots and stalks through the clusters of our guests as they watch demonstrations on the smaller platforms. Some of them have never been to LEVELS New York or any BDSM club. They watch in awe as Malcolm—a Dom and a Shibari master—prepares to bind Starr in white silks. I recognize them despite their masks, especially since Malcolm is bare chested. A sexy as sin, intricate tattoo wraps around his well-defined pecs to span across his back to form wings.

I only get a glimpse before My Sexy Rogue moves on.

Then do a double take when we approach another platform. A St. Andrew's Cross stands in the center. A sub in a playsuit stands bound by wrists and ankles to the cross. Her barely there lingerie has three thin black studded strips wrapped around her throat, outside the cups of her black lace demi-cup bra to crisscross over her torso to form a pattern over her lower belly, then merge with lace to cover her mons. She moans as her Dom traces one stretched arm with a peacock's feather. Lola and Sebastian!

Once again, the masks cannot hide their identity from me. While at the boutique, Lola showed us the playsuit she designed to wear for the party. I love how it resembles bondage. Perfect for the St. Andrew's Cross demonstration she takes part in with Sebastian.

"Where are you off to in such a hurry? Not sneaking away from your own party, are you?"

I bump into Harris' back as he comes to an abrupt stop. A peek around his massive frame, reveals Haley with an impish grin on her face. Only the bottom half shows beneath the elaborate red and gold mask she wears. The long red feather bobs as she giggles.

"We supplied the activity and venue. We will not play with our guests, too," Harris responds wryly. Then he counters her questions with his own. "Shouldn't you partake in all the night offers, my dear twin? Or is Little Lord Fauntleroy not enough for you?"

Lachlan growls from beneath his tiger's mask. His emerald green eyes flare.

"Surely, *you* jest. Or did your Joker's mask warp your brain?" Lachlan all but snarls at Harris.

"Oh, for fuck's sake! Enough with the pissing contest, mates."

We shift our gazes towards the Scottish accent.

A man raises his full mask and flicks his green eyes between Harris and Lachlan. Patrick!

"Put your knobs away or go find an alcove and put them to better use," he tells them. He nods at Haley and me, then continues past us with Billie holding back giggles trailing behind him. The Alpha Dom's sizable hand clasps a diamond chain connected to a diamond collar around her neck.

Our friends hold nothing back tonight. And I am all for it!

I bring my gaze back to Harris and Lachlan.

"I agree. Use all of this testosterone for the better good of womankind—Haley and me," I tell them as I take Harris by the arm and tug him along.

Haley concurs and does the same to Lachlan as the Alpha male and Alpha Dom mutter under their breath. A fucker here, a wanker there, and they're back to loving, loyal cousins. Men…

My Sexy Rogue and I weave our way towards a darkened alcove. The erotically enamored couples, ménage à trois, and other combinations of polyamory we encounter, the higher my arousal peaks. The carnal electricity from the scenes playing out around us sparks.

It skitters across my skin, leaving a wake of tingling nerve endings. The fine hairs on my arms raise. Puckered nipples tighten to the point of pain. Juices dampen the gusset of my panty. The need for My Sexy Rogue to take me heightens. I increase my pace.

At last, we reach an empty banquette shrouded in shadows. Many others occupied by guests in various stages of sex and clothing. However, their masks remain fixed on their faces. Everyone enjoys an air of intrigue.

My Sexy Rogue sits on the vamp red leather seat. He widens his muscular thighs and settles me between them— my back to his front. His hands skim the tops of my thighs as he spreads, then drapes them over his legs. Fully exposed an additional round of carnal electricity zings through my body.

"I want you to pick a scene and describe what you see,

then how it makes you feel," he says. I shudder as his lips trace from the curve of my shoulder up the side of my neck. "And do not skip one detail."

The solid rod of his massive erection as it presses against the crack of my ass proves a pleasurable distraction. But I snap to with a yelp when he plucks my engorged clit. The sopping wet gusset of my panty does nothing to limit the sting of his reprimand.

Quickly I scan the floor of Peepshow. Our guests mingle with staff subs and Doms/Dommes while voyeurs linger on the fringes, greedily absorbing bacchanalia before them. All kinds of kinky demonstrations occur. The moans, groans, and occasional scream blends with the sensual throbbing of the bass in music as the deejay spins. The air ripens with the scent of sex.

A blindfolded, naked woman astride a Sybian surrounded by four bare-chested men in tight leather pants makes my pulse race. Her full, round breasts jiggle as the vibrations from the dildo attached to the saddle jolts her pussy. A sheen of sweat glistens on her warm honey colored skin. Rainbows shimmer around her from the crystal-embellished mask she wears.

The man behind her grips her stacked forearms bound to her back by a black cord. He uses the handle to tilt her backwards. As she cries out from the dildo, rubbing her G-spot, he slams his mouth over hers. On either side, two men take advantage of the deep arc of her shuddering body to engulf her pebbled brown nipples with their hungry mouths. Her thighs quiver when the man in the front laps at her engorged clit. None pay any attention to the cluster of guests around them. The beautiful woman commands their attention during their erotic play.

My body reacts to each of their ministrations as though I wear their toy. My swollen nipples ache as they strain against the molded demi-cups of my corset. Inside my belly, excitement swirls. It reaches down into my core to set it ablaze. More cream gushes. I feel it seep beyond my panty to pool onto the leather seat.

After I share all details, I close my thighs for friction. But My Sexy Rogue widens his opening me further. The coolness of the room touches the heated flesh of lower lips as they slip from my panty. I moan in frustration.

"I did not tell you to relieve yourself. That's for me to do," he chides. A smack to my pussy lips furthers his disapproval.

However, combined with my heightened arousal, my punishment provides enough contact to elicit an orgasm. I shudder and lean limp against his powerful chest.

He growls and lifts my hips. The pinch of lace against my clit dispels the brief moment of orgasmic bliss. One-handed, My Sexy Rogue unzips his leather pants. His turgid cock bounces free heavily against my ass. He groans in relief. The rumble in his chest vibrates against me.

"I'm going to fuck you right here. Right. Now."

With one brutal thrust, he impales me on his velvet-covered steel. Its tip breaches my slippery folds and prods my cervix. I climax upon impact. He hisses in my hair.

"So fucking good, Siren. You make it hard not to cum,"

he grinds out through clenched teeth as my pussy walls flutter along his solid length. "Do. Not. Move."

Despite his command, I swivel my hips to encourage him to fuck me now. My disobedience earns me a quick succession of smacks to the outer lips of my pussy stretched around his impressive girth. I buck against the onslaught of spanks.

When the pain lessens, the pleasure takes its place.

My Sexy Rogue grips my hips and thrusts up repeatedly. He doesn't stop, even as two more orgasms rip through my pulsating core. His feral grunts and growls fill my ears. I bite my lower lip to prevent my carnal cries from bursting forth. He fucks me until spots dance before my eyes.

When he explodes a torrent of hot cum deep within my pussy, his release triggers another mind-blowing one of mine. He pulls my head to the side and captures my mouth. We swallow one another's cries of ecstasy with our bodies connected as one.

This is one night of Halloween Erotic Eve debauchery with My Sexy Rogue I'll never forget and look forward to many more ahead!

HARRIS

"Kat! Open your eyes!"

"You're missing the view of the mountains!"

"Don't be a baby! You won't have to ski back down from up there."

My Kitty Kat ignores her girls and burrows her face deeper into the partially opened front of my Moncler Grenoble parka. Her arms tighten around my waist as she tries not to tremble in fear.

I press my hand against the back of her head covered by her hood and tilt it back, so she peeks up at me with one eye closed.

"Kitty Kat, do you trust me?" I ask as my other hand bands around her waist to pull her flush to me.

She bites the corner of her mouth as she continues to peek up at me with one eye. I wait patiently for her to respond. The other eye opens. Nerves battle with trust in the emerald green depths as she flicks her eyes from my face to the window of the gondola. They widen and rush back to me. Her body quakes.

Her reaction is so cute, I want to kiss the tip of her nose —red like Rudolph. She swallows thickly and blinks.

Still, I wait.

Her inner battle ends when she nods, then catches herself and vocalizes her response.

"Y—Yes," My Kitty Kat stammers, then clears her throat. "Yes, I trust you, Harris Steele."

An intense wave of satisfaction floods my system at her trust in me, despite her fear of heights. Made even more endearing since we're riding up in a gondola with over-sized windows to the highest point of the Rocky Mountains in Colorado. The majestic snow-covered peaks dominate the panorama. While below, the town spreads beyond STEELE Aspen Resort. At this distance, they appear miniature. Colorful dots in the snow.

It's Thanksgiving weekend and Baz and Lola's holiday to host for our family.

Since we're spending Christmas through New Year's in Sydney for the wedding, we'll miss being at *Chalet de la Joie* —Roger and Leonie's residence in Verbier, Switzerland. Baz and Lola decide Aspen would make up for our skiing in the Alps and chose here over their private island— Bougainvillea Cay in Exumas, Bahamas.

My Kitty Kat never skied, so I promised to teach her on the bunny trails. This gondola ride up to the top of the mountain doesn't exactly match the smaller hills. However, we won't ski down like the others after breakfast in the Peak Lodge. We'll ride back down on the gondola with her family since they're not skiers, yet.

I thought she'd enjoy the expansive view. Guess not…

My forehead presses against hers, hidden within her hood. Our eyes lock. I slow my breathing to encourage her to follow. She does and begins to calm. Her body stills as she relaxes in my arms.

"Good, lass," I croon.

She sighs and leans against me heavily.

Lost in our own bubble of trust and love, our family and their conversations around us fade. I rock My Kitty Kat gently.

"Now, I want you to look through the front window of the gondola. Up towards the mountain peak, not down. Focus on its beauty and know I'll let nothing happen to you, Kitty Kat," I tell her.

Her eyes scan mine, then she nods and looks behind me. I move around her and hold her back to my front. My hands rest protectively beneath her breasts. A small gasp escapes her lips as the mountaintop looms ahead.

I whisper words of encouragement and smile as she settles enough to appreciate the view. Oohs and aahs warm my heart. Her level of trust in me means the world to me.

By the time we reach the gondola house, My Kitty Kat chats easily with everyone as we disembark. We make our way to the restaurant en masse. The hostess greets us by name and leads us to reserved tables beside the wall of windows facing the surrounding mountains and Aspen below.

At this super safe distance, My Kitty Kat plops onto a chair closest to the expansive view. Her smile could rival the brilliant sun in the cloudless blue sky above.

"That was beyond incredible! Well… Once you calmed me down," she says with a giggle. "Had I known we were riding in a sardine box with windows up the steepest incline in the world, I would have stayed at the base lodge!"

Her Mum laughs and pats her hand. Then, Mum Allison smiles at me.

"Harris, you really helped my wee lass. She used to be afraid of the sliding board at the park. After she got to the top of the ladder, she cried until her father scooped her off!" Allison says with a shake of her head.

"I don't regret the ride up. It feels like we're in the heavens all the way up here," My Kitty Kat exclaims.

"On the ride down, you can see what you missed," I tell her.

She faints dramatically and waves a hand over her face.

"Give a lass a minute, will ya?" She says.

Everyone at our table laughs.

The conversation turns to the day's activities. Some will continue to ski while others will sleigh ride, ice skate, or snowboard. My Kitty Kat and I will hit the bunny hill for lessons. If she picks it up quick enough, we can try an easy trail.

While we enjoy a hearty breakfast to fuel our day, the girls chat about the wedding planning. I've stayed on the periphery. Not interested in the choice of flowers or music selection, table assignments or order of speeches. Ah, no.

As long as My Kitty Kat walks down the aisle to me, I'm all good.

I took advice from my brothers for the honeymoon. They went all out for theirs and wowed their new brides. I will do the same for my Mrs. Steele. A grin spreads across my face. I cannot wait for her reaction. Priceless, I'm sure.

My parents—along with Uncle Connor, Aunt Lucie, Mum Allison and Henry, Leonie's parents, and Starr's parents—plan on dinner after an art gallery opening. The rest of us—including Payton, Michael, and Charlotte—will go to Escobar. The après-ski nightspot has a sleek vibe with popular deejays and creative drinks.

After breakfast, My Kitty Kat, her family, and I watch as the rest gear up for their trip down the mountain. They choose a double black diamond piste. All advanced skiers, they'll thrive on the challenges the extremely difficult trial offers. We bid them good luck and take the path to the gondola house.

My Kitty Kat squeezes my hand when the gondola moves beyond the opening. The expanse of the Rocky Mountains, Aspen, and beyond lies before us. She steals a peek at me. I smile and rub her back to soothe her nerves. She takes a deep cleansing breath and faces her fear head on.

To distract her, I point out key spots and talk about the fun I had spending Christmas here. They get a kick out of my mishaps on the slopes when I was younger. Particularly the time I thought I started an avalanche. Only to find out the snow from the trees above fell on me, not a horrific wave of snow down the mountain. I learned the lesson to not go off-piste alone.

When we disembark from the gondola, My Kitty Kat announces she no longer fears heights and plans to learn to ski well enough for the advance pistes. We cheer her on with claps and wolf whistles. She curtsies, then thanks me with a mind-blowing kiss.

"I do not care to see my sister in a lip lock."

Payton's grumbled remark breaks us apart. We stare at him. He grins and adds for us to get a room. Relieved he's not being an asshole, I clap him on the shoulder and laugh. The others join in, equally pleased he was joking.

Mum Allison and Henry leave us to take a sleigh ride.

I lead the rest to the base lodge where our ski butlers await. They help us with our gear while the instructors for Payton, Michael, and Charlotte talk to them about their goals. Sure, My Kitty Kat could have an instructor. But I'll be the only one to ever pick her up when she falls, not some hotshot. Mine!

We get to the T-bar lift and the lesson begins. I explain how to lean against the upside-down T to avoid pulling it down and landing on her ass. She masters it on the third try. First victory!

At the top of the bunny hill, part two of the lesson begins. I show her how to fall to the side to avoid injury. She tries and laughs as she struggles. I demonstrate the V formation with my skis and slide down the slope, going left and right a few feet. As I sidestep up to her, she practices the V. I go down again, then call for her to try.

My Kitty Kat skis a few feet before she wobbles, flails her arms, and plonks to her ass. She laughs and falls back on the snow. Her arms move to create a snow angel before she sits up.

A little girl zips by, and My Kitty Kat laughs harder.

"Great, even a wee lass has me beat!" She says as she throws her hands up. "Help me, Harris."

I chuckle and sidestep up to her. I angle her to face parallel to the bunny hill, then grip beneath her arms and lift her. She stands on her skis and dusts the snow from her ass.

"Oh, no you don't. Part of my payment is to swipe snow from your body," I say as I replace her hands with mine.

She wiggles her hips and asks, "What's the other part?"

I rise to my full height and smirk down at her. Not wanting a single soul to hear my carnal plans, I lean down to murmur them in her ear.

She gasps and darts her eyes around to confirm no one heard a word. Below the Dragon mirrored ski goggles, her face turns a darker shade of crimson.

I chuckle wickedly, smack her on the ass, and tell her to try again.

Two and a half hours later, we're cuddled up on the sofa beneath a cashmere blanket before a roaring fire in my family's lodge.

My Kitty Kat loves the contemporary timber and stone, twelve-bedroom mountain lodge we have within the

STEELE Aspen complex of hotel, restaurants, spa, and residential properties. The gated private homes surround the hotel and have access to its amenities as a perk of being a part of the luxury resort. From our lodge, it takes only minutes to arrive in the center of Aspen or at the ski lifts. Outside the double-story wall of windows beyond the heated deck, more panoramic views of Colorado's majestic snow-covered Rocky Mountains and of the ski resort leave one breathless. It's also one of my favorite residences.

Our moment of peace ends when my nieces and nephews return from their ski lessons. They barrel into the great room after depositing their gear in the equipment room and their outerwear in the mudroom. They head straight for us with cries of *Oncle* Harris, *Tante* Kat for Roger's children and the English equivalent of uncle and aunt for the rest of the little monsters.

My Kitty Kat and I make room for their invasion after we tell the nannies we got it under control. The children regale us with tales of their exploits for the day. They remind me of myself at their ages—busy, adventurous, curious. We listen raptly and laugh along with them or offer words of support and encouragement.

Next to arrive, the skiers stride in. The parents scoop their children into their arms, and the stories begin again. Lucien goes to the chef's kitchen and returns with mugs of hot chocolate and a tray of tasty chocolate chip and sugar cookies. It becomes an impromptu party. We spend time together before dinner, then clubbing.

Haley catches my eye and cocks her head with a smirk.

I frown, confused. She purses her lips and jerks her chin to my left. I turn to find My Kitty Kat glowing as she holds Dione and Iris on her lap. Malcolm and Starr's twin daughters chatter on about the snowman they want to build in the morning.

Kat tells them she'll help since she has a wee bit of fairy dust she can sprinkle on it. Their eyes widen and ask if it's like Frosty. She tells them it's a secret and they'll see in the morning if they promise to be extra good tonight.

Mini Malcolms 2.0—as we affectionately call their second set of twins—sit stunned. Then Iris leans forward and wraps her arms around Kat's neck for a hug. Her eyes shimmer before she closes them and hugs both Iris and Dione.

My heartbeat quickens.

Does Kat want children now? Am I being selfish in not wanting them for a while? Do I want to hold off for real? Fuck!

I sit back against the sofa with my mind churning. Haley—who stared at me the whole time—starts to laugh uproariously. I throw a glare at her, which only makes my twin double over. She wipes tears from her eyes as she shakes with mirth. I groan.

Just fucking great…

KAT

armth cocoons me as I float on a cloud of bliss. Memories of Harris worshipping my body for hours cause tingles to ignite along my heated skin. His talented mouth brings me to climax again and again before his beautiful cock makes me explode. I tremble at the thought.

My hand stretches out to caress my lover.

I roll over and open my eyes to find his side of the king-size bed empty. My palm strokes cold sheets instead of his hot body. My head cocks to listen for him in the en suite bathroom since the double doors to the living room remain closed.

Not hearing any movement or water from the shower, I sit up. My eyes scan the bedroom, then land on a cream notecard set on the nightstand. A crystal vase overflowing with gorgeous blue roses stands beside it. Then I notice their delicate scent. I inhale deeply and scramble across the bed.

My True Love Kitty Kat,

As much as I love waking to your beautiful face, this morning I must wait until I see you walk down the aisle to become my wife. My heart races at the thought.

These Blue Roses symbolize trust, commitment, and relationship. All that you have given to me, and all I have given to you willingly. Blue is the rarest color of roses just as life doesn't always provide a True Love. Tonight, we become one, Mrs. Harris Steele.

Love your Husband forevermore,
Harris

Tears fill my eyes and spill to my cheeks as I finish Harris' touching love letter. Seventeen months after we first met, three months together, fourteen weeks apart, three weeks salvaging our relationship, eleven months back together, and here we are on the morning of our wedding. I fulfilled my vow to get my man back while in this very city last New Year's Eve.

Life may have been a rollercoaster with highs in love and lows in despair. But we made it this far. This day, we vow to never part from the other. Husband and wife. Forevermore.

I dab my cheeks with the handkerchief Harris had so thoughtfully left on the nightstand beside the note card. Through my tears of joy, I smile. I love my man.

Once again, I scramble across the giant bed to the nightstand on my side. I grab my mobile to call Harris.

"Good morning, Siren. Your call enthralled me to marry you and only you. How do you feel on this momentous day?" He asks as his smile shines over the airwaves.

I open my mouth to speak, but emotions overwhelm me again. I lean back against the fluffy pillows and close my eyes. The lids help to staunch the flow of more tears.

"Babe? Are you still there?"

Harris' worried voice filters through the rising tide of my emotions. I take a deep, cleansing breath and try again to regain my ability to speak.

"Y—y—yes, my love," I start, then clear my throat thick with tears. "I feel wonderful, especially after reading your love letter. The Blue Roses are incredible. You are incredible. I—I love you, Harris Steele."

Now, his end of the call drops into silence.

I strain my ear to hear what he's doing.

A soft rustling sound, then a door closes. Harris clears his throat.

"I love you, too, My Kitty Kat," he murmurs in a raspy voice. "It's incredible you love me. Me. Not just who I am and what I have. I can't wait for you to be my wife, Kat Jackson soon-to-be Kat Steele."

"Listen, lover boy, we have to go!"

"Yeah, up and at 'em!"

Roger and Laurent call to Harris. He tells them to fuck off before more rustling.

"I presume this is Kat. So, good morning, Kat," Roger says, then continues. "I'm quite certain my mother has plans for you, and we have plans for Harris. He'll be nice and ready for you. Much love. But… Ciao!"

Roger *The Responsible* ends the call chuckling while Harris growls in the background.

As if on cue, a knock on the bedroom doors startles me. I squeak and lift the sheet over my bare breasts. The door opens.

"Rise and shine, Kat, sweetheart!"

"Yes, time to start your wedding day, honey!"

"Come along, darling. We have much to do!"

Through the now open double doors, Sergeant Shelley, Major Mum, and Lieutenant Lucie stride inside. They tsk at me still lying in bed and urge me to the bathroom for a steam shower. They allot me twenty minutes before they expect me in the living room.

I can't help my giggle but follow their command without hesitation.

Emerged from the dressing room in the flowy maxi dress and sandals they set aside for my attire, they hustle me out of the suite. One of the two wedding planners greets us when the lift opens on the lobby of STEELE Sydney.

As my future sister-in-law said, the view from their

property is far superior to the one from the Park Hyatt Sydney. As we move through the lobby, I steal glimpses at Sydney Harbour. The sun shines brightly on the azure blue waters. Boats of all types float along its surface. The Sydney Opera House's distinctive series of arched white roofs shaped like the sails of boats rises above the Harbour. A magnificent day for our wedding!

My heart skips a beat knowing in only a matter of hours, I will be Mrs. Harris Steele. OMG!!!

"Don't dawdle, Kat, honey!"

Major Mum's chiding words hurry me along.

We enter the spa. Instantly, the tranquil environment slows my breaths. I close my eyes and allow the soothing scent of lavender and the calming sound of wind to wash over me. Be still my beating heart.

Arms band around me from the front, back, and sides.

My eyes fly open to find myself engulfed by Vivian, Charlotte, and all my future sisters-in-law. They swap with Blair, Billie, Adrienne, Márcia, Anita, and Isla Ritchie—my friend and the former administrative assistant to Lachlan.

They're swathed in fluffy terrycloth robes with matching slippers on their feet. Hair pulled up in topknots. Makeup-free faces beam at me.

Soon we're whisked away by aestheticians for a plethora of treatments. By the time we meet up again, we're pliant, buffed, and waxed to perfection. I'm so at ease, my feet barely touch the ground as we walk to one restaurant for my bridesmaids' luncheon. Or more like maid of honor and my girls' luncheon since only Vivian is in the wedding party opposite Laurent as Harris' best man.

As we go along, Mum Shelley and Aunt Lucie remove their military command helmets to introduce me to various wedding guests we pass.

After we went through the numbers, we found between the Steeles and the Jacksons, we had four hundred—about two hundred each. My handful put us over the four hundred number. Since the wedding is so large, our party dominates the hotel. Malcolm—as STEELE International, Inc.'s President of Entertainment Properties Division—closed the hotel for our private use during the duration of our time here.

After the hostess leads us to a table with views of Sydney Harbour and the server takes our order, I present gifts to everyone. The Mums receive sterling silver frames with a photo of Harris and me taken from our sitting with the engagement announcement photographer. Their eyes well with tears as they thank me.

Even though they're not in the wedding party, I give my sister, sisters-in-law, and friends gifts. Their contribution to the love Harris and I share makes them invaluable. Each ooh and aah over the vintage diamond brooches I collected from auctions at Sotheby's. I worked with a representative who scoured the auctions at their houses in New York City, London, Geneva, and Paris to find unique pieces befitting each one.

As we dine on tasty food, guests stop by our table to offer words of congratulations and best wishes. Mum

Shelley and Aunt Lucie make more introductions. I try my best to remember names. Lola leans over and tells me not to worry. No one expects the bride to know everyone. I smile at her gratefully.

Soon it's time to take a nap before we change for the ceremony.

My nerves amp up again. Even though I ate a light lunch of grilled balsamic vinaigrette chicken over a bed of butter lettuce, my stomach roils.

Starr must sense my distress because she takes both of my hands between hers and makes me focus on the sound of her voice.

"Slow inhalation. Pause for a beat. Slow exhalation. Slow inhalation. Pause for a beat. Slow exhalation. Continue while you listen to me only," she says, then takes me through a restorative mediation.

The sounds of the other diners' chatter and cutlery on dishes fade away. My mind latches on to Starr's soothing intonation. She tells me to open my eyes on my next exhalation.

At once, a sense of peace blankets me. With a smile, I squeeze her hands. She nods, and we rise along with the others. Once again, I float through the hotel, smiling at those I meet.

Major Mum, Sergeant Shelley, and Lieutenant Lucie escort me to my suite. They encourage me to rest in bed even if I don't sleep. My body will relax naturally.

When I step inside the bedroom, I smile. They had the maids close the drapes, turn down the bed, dim the lights, and turn on Zen music with water sounds. I step out of my sandals and strip my maxi dress over my head. The soft sheets swaddle me. Moments later, I fall fast asleep.

THE SOUND of my name rouses me.

My eyes pop open to find my Mum sitting on the edge of the bed. She smiles with tears in her eyes. I sit up and throw my arms around her. We hold one another in silence. Emotions roll over us.

"Oh, Kat, honey. I'm so proud of you. My wee lass all grown up about to marry her love—" A sob cuts her words off, and she squeezes me tighter. She takes a breath and pulls back to stare into my eyes. "Your father would be so proud of you, too, Kat. Know he is with you. Always. Although Connor will walk you down the aisle, your *Da* will be right beside you, honey."

I nod vigorously as tears stream down my cheeks. The anger I had with my father over him dying so young and leaving us with only our Mum to raise us ebbs away. In my heart, I know he did his best and loved us dearly. I send a silent prayer of love to him. It's my wedding day. I will not hold on to any negativity. Only love and light surround us.

My Mum pats me on the back and rises.

"Time to get dressed, Kat, honey," she says with a smile. "Mr. Valentino wants to make any final adjustments before you walk down the aisle."

Before we leave my suite, I freshen up in the bathroom. I check my mobile for a text message from Harris but find none. Well wishes from colleagues not invited to the wedding make me smile. I follow my Mum to the suite beside the ballroom where the ceremony will take place. One of the wedding planners guides us through the hotel where guests won't have the chance to cross my path.

In the suite, my wedding gown hangs in the middle of the room. My breath catches in my throat. I clutch my chest. Butterflies like those embroidered amongst the flowers on my gown and my cathedral veil flutter in my belly.

The white sweetheart neckline gown floats like their gossamer wings with its layers of sheer tulle. The veil hangs beside it. Monsieur Valentino commissioned a pair of Manolo Blahnik shoes to match my gown flawlessly. They sit below the gown while my Lola's Coterie white silk panty and pale blue silk garter belt rest on a table. The entire ensemble designed to awe my future husband.

Both the videographer and photographer who followed us throughout the day capture the moment. The glam squad fixes my hair and makeup. I smile at the atelier dresser assigned to help me and step behind the screen. I re-emerge like as my fantasy bride.

Now dressed in her Valentino mother-of-the-bride dress, my Mum's eyes widen. She dabs at them with a handkerchief as she approaches me.

"Honey… Extraordinary… Oh, Kat," she says softly.

I fan my face and glance up at the ceiling to stop the tears from falling. Then often a watery smile to Monsieur Valentino when he enters the suite. His words of praise thrill me. Me. Kat Roberts—the poor Scottish lass—now dressed in her wedding gown by a master about to marry a multibillionaire. Unbelievable.

Uncle Connor walks in as Monsieur Valentino leaves with the dresser and glam squad. He greets them, then stops speechless when his gaze reaches me. He shakes his head and smiles.

"Kat, lass… You are simply stunning. As gorgeous as my Lucie on our wedding day. It is an honor to walk you down the aisle," he says, then holds out a navy blue bag to me. "From your betrothed."

I reach inside and remove a large square blue velvet jewelry case. The click of the sapphire cabochon closer reveals a suite of diamonds nestled on silk. My jaw drops.

"Here, I will help you," Uncle Connor says as he sets the bag and case on the table.

He places the bib necklace on me. It glitters from my neck to above the swell of my breasts. Each of the drop earrings slip into my ears. I hold my wrist out for him to close the bracelet around it. My Mum slips the brooch in my hair so it shows when I remove the veil. Last, I slip the ring on my right hand. My gaze goes from the priceless jewels to Uncle Connor.

"Exquisite," he states. At the knock on the door, he raises his arm. "Shall we?"

I nod, too overcome for words.

He cocks an eyebrow.

I bite back a giggle at his Alpha Dom reaction and

verbalize my response. He leads me from the room and to the man I love with all my heart, body, and soul.

No more nerves. The only butterflies that swirl about remain on my wedding gown and veil.

Mrs. Harris Steele, here I come.

"No turning back now, Harris!"

"You sure you've given up your player's card? For good, bro?"

"Remember what you told me when before I married Lola?"

"Yeah… Exactly!"

"You know that's right, cuz!"

I roll my eyes at my brothers and cousins as they continue to rib me.

After I left My Kitty Kat sated and passed out from hours of toe-curling orgasms, I went to the suite Malcolm reserved for me.

My Kitty Kat is traditional and didn't want to see me but didn't want to put me out of our suite. I saved her the discomfort of asking me to leave and left of my own accord. Plus, I don't want to start our new life with any chance of bad luck. We've been through enough shit to last a lifetime. The rest of this one and forevermore, I want to spend happily with My Kitty Kat—the future Mrs. Harris Steele. Thank you very much.

I showered, then went to the gym to burn off nervous energy. Not that I'd tell these clowns…

They showed up as planned, and we got in a workout before my bachelor's brunch. No, I didn't opt for the whole get drunk at a strip club and fuck some broad. Not my style, nor my boys. Hard pass.

After the wedding rehearsal last night, we hung out at the Jackson Smoke&Scotch Sydney. Lachlan did a tasting while Laurent handed out a new cigar he created. We just talked shit as usual, enjoying each other's company for a few hours. Sure, some women ventured over. But we deftly avoided their advances. They got the message and moved on. With a warmth in my belly from the Scotch, I returned to my fiancée.

Until the sun rose, I ravaged her tight, curvy body. She'll wake up sore. Hopefully, she'll be able to walk down the aisle without leaning too heavily on Uncle Connor's arm. I chuckle at the thought even as my cock threatens to swell uncomfortably in my gym shorts. Calm down, big boy. Later.

"Oh, man, leave Harris alone. He was bound to fall, eventually."

Norman's words draw me from my musings. I smile and nod my thanks to the Champ. He claps me on the back as he heads to the weight rack.

"True, I'll give him that. Besides, it's always the most

vehement ones who fall the hardest," Chase Wentworth—Lydie's love—says, then continues. "Besides, I have to give him some credit for having his wedding in my hometown."

Lachlan clears his throat. We turn to face him.

"Harris, now is a good time to remind you to treat Kat with the utmost respect. She is a Jackson. Thus, my responsibility. Don't fuck with her or answer to me," he says.

The gym erupts.

Baz grabs Lachlan into a headlock.

Malcolm throws his water bottle at him.

Roger swipes his legs from beneath him. He and Baz fall on top of him.

Lucien and Laurent jump in. To save their brother or to help take him down, I don't know.

I just throw my head back and laugh.

Eventually, we finish our workout and head for the sauna, then shower. My stomach rumbles when we enter the restaurant. With all the energy I burned off fucking and lifting, I'm famished.

Several heads turn as we follow the hostess to our table. Guests offer their well wishes as we pass them. Others stop by the table. I thank them all.

After we order our food, I signal to the server. The manager returns with bags. He sets them on the floor beside me. I grin at my boys.

"Well, brothers, I want to thank you for your words of wisdom, support, and love. Without you, who knows? Maybe I'd still be shooting my load at LEVELS with some willing female," I say with a chuckle. The very idea turns me off.

"Here's a little something to remember this momentous occasion," I add as I hand a bag to each of them.

"Hot damn!"

"Shit, man, thanks!"

I sit back and fold my arms over my chest with a smirk as they open the wooden boxes.

Inside of each rests a Patek Phillipe 6301 Grand Complications watch. The platinum case with hand-stitched, shiny platinum gray alligator strap engraved with Kat's and my names and the date of our wedding. I choose the color combination to represent STEELE. They'll always remember this day when they put on the luxurious, complicated dress watch. As fine watch collectors, they'll appreciate the gesture.

For the rest of the meal, the married ones offer advice. I take mental notes. Their trials and mistakes will help me avoid similar pitfalls. Their successes will make me a rock-star to My Kitty Kat. Without a doubt, it's a win-win situation.

Laurent calls time on our bachelor's brunch. He reminds us it's time to rest up before my big moment. His tone brokers no argument. My best man takes his duties seriously.

We part as the elevator takes us to our floors. I walk into my suite and straight to the bedroom. The workouts and food knock me out. As I head to the bed, I notice a gift box in the middle of it. I grin in anticipation of something fantastic.

I plop down on the bed and tear into the white wrapping paper of the rectangular box. Beneath the tissue paper, my finger grazes a textured surface. I move the paper aside. A dove gray leather-bound album appears. I lift it out of the box and set it on my lap.

A note from My Kitty Kat catches my eye on the first page.

My Dear Love,

You bring me such joy. Each and every day, I give thanks for you being in my life. Often, I reflect on the time we have spent together. No matter what, I find the good in it all. I pray you do, too.

This album holds memories we will cherish for years to come. Some moments you may recognize, while others will surprise you. You will never know when I capture a moment we share. It is just the start of our life together. We have many more pages to fill.

I love you.

Your Kitty Kat and Siren forever,
Mrs. Harris Steele

Tears blur my vision. And no, I'm not too manly to cry.

Especially when I flip through the pages to find My Kitty Kat documented so many moments in our life together. From our first getaway to the Channel Islands to me asleep at LEVELS London and most recently building a fire in Aspen.

As I close the album with several empty pages for our future moments, my heart soars. I love this woman so much it frightens me. To give my heart to someone else was not on my mind. And here I am, a few hours away from spending the rest of my life with another.

A smile of pure happiness obliterates my tears.

"I love you, Mrs. Harris Steele!" I shout.

"TIME TO WAKE UP, SLEEPING BEAUTY!"

A nudge, and I jolt awake. Laurent—dressed in his bespoke Tom Ford tuxedo—stands beside the bed, grinning at me like the Cheshire Cat.

I sit up. Yup, time to do this, like Brutus!

In no time, I'm dressed in my custom tuxedo and groomed to perfection. Can't meet my beautiful bride looking like a schmo. I walk into the living room of my suite and find Laurent and a wedding planner waiting for me. I give a nod I'm ready, and we head to the ballroom.

We take the back route and avoid wedding guests. STEELE Sydney staff offer their congratulations as we pass, and I thank them heartily. By the time we reach the ballroom, I'm euphoric. Laurent and I enter from a side door straight to the altar.

I greet the officiant. Then my eyes scan the crowd. I

nod at our guests and grin at my family. When the music from the quartet changes, I face the double doors of the main entry to the ballroom. They open and Vivian walks in.

She's absolutely stunning in her gown. Her smile lights the ballroom. If she's this happy, my bride must be ecstatic. I smile at Vivian when she stands across from Laurent and me. She beams.

Once again, the music played by the quartet changes, and all guests rise. My heart pounds in anticipation. I stare at the closed doors. They open, and it's as though Heaven sent an angel.

My Kitty Kat floats down the aisle on Uncle Connor's arm. She's beyond radiant, even through her sheer veil. The diamond suite glitters in the light, adding to her brilliance. The layered skirt of her wedding gown billows around her like a cloud. I stare at her in awe.

When Uncle Connor agrees to give this woman, I force myself not to grab her and run. Instead, I shake his hand and take hers in mine.

She beams up at me. Tears shine in her emerald green eyes. Intense love flows from her to hit me in the chest at full force. I rock on my feet, then stand firm.

As we listen to the officiant, we only have eyes for each other. Laurent has to nudge me to recite my vows. My Kitty Kat follows with her vows. Laurent opens the rectangular jewelry box, and My Kitty Kat gasps.

I lift the hand harness made of a chain of diamonds connected to her eternity band on her middle finger to a princess-shaped diamond that rests atop her hand connected to a diamond double bracelet. Her engagement ring sits on her ring finger. The harness is removable. So she can wear her band and ring together.

A murmur rises from the guests, impressed by the incredible jewels and their symbolism. Kat Roberts-cum-Jackson is now Katrina Steele. My wife. MINE!

Tears shine in her eyes as she places my classic platinum band on my left ring finger. She holds my gaze as she brings my hand to her mouth to kiss my ring. She whispers, I am all yours and you are all mine.

Hell to the yes! My cock jumps to attention.

The officiant pronounces us husband and wife.

With a smirk, I lift her veil and kiss Mrs. Harris Steele until she's breathless.

The guests stand and clap. Our family whoops.

Vivian places My Kitty Kat's bouquet in her hand and rearranges her veil and gown as we turn to face our jubilant guests. Their cheers follow us as I clasp her hand and walk with her by my side down the aisle. Our future as husband and wife begins. And may it never end!

As soon as we enter the suite beside the ballroom, I pull My Kitty Kat into my arms. One kiss of my new wife will not suffice. I draw her close to me, melding our bodies together, and cover her mouth with mine. She moans into the possessive kiss as she leans against me heavily.

The weight of her body reminds me she is mine to protect, provide for, cherish, and love forevermore.

Only the knock on the door makes us come up for air.

My parents, Uncle Connor, Aunt Lucie, and Mum Allison with Henry rush inside. They embrace us before we take family photos. A photographer and videographer followed my boys and me around earlier, so we have but a few more images to do.

Then it's time for the reception. As we wait for the emcee to announce our arrival, I turn to my wife.

"Are you happy with everything so far, babe?" I ask, already knowing her answer since she hasn't stopped smiling or laughing.

She doesn't disappoint. With a giggle, she rises to her toes and presses her soft mouth to mine.

"Oh, so happy, husband of mine," she murmurs against my lips.

I pull her closer to me, making sure she feels the thick erection I've had from the moment we kissed at the altar. I do a grind against her belly.

She mewls and matches my fervor with her own.

The wedding planner coughs politely, and my bride and I part with a laugh as the doors open.

"Ladies and gentlemen, presenting Mr. and Mrs. Harris Steele!" The emcee's voice carries over the throng of voices.

We stride inside, arms held high, faces lit up with dazzling smiles to rival my wife's new jewels.

Our guests cheer.

We make our way to the dance floor for our first dance. The opening chords of "Truly Madly Deeply" play as I sweep my wife into my arms. Her eyes widen and she glances over her shoulder as Darren Hayes' voice blends with the music. She squeals when he steps onto the stage to serenade us. Then she throws her arms around my neck.

Our bodies rock to the romantic song as I murmur the words in her ear. She trembles and holds back her sobs as the words evoke a wellspring of emotions in her. I bury my face in her silky Titian hair and forget all around us except for the touching words of our anthem.

When it ends, we bow to Savage Garden and make our way to the head table. I help my wife into her chair and sit on mine. My thumb brushes over the diamonds on her hand harness and eternity band before I entwine our fingers. I rest our joined hands on my thigh and lean over to kiss my wife.

"I love you, Mrs. Harris Steele," I murmur as I nuzzle the delicate shell of her ear. A lust-filled smile spreads on my face when she trembles. "Never forget. You. Are. Mine."

She nods, then catches her faux pas.

"I love you, Mr. Harris Steele. We are one for all time," she whispers.

Our attention turns from each other to Mum Allison. She makes a heartfelt speech as the parent of the bride. Her references to Kat as a child and how proud her father would be of her make my wife sob softly.

I wrap my arm around her and murmur words of love to soothe her. She cuddles against me while she listens to the rest of her Mum's speech.

The emcee announces dinner.

My wife excuses herself and disappears with Vivian.

While they're gone, I enjoy the first dish of our four-course meal. My mother comes over to check on me. Her face lights up, and I follow her gaze.

My wife returns as the redheaded Siren.

She changed from her ethereal wedding gown into a long-sleeved reception dress with a plunging, wide v-neck and fitted bodice that skims her hips and thighs to flow to the floor. The vavavavoom silhouette has a touch of demure by way of tiny pearls forming flower shapes over the subtly sheer fabric. Her flaming red hair cascades down her back in soft waves. Matte red lipstick dominates her alabaster face.

My unsatisfied cock weeps.

Enthralled, I rise from my chair and make my way to her as she crosses the room like a goddess. Those on the dance floor part. Others seated stare. My Redheaded Siren's call enchants them all.

"Hello, Mr. Steele. Will you dance with me?" She purrs as her fingertips glide up the lapels of my tuxedo jacket. Her emerald eyes smolder from an internal fire.

"It would be my pleasure, Mrs. Steele," I respond, eyes locked on hers.

After our dance, we circulate amongst the guests. Up close, My Redheaded Siren charms them with her smile, gracious words, and affectionate touches. The man all but drop at her feet. The women wish to be her.

I want to fuck her. Now.

However, the wedding planner has other plans for us. It's time for toasts. One by one, our family and friends speak stories and offer their best to us. We laugh and tear up. Especially when my father gives a deeply felt speech in recognition of his last son moving forward to add to the next generation of Steeles.

I freeze.

Children?

Everyone wants children for us like yesterday.

Me?

I'm still ambivalent. At this time, at least.

A sneak peek at my wife lets me know she may have succumbed to the enchantment of the wee ones. Her emerald eyes shine. Undoubtedly visions of little Harrises and Kats play in her mind. She lifts her head to gaze at me. But my eyes slide away. She doesn't notice and kisses my cheek.

Damn.

However, I refuse to dwell on thoughts that dim our momentous day. We move on to through the reception activities.

It's Uncle Connor's time to glide my wife across the floor. My wife tosses a replica of her bouquet to the eager single women. The bachelors prove less inclined to catch her garter. I may be a caveman, but we keep the cake cutting civilized. I place a forkful in her mouth, and she does the same for me. With a wink, she reaches up and licks icing from the corner of my mouth.

I'd rather have her ambrosial cream coat my lips than the sour cream icing. My cock aches.

Once again, Vivian links arms with my wife, and they

leave the reception. I watch after them and wonder what she'll reappear in this time. I don't have long to speculate.

In My Redheaded Siren walks. She shimmers in a mini dress made of crystal strands in varying lengths. They sway and catch the light with each step she takes. Her long, toned legs end in sky-high crystal embellished sandals. Now she collected her thick tresses atop her head in a sexy bun. Fresh, matte red lipstick completes her seductive look.

Hot. Damn.

With the way she oozes sex, I don't know if we'll make it to the New Year's Eve countdown. We may just ditch it and celebrate with our own fireworks. So powerful, they'll rival those above Sydney Harbour.

But I can't deny her the night of her dreams. Instead, I rise and lead her to the rooftop dance floor where Janet Jackson steps onto the stage and sings "Escapade." It's perfect for the honeymoon I have planned for my wife. I tell her it's a clue for what's coming, and she begs me to tell her more. But I smirk and spin her out with no response.

The original Ms. Jackson performs all the way up to the countdown. The servers circulate trays with flutes of Dom Pérignon amongst the guests—all have moved to the rooftop. With Sydney Harbour as her backdrop, Ms. Jackson leads us down from ten. At one, we yell Happy New Year!

The night sky explodes with an array of fireworks. The closest to the hotel displays *Congratulations Mr. and Mrs. Harris Steele!*

My wife throws her arms around my neck as she squeals in delight. I chuckle at her exuberance and squeeze her tight. Then I press my mouth close to her ear so she can hear me over the surrounding celebration.

"Time to consummate our union, Mrs. Harris Steele."

We take nearly an hour to extricate ourselves from the reception turned nightclub. Everyone wanted a chance to congratulate us. We couldn't possibly ignore them. So I consoled myself with the knowledge we have the rest of our lives together. A few minutes won't break us.

They give me blue balls though…

We sigh in relief when the elevator doors close and separate us from the excited partiers. Suddenly shy, my wife's gaze skitters from mine in the reflection on the metal doors. I turn to face her and cup her cheek.

"Alone at last, Mrs. Harris Steele," I murmur as my thumb brushes her lips. "Your Siren's call enthralled me from the moment you walked down the aisle like a sweet angel, to now you stand before me like a seductive goddess. I can barely contain myself."

My forehead drops to hers. The floral aroma of Champagne on her breath mingles with mine. My mouth lowers to capture hers. The tip of my tongue swipes across her lips to demand entry. On a sigh, she lets me in.

Our tongues caress. The delay in our carnal satisfaction urges us on. The gentle kiss bursts into an explosive ball of passion. Lips press harder. Teeth clash and nip. Tongues tangle. We groan hungrily.

The elevator doors ding open.

I grab my wife's hand and all but drag her from the car through the lobby and onto the elevator to reach our suite. We can't keep our hands off each other on the ride up. In the hallway, I scoop her up and rush toward the suite. She throws her head back and laughs throatily.

Inside, I don't hesitate and go straight to the bedroom. The romantic sight of Blue Rose petals, lit candles, and an ice bath of Dom Pérignon only serves to make us pause briefly. With a nod, I stand my wife on her feet beside the wall of windows. My thumb and forefinger lift her face up to align our eyes.

"First, I will claim you. Then, I will make love to you until the sun rises. By morning, there will be no mistaking you are Mrs. Harris Steele. You. Are. Mine. Do you understand?"

Her eyes widen, then half shutter with lust. The tip of her little pink tongue darts out to moisten her full lips.

"Yes, Mr. Steele," she responds huskily.

My cock throbs along my inner thigh painfully hard.

I spin her around to unzip her mini dress. It drops from the weight of the crystal strands to a puddle on the floor. I offer my hand. She slips hers into mine, and I hold her while she steps from the dress.

The skimpy silk of her G-string proves no match to the flick of my wrist. The fabric flutters atop the mini dress.

Bared to me in only her wedding jewelry and fuck-me sandals, My Redheaded Siren's song increases to a scream. I answer her call with a hungry growl of my own.

She shudders. Her DDs jounce. The rosy pink tips darken to mauve as they pebble beneath my carnal stare.

I like my lips. My hands reach out to cup her voluptuous tits. Their heaviness increases by her arousal. I pinch both nipples and tug. A guttural groan responds to her sharp cry of pain. My head bows to lavish her delicious tits.

Licks, nips, and sucks cause My Redheaded Siren to fist my hair as she writhes. Her breath comes in pants. Warmth suffuses her alabaster skin from the tips of her tits to her hairline.

"Fuck me already, Harris…" she wails.

I chuckle wickedly against her damp skin, wet from my ministrations. My tongue traces her areola, then along the lower curve of her tit. I bend my knees to continue the scorching trail over the planes of her body. Her belly, the curve of her hip, the apex of her thighs.

She yanks my hair when the tip of my tongue laps at her seam coated with her ambrosial cream.

So much better than our wedding cake.

"*Bloody…* HELL!" She screams. "Don't stop… Oooh… Right… there!" She cries before an orgasm seizes her body. It convulses with erotic pleasure.

Like a starving alley cat, I lick her cream voraciously. She rides out her orgasm on my tongue. Her pussy walls clench. She breaks again when I force another orgasm from her molten core.

I need her soft and soaked. Ready for my claiming.

One hand bands around her thigh to lock her in place. The other hand reaches up to tweak her puckered nipples. They grow more taut. She hisses from the bite of pain. My thumb brushes them to ease the sting.

She rewards me with another gush of cream.

I lap it up then rise to my full height, kissing my way up her trembling body. My mouth slams over hers for a brutal kiss. She pulls away. I smack that ass and groan when it jiggles beneath my sizable palm. She rises to her toes with a yelp.

"Mine!" I growl as I nip her lower lip. "Take what I give you, Siren."

She mewls but doesn't move again.

I finish the kiss with another smack to her ass and lift her under her with ease. Automatically, she wraps her legs around my hips. Her ankles lock under my ass. Her back slams against the window and she shudders.

My mouth drops back to her tits for a quick suck. Her nipple pops from my mouth as I slide her higher. My cock stands tall between her lower belly and my eight-pack abs. Its bulbous tip—purple from denial—leaks pre-cum. The entire ten inches disappear inside of her tight, dripping pussy with one thrust.

She cries out in wild abandon as the brutal invasion

triggers another toe-curling orgasm. Eyes squeezed shut, her head thrashes from side to side.

"Fuuuck! You like how my colossal cock claims every inch of *my* tight pussy. Every part of you is mine. Tell me you belong to me!"

I pummel her pussy while she screams my name. My relentless claiming drives her wild.

"Keep cumming on my cock, Siren," I growl as the first sign of my release tingles along my spine. Electricity zings down to my cum-filled balls. They draw up. "That's it, Siren. Give it to me, and I'll give it all to you!"

Her pussy clenches hard along my dick from root to tip.

I snarl from the carnal pain. No longer able to hold back, I throw my head back and roar my release. A torrent of jizz shoots from my cock straight into her womb. Her pussy milks every drop.

Lights brighter than the fireworks that still illuminate the inky sky outside the window blind me. My knees buckle. I lower us to the floor, twisting around to sit with My Redheaded Siren on my lap. My semi-flaccid cock glistens with her cream as it lies against her hip.

"Bloody hell, Harris. You'll kill us before we're married for a day!" My wife says between pants. Her Scottish accent is thick.

I squeeze her outer hip, and she squirms. My mouth goes to her ear. She trembles from my hot breath.

"Oh, no, Mrs. Steele. Now that you are mine forevermore, I have so much more to do to you and with you before either of us leave this Earth," I croon.

She tilts her head to the side and peers up at me through the thick fringe of her golden-tipped eyelashes.

"Well, in that case, you did say you'd make love to me until the sun rises, Mr. Steele," my wife purrs.

I growl and hop to my feet with her cradled against my chest.

"Indeed, I did, Mrs. Steele. Indeed, I did," I rumble.

"WELL, good morning, Sunshine. I wonder what has you to vibrant…"

My wife stretches her arms towards the headboard. Like a cat, she arches her back and purrs. Emerald green eyes flutter open. Lust sparks in them as she spies me naked, toweling my hair dry from the shower. She licks her lips at the sight of my cock—though flaccid—still reaches my thigh. She mewls in appreciation.

"Well, good morning to you, Adonis," she replies, then tsks. "Started your day without me? Naughty husband."

I toss the towel over my shoulder into the en bathroom. Then, like a wolf with his prey in sight, I stalk my wife. Thigh muscles flex with each stride. My cock grows.

"Naughty husband, you say?" I growl.

She nods and throws the bedding off her glorious body. Thighs part in welcome. Pussy glistens. Her hips cradle mine as I lower myself over her body. I thread our fingers as my mouth claims hers. She moans.

I rock against her seam, self-lubricating with her cream. Fully erect, I fist the base and align the tip with her pussy.

Slow two inches in, one inch out, until I fully seat myself within her wet warmth. We groan in unison. I continue with the long, languorous strokes.

My wife tugs at my fingers, still entwined with hers above her head. Her eyes narrow in frustration at my slow pace.

"Fuck me, Harris!" She demands, then lifts her head and nips my bottom lip. "Don't tease me!"

Purposefully, I slip the shaft free. Only the mushroom tip remains embedded in her greedy little pussy. I hover until she brings her eyes back to mine. I smirk.

She growls as she throws her head back onto the pillow.

"*Bloody* hell, Harris Steele!" She snarls.

My Kitty Kat turns into a fierce tiger when not fed my cock.

I snap my hips and impale her on my entire length.

She yowls.

I plunder her pussy with relentless abandon. I grunt as her inner walls clamp down on my cock. The vise-like grip sucks my cock deeper into her spasming pussy as she cums for me. I drive her into the bed repeatedly.

"Oh. Oh. OH!" She screams with each thrust. Another orgasm rockets through her core, choking my dick. "Just… like… that—OH!"

"Who exactly is naughty, Mrs. Harris Steele?" I ask as her entire body vibrates. "Your husband who just fucked you mindless?"

Lost in a state of sheer euphoria brought on by multiple mind-blowing climaxes, she can't answer verbally. However, her core clenches once again on my cock.

I chuckle wickedly.

"Yeah, thought so, Mrs. Harris Steele," I answer for her smugly.

In one swift move, I flip her onto her hands and knees. I place a palm between her shoulder blades and press down. Lowered to the bed with her arms stretched out and her forehead kissing the sheet, I grip both hips and raise her ass to my crotch. A throaty growl rips from my mouth when I sink balls deep inside of her dripping, pliant pussy.

Booted from bliss as I breach her swollen folds, my wife keens. Her palms slap the mattress. Fingers shred the rumpled sheets.

"Do you feel every ridge, every vein, every Fucking. Inch. Of my cock?" I ask in her ear as I pummel her fluttering pussy.

"Y—Y—Yeah… Unnnhhh…" She responds.

I swivel my hips and lift her ass higher in the air. The change in angle and position satisfies both of us. My dick dives deeper. It strokes her G-spot while my heavy cum-filled balls slap her engorged clit. We groan. Harris for the win.

"Now, take what I give you, wife," I bark.

She mewls in submission.

With plundering thrusts, I chase my release. My cock swells achingly bigger. My balls draw up. Three senses fade, leaving me with only sight and touch. My long, thick shaft disappearing into her glistening pink pussy makes me harder. The sensation of her tight pussy engulfing my dick, then spasming around it as she climaxes again finishes me off.

A feral growl rips from my mouth as I throw my head back. Cum explodes from my cock. It overfills her pussy and drips between her spread thighs to the sheets. I continue to thrust until my balls empty.

I collapse atop her to feel my weight. My claim of her. Her sigh signals her acceptance.

"Now, we started our day together, Mrs. Harris Steele," I say hoarsely against the side of her neck.

* * *

"Good morning, Sunshine! Don't you look radiant!"

My wife blushes as she giggles at Haley's teasing. Our tendency to think alike or finish one another's sentences is eerie.

My twin goes on to rib me. I let her have her fun. She certainly took enough shit from me when she married Little Lord Fauntleroy.

We're seated at a table for the post-wedding day brunch. It's not with all four hundred of our guests. This is for about half of them. Close friends, prominent politicians, business tycoons, and celebrities mingle with our family.

With this being the last Steele wedding of our generation, my parents went all out with the guest list. As I said from the beginning, as long as My Kitty Kat was happy, she could do as she pleased.

I glance over at her and she does glow—pat on my back. She enjoys the attention of all gathered. Not egotistically. No. She's living her dream. And I'm here for it.

I catch Payton's eye.

With a smile, he raises his Mimosa in salute. He's come a long way from the surly tosser to the loving older brother he should have been. But hey, no judgement. He's fine as long as he doesn't upset my wife.

I acknowledge his gesture.

A gasp from my wife jerks my head in her direction. I relax when she shows me a photo of us kissing on the altar from some media website. I nod and kiss her temple as she scrolls through more images.

At a nearby table, Baz holds court. He and Lola sit with some of our business partners. Whatever the event, an opportunity to benefit STEELE International, Inc. takes precedence. As CEO, Baz balances business with pleasure easily. He's a boss and Lola flows amongst the conversations like a pro. They're the power couple of the Steeles.

Malcolm sits with the entertainment crowd—including the head of a major film studio and her husband and a music mogul with his chart-topping singer. He's in his element as he converses with the owner of a Las Vegas casino he wants to acquire. Starr—her Zen to his bad boy —acts as his counterpart and charms everyone at the table. They're the rockstar couple.

My gaze lands on a table on the other side of the ballroom. I smile at the sight of Michael using his hands to speak enthusiastically with someone in Roger's group. I recognize the editor of *Architectural Digest* and the owner of a major textile company. Leonie chats with the editor of *Vogue* and Monsieur Valentino. Together, they straddle the worlds of design and fashion. They're the celebrity couple.

Then I spy where my twin and Lachlan—the Countess and the Earl of Aboyne—hold court. A prince and his American actress wife chat with a king and his queen of an African nation. Haley reigns supreme and serves as the perfect partner for Little Lord Fauntleroy. They're the noble couple.

My gaze shifts back to my wife.

And what couple are we?

I'd say we're the best!

I chuckle at my declaration. But it's absolutely true.

"What's so funny? Or are you giddy from being married to my fabulous best friend?"

Vivian's question draws me from my musings.

I glance at her and smile as I respond, "Most definitely."

"Good, because she's a keeper," Vivian says.

During the rest of brunch, my wife and I walk around the restaurant. We want to speak with as many guests as possible. It's major they flew from around the world to share in our nuptials over a span of four days. We provided all attendees with luxurious gift baskets and paid for their hotel stays and activities. But a personal touch proves we appreciate them.

It's time to leave for our honeymoon, so I tell My Kitty

Kat we need to say goodbye to our family. She beams and wraps her hands around my upper arm. A kiss to my cheek and we make our way to their tables.

"Oh! Have fun!" Haley squeals as she hugs Kat, then me. "And don't worry. I have you covered at the offices. Focus on your new bride!"

As my siblings before me, my Kitty Kat and I will spend two months on our honeymoon. A nice long time to just, as Haley says, focus on each other without distractions. Sure, I'll be available if it's an emergency. But my twin can handle anything and has the support of our brothers. No worries.

We save our parents for last.

A teary Mum Allison pulls Kat in for a tight embrace. She whispers something to her daughter that makes her smile. An equally tight embrace for me and the reminder to take care of her little lass. I promise.

"Congratulations again, son. You fill your mother and I with pride. You followed your heart, and your instinct served you well. Now, you have the responsibility of another, and in the future, your children. Always do well by them," my father says.

"Thank you, Dad. I will," I respond.

He turns to Kat, who gives my mother another hug. We switch.

"Oh, Harris, sweetheart! We're so happy for you and love you so much. Start your new life with Kat knowing you have so much more ahead of you as a couple. Enjoy your honeymoon!" My Mom says as tears shine in her brown eyes.

"I love you more, Mom. Thank you for an incredible wedding celebration," I respond.

I take my wife's hand and lead her from the restaurant to the start of our new life.

KAT

"No. I still won't tell you our destination. Have patience, Mrs. Steele."

I purse my lips and narrow my eyes at my husband's chiding.

Despite my best efforts, he refuses to tell me the top-secret location of our honeymoon. I didn't even pack my luggage. He asked my sisters-in-law to shop, then pack for me in my new set of Bottega Veneta Intrecciato hand-crafted luggage. And I just glimpsed the bags as the crew loaded them onto Harris' private jet.

I only know there's lots of Lola's Coterie lingerie and loungewear since Lola told me she'd gift my trousseau. I attempted to pry the honeymoon details out of them since they know the type of attire I'd need. But no. They wouldn't even give me a clue. Not one. Bah!

But if no knowledge of our honeymoon is the only stroppy situation of our wedding extravaganza, I'm thrilled. Just the thought of our momentous day—as Harris calls it—makes my heart swell with love and puts a giant grin on my face. It was extraordinary!

I glance down at my left hand. Sunlight from the jet's window makes the crazy amount of diamonds sparkle. Whether it's my ginormous engagement ring or the dainty stones of my eternity band or the varying sizes of my hand harness, no one can mistake me for a single woman. More than likely Harris' reason!

Not to mention the extravagant suite of diamonds he gave to me. Then this morning, I awoke to find the Cartier Love bracelet on my right wrist. More diamonds paved in platinum adorned my body. It's as though I won the jewelry lottery!

My Valentino gowns awed everyone. I received so many compliments. The editor of *Vogue* did a cover feature for their upcoming wedding issue. I was so nervous about the interview and the video. Harris was unfazed. Accustomed to the spotlight, he was the consummate pro.

The next morning, Viv and Charlotte showed me websites from around the world. Major media outlets to social media to blogs. Photographs and even some video footage from guests' mobiles—even though we asked them for privacy.

Leonie gave a Gallic shrug and said it's expected since people want to know about our lives. Live the fantasy and all. Said so nonchalantly by someone who's had cameras in her face since she was a teenager. Another pro—or megamodel.

The coverage reminded me of the socialites I admired. Who would have thought I'd join their ranks? Our wedding was even more fabulous than many I recall. Not that I'm being obnoxious!

Then there's getting used to being addressed as Mrs. Steele.

When the hostess at brunch greeted me as such, I almost didn't respond. It's usually Mum Shelley or one of my sisters-in-law who answers automatically. Starr giggled when I told her. She said it'll come naturally quickly. She added the special treatment we received as their girlfriends will triple with marriage.

So far, Starr isn't exaggerating.

Most notably from the flight crew. Oh, they were polite pre-wedding. But today, they all but fell over themselves for me. All immediately greeting me as Mrs. Steele. Asking if I preferred the window shades up or down. They checked the temperature was fine. Normally, questions posed to Harris they asked of me. Wow. Just wow.

Although one of the flight attendants—who was luke-warm towards me previously—has a less than cheerful face. More of a pinched, I-sucked-a-lemon face.

Now that we're airborne, the other flight attendant asks if I care for water or Dom Pérignon Champagne. I smile warmly and accept the Champagne. Then she asks Harris, who agrees. Subtle differences. But difference none the less. Meanwhile, Ms. Lemonhead prepares a snack in the galley.

I'll take all of it as Mrs. Harris Steele!

My husband shifts in his chair and raises his Waterford Crystal flute.

"You are neither a Roberts nor a Jackson. You are a Steele. Katrina Steele. My wife. Mine to protect, provide for, cherish, and love forevermore," he proclaims.

Tears of joy fill my eyes. His words, so sweet, yet so possessive, make my curiosity over our honeymoon insignificant. We matter. Nothing else. Period.

Hours later, we disembark the private jet for a helicopter. I guess the mode of transportation by the sound of rotors since my husband placed a red silk blindfold over my eyes. Of course.

The short flight ends with my husband removing the blindfold. I blink at the sudden brightness. Once my vision clears, he points out the window.

I peek around him and my breath catches.

Ahead of us floats a five-hundred-foot megayacht in sparkling azure waters. Beyond it, the water crests on golden sandy beaches of a large tropical island. As we circle around the megayacht, the glossy, jet black, sleek hull gleam in the sunlight. Four white tiers with walls of windows sit on the topmost tier. An impressive row of three-deck-tall windows command the megayacht's center. Cutouts on both sides provide several spots to soak up the sun. Bold white letters emblazon the name *Temptation* on its rear. Yeah, well, I can see why.

Moments later, the helicopter descends on a circular pad at the rear of the third deck. My husband helps me to the deck. He pauses and stretches his hands out wide.

"Our wedding song inspired our honeymoon theme to stand on a mountain, bathe in the sea, and lay like this forever with you. Prepare to enjoy two months cruising the South China Sea, Celebes Sea, and Sulu Sea. Behind us is the Malaysian island of Borneo. Sabah is our first destination to visit its highest peak—Mount Kinabalu. Let us begin with a sunset dinner, Mrs. Steele."

My husband grins like the Cheshire Cat while my eyes widen, and my mouth gapes as he speaks. He scoops me up in a bridal carry.

I wrap my arms around his neck and pepper his face with kisses.

"You always amaze me, Mr. Steele! But you've outdone yourself this time. Unbelievable!" I squeal as he strides along the deck.

We pass the crew dressed in immaculate white formal uniforms lined up to greet us. One holds a tray with Champagne. I smile and snag two crystal flutes.

"We'll have time for an official tour of *Temptation* tomorrow. In brief, it belongs to Haley, has ten oversized staterooms, sun decks, pool, spa, salons, game room, and more. Totally tricked out for pleasure. All kinds of pleasure," my husband says as he waggles his eyebrows.

I giggle at his innuendo.

He steps onto an elevator. I hold a flute to his lips. He finishes it off in one gulp.

"Caveman!" I tease, before I take a sip of mine.

He nuzzles my neck and murmurs, "And you love every bit of me."

"Without a doubt, oh caveman of mine," I respond as the elevator doors dings open.

My husband carries me down the modern decorated hallway and stops at the last stateroom towards the bow. I open the door and gasp.

Across from the door, floor-to-ceiling windows in a horseshoe shape account for three walls of the stateroom. Based on an open-concept design, a bedroom area marked by a thick white carpet where a king-size platform bed dressed in opulent white with black piping linens and loads of pillows dominates the space close to the windows facing the front of the megayacht. A platinum vase of Blue Roses. The rest of the space has a sitting area in the middle on more carpet and a glass-enclosed white marble bathroom with a dressing room. Various types of lighting placed throughout. Ritzy, to say the least.

"This is my stateroom. It's a mini version of Haley and Lach's full floor suite upstairs. As her favorite brother, I get the best digs. I've spent many a great night in this bed," my husband says as he toes off his Berluti sneakers.

I stiffen in his arms.

Who did he fuck in this bed? Why would he tell me about his sexcapades?

While my mind reels from jealousy, a nudge to the side of my neck refocuses my attention. I sigh, disheartened.

"Mrs. Steele… What's going on in that pretty head of yours? Hmmm?" He murmurs against my skin.

Get it together, Kat Jack—Steele! I tell myself.

"Nothing," I respond aloud. I squirm in his arms to get

down. Without looking at him, I tell him I need to use the bathroom.

He hesitates and dips his head to see my face. But I let the curtain of my hair block his view. He sets me on my feet. With bent knees, he lowers to my eye level. His thumb and forefinger grasp my chin to force my gaze on him.

"We vowed honesty, Kat," he says, no sign of the jokester in his dove gray eyes. "Now, answer truthfully."

My eyes skitter away. But he's not having it. He shifts my chin until my eyes meet his serious gaze. I swallow to moisten my dry throat. Honesty. Fine.

"I hate to sound like a jealous shrew. But I do not want to know about your past lovers. Especially on the second day of our marriage. And I do not want to sleep in a bed where you fucked someone other than me and rave about it during our honeymoon."

My voice catches on the last word. Embarrassed by my lack of self-esteem, I jerk my heated face from his hold.

Surprised, he releases me.

I rush towards the bathroom. Head bowed and tears blurring my vision, I make my escape. Only to squeal when my feet lift from the floor.

"No running from me… from us, Kat! You can't say shit like that and run off. Talk to me, woman!" Harris growls as his front crashes into my back. His arms band around my hips and he carries me to the bed. Where he sits and positions me on his lap.

"You know, now I get why Doms spank their wayward subs," he continues with a shake of his head.

I squirm, not wanting to be on his lap and definitely not on the fuck bed.

Suddenly, I'm hoisted into the air. A succession of three resounding smacks lands on my upturned ass. The pain reverberates through my entire being as it jiggles beneath Harris' sizable palm. I yowl as much in frustration as in pain.

"I've never fucked a woman in this bed. Nor would I discuss the sexual activities of my past with you," he says. Then he adds with a snarl, "And unless you want me to go on a hunting spree, do not tell me a damn thing about your past."

The ferocity of his words gives me pause. Perhaps I'm overreacting. But I have one question.

"What about your flight attendant?"

Harris' face scrunches in confusion.

"Which one, and what about her?"

I clear my throat before I bring my gaze to meet his stormy gray eyes.

"The blonde. Have you had sex with her?"

Harris' head snaps back and his eyes bulge, then narrow.

"What the everlasting fuck, Kat?! No! I never had sex with her or any other STEELE employee. Hell, you're the first and only Jackson Corporation employee I've said more than hello to as I passed them by. Where do you get that ludicrous idea?"

Chagrined, my eyes dart away. But again, Harris won't tolerate my avoidance.

"Eyes on me, Kat," he growls.

I return my gaze to him. Then shrug before I respond.

"She was always a bit standoffish towards me. Never rude, just cool. When we boarded your jet, she greeted me as Mrs. Steele, like the others. But she wore a sour expression. I assumed she was mad I went from girlfriend to wife, and she lost her chance."

Gobsmacked, he scans my face for a moment.

"You mean to tell me you were uncomfortable because of my employee in my presence and didn't tell me?" He asks incredulously.

I nod, and his nostrils flare. He answers in a none-too-pleased tone of voice.

"In the future, tell me any issue that concerns you when it happens, not months later. I'll have her spoken to by Human Resources and placed as a crew member for the corporate fleet immediately. They will monitor her behavior."

Now, my eyes widen. Even though I like his solution, I didn't want to cause trouble for her. I tell him so, but he reassures me it won't impact her career and my happiness tops all. I sigh in relief and apologize for ruining the start of our honeymoon with nonsense.

"Oh, you will make it up to me, Mrs. Steele. Every single day," my husband rumbles deep in his chest. "Starting. Now."

I squeal when he flips me over his muscular thighs. My hands fling out to brush the white carpet with my fingertips. Behind me, my legs flail. Cool air kisses my ass exposed with two flicks of my husband's wrist—one to raise my maxi dress and the other to shred my G-string.

Without hesitation, he peppers my bare ass with a round of smacks. He never hits the same spot in a row. When my ass burns from the sting, his palm connects with the delicate area of my sits bones.

I buck. My hands fly behind me to block the painful blows. Then scream in frustration when he grips my wrists in one hand at my lower back. A second later, air leaves my lungs in a burst. Pain radiates to pleasure as my mind, then body reacts to three smacks to my pussy lips and clit. My hips jerk away even as my thighs spread.

My husband chuckles wickedly.

"You like a good spanking, naughty lass. Your cream drips from your pussy. It soaks my joggers and sticks to my fingers."

His hand leaves my throbbing pussy and swollen clit. Slurping and a groan fill my ears. The cheeks on my face heat and turn as crimson as I imagine my ass.

"Ambrosia, Siren," he sighs, enraptured.

My pussy clenches as it begs for his giant cock, now fully erect against my hip. I wiggle for attention. Even the burn of his palm would trigger the orgasm hovering on the edges.

"Hungry for satisfaction, Siren?" He asks as he leans over to press his lips against my ear. The warmth of his breath makes me shiver. "I'll take your response as a yes."

I explode with a primal scream when his thick fingers plunge into my pussy unexpectedly. My toes curl as my legs jerk. I writhe on his lap, shamelessly riding out the vestiges of an epic climax. Before my body can dwell in the aftermath, I'm flipped up.

My jellied thighs straddle his muscular ones. He grips my hips, then slams me down onto his turgid dick. His hips ratchet up to slam his velvet-covered steel into me.

I throw my head back and keen.

"So fucking snug… So soaking wet… This cock is yours, Mrs. Steele… Only. You…"

Harris' declaration—punctuated by powerful thrusts—trigger another orgasm. He doesn't stop until I beg him for no more. Then he whips us around.

My back slams onto the mattress. Hands fly to his forearms. He drags me up his body. The backs of my thighs press against his chest. Still carnally connected, he leans down. Unable to move with my legs trapped between us, Harris drills me into the bed.

"Do… You… Understand…"

I nod, delirious from the onslaught of carnal pleasure.

He lets my wordless answer go unchecked as he chases his release.

We rock more powerfully than the waves against the megayacht. I swear the bed shifts on the plush carpet. Our combined grunts and strangled cries bounce off the wall of windows.

Head thrown back, my husband's roar punches the air. His massive cock swells impossibly larger and fills my pussy with his cum. He growls when my inner walls clamp on his dick to milk him dry.

"FUUUCK, KAT!!!" He bellows as I take him deeper into core.

With a satisfied groan, he collapses to his side and pulls me with him. Our sweaty bodies slide against each other as I drop against his heaving chest. I place a kiss over his pounding heart.

"Only you and only me, Mr. Steele," I whisper.

HARRIS

"*O*ur results for the first quarter please me. Each division and subsidiary performed at or above expectations. Keep this pace up for the rest of the year and we'll blow through projections. Well done!"

Baz claps as his platinum gray gaze meets our varying shades.

We're in his conference room for our quarterly team meeting. Malcolm, Starr, and I sit around the table with him. Roger, Leonie, and Haley join us via video conference on the giant center screen. Each of us gave our reports, followed by questions. Haley gave ours since I missed the first two months of the year on my honeymoon.

I grin as memories of adventurous days hiking, surfing, and lovemaking followed by incredible nights of delicious dinners, gorgeous sunsets, and lovemaking. Oh, did I mention passionate lovemaking? Uh, yeah, baby!

After the initial hiccup and I settled my wayward wife

down, we had a perfect time. So many moments captured on camera—still and video. My favorites of us on the mountain peaks with any of the seas below. While my wife slept in *our* bed, I took photos of her beautiful face—and that hot as fuck body when the sheets didn't cover her tits or legs.

Most importantly, she loved every minute of it. When we returned, she went to dinner with her sisters to tell them all about it. I'm sure they compared notes. And without a doubt, our honeymoon was the best!

Now that we've been home for a month, the honeymoon seems so far gone. Last night we watched our wedding video while we ate dinner from Wayan—the Malaysian restaurant in Nolita. Our emotions ran high again, and we ended up making love on the sofa.

The only downside is My Kitty Kat awoke puking her brains out. One minute I had her curled in front of me and the next she ran to the en suite bathroom. I raced after her and held her hair back while her head hovered over the toilet bowl. My poor baby came up paler than usual. Emerald green eyes dim.

I only left her when she promised she'd have our family doctor come over if she wasn't better by noon. It must have been the Lobster Noodles since I ate the Crescent Duck and didn't get sick. Then again, I have a cast-iron stomach as my Mom says.

While the meeting wraps up, I check my mobile. No text message or voicemail.

"What's got you frowning?"

I glance up to find my twin leaning over to see the screen of my mobile. Nosy bird.

"Kat was sick this morning after we ate Malaysian food last night. I want to see if she went to the doctor or—"

My mobile vibrates—I had the ringer off for the meeting—and cuts off my answer. I smile when My Kitty Kat's photo pops up.

"Hey, bab—"

Muffled sobs carry over the line.

I jump to my feet. Crazy thoughts of her being kidnapped again or of her hurt somewhere fill my head. The chair rolls back so hard, it hits the console against the wall.

All heads turn to me.

"Kat! What's wrong?!" I yell in a complete panic as I stride to the double doors of the conference room. I put her on speaker while I pull up the tracking device app.

She mumbles something indecipherable.

She's not at home, and I don't recognize the address. Where the hell is she?!

I ask just that as my pace increases.

"I'm pregnant!"

The mobile falls from my hand.

"I'm so s—s—sorry!" Kat's wail continues from the floor. "It's been s—s—so bus—s—y. I forgot my shot—"

Haley grabs my mobile while I stand frozen. She shoves it in my face and hisses my name at me with a glare. She mouths, *don't you dare upset her further!*

Kat's still babbling as I take the call off speaker and raise the mobile to my ear.

My head spins. But Haley is right.

"K—" I start, then clear my dry throat. "Kat, don't cry. Are you at the doctor's office now? I'll come to you."

She hiccups and thanks someone, then blows her nose.

Oh, great. They're going to think I'm an ogre making my pregnant wife cry. Scared I'll be pissed.

Although technically… Well, pissed isn't quite the right word. It's more disappointed… shocked… upset? Or plain old, fucked. No pun intended.

"Y—yes. The address—"

"I have it on the app. I'm on my way now," I interject, then end the call.

My shoulders slump. A sudden pain shoots behind my left eye like someone jabbed me with an ice pick. I scrub my hand over my face.

"Damn, bro! Get a fucking grip! Be a man!"

Roger's blunt chastisement breaks through my pity party.

He, too, is right.

Gah!

"Listen, Harris, Kat is upset enough. Obviously, you expressed not wanting children—I guess for now. But the situation has arisen. On your way to get her, think of what you will say and how you will behave. The last thing you want is a fight over children with your pregnant wife," Baz says as both brother and a father.

"Exactly! You do not know what it's like to be pregnant. Do not make her feel worse than morning sickness!" Haley says heatedly.

Leonie and Starr agree wholeheartedly with my twin. The girls band together. A reminder not to get on their collective bad side.

Malcolm strides toward me.

"I'll walk you to the elevator," he says as he opens the conference room doors.

I nod mutely.

The others stream out behind us. I can feel Haley's glare on my back.

"I can understand your point of view. When Starr told me she was pregnant, I wasn't in the right place to show joy. And I almost fucked up our relationship, letting my ego get in the way," Malcolm starts, then glances at me. "Things have a way of happening when they should and being the appropriate outcome despite what we think. A lesson I learned from My Angel. Heed her words of wisdom and learn from my mistake."

We reach the private elevator for our family's residences that leads from them to the STEELE International, Inc. offices and the lobby of The STEELE Tower. Malcolm presses the call button and puts his hands in his suit trouser pockets.

I look at my older brother. He works hard, plays harder, and loves the hardest. I recall the stress between him and Starr. He pretended it didn't impact him. But he hurt badly.

Now they're happy as all fuck with two sets of adorable twins.

He's right, too. I appreciate my siblings' concern and input.

The elevator doors open. I step inside, turning to face Malcolm before they close.

"It all works out, Harris," he says, then continues with a nod. "Make sure you don't lose her before your great adventure gains traction."

I return his nod as the doors shut.

I pull out my mobile to send a text message to my driver for him to bring my Black Badge Rolls-Royce Cullinan around the front. He replies Roger already contacted him. I smile as I put my mobile in my pocket. Roger *The Responsible*.

The ride across town takes some time with Manhattan's never-ending gridlock of traffic. Enough for me to come out of shock. The fog lifts. I consider my family's words of advice. Sure, they're right. But I'm not ready for children yet. And I've said it thousands of times—to them and to Kat, most importantly.

Does it make me a monster? Selfish?

Some may say most definitely.

Others may understand.

But here we are at this moment I wasn't expecting for at least three or four years. I wanted time to spend with Kat. Travel every chance we get. Go to LEVELS clubs. Just be us. Not happening now.

Damn.

Kat seems pretty noncommittal one way or the other. At only twenty-eight, she's still young. However, she enjoys my—well, now, our—nieces and nephews. Giving my siblings date nights as sitters. No need for the many nannies. Uncle Harris and Aunt Kat step in happily.

But one of our own. So soon? How happy will we be then?

The chaos in my mind doesn't stop even when Alonso stops the SUV in front of the address on my app. I follow the tracker up the steps of an impressive townhouse, then through the front door. A second door leads to the foyer where a receptionist sits behind an ornate wooden desk.

"Good afternoon. How may I help you?" She asks.

I clear my suddenly parched throat and reply, "Yes, my wife Mrs. Harris Steele is here. Kindly take me to her."

As I follow the receptionist, we pass the waiting room. A man with an affectionate smile has his hand on the significant baby bump of the woman he sits beside. She beams at him. He glances at me and gives a nod of one father-to-be to another. I blink.

The walls display multiple photos of newborn babies. Some posed on photography sets as pumpkins and such. Others asleep or awake in their cribs or close ups in their parents' arms—parents like the couple in the waiting room. All oh so sweet.

The receptionist knocks on a door, then gestures for me to enter after the doctor acknowledges her knock.

I scan the room for Kat. She sits on the examination table in a gown. Her eyes seek mine. Unable to determine my frame of mind from my blank expression, her chin wobbles. She averts her gaze and pulls the open-front gown closer around her body in a protective motion.

The doctor must sense the tension in the room and addresses me.

"Mr. Steele, I am Dr. Oscar Rice and Lola's OB-GYN. Your family doctor suggested your wife see me. Obviously, food poisoning does not ail her. She is fourteen weeks pregnant based on my calculations. She wanted to wait for you before we proceed with the ultrasound. Would you care for a moment alone before we begin?"

Damn. So this is happening.

I shake my head mutely and approach the examination table when he waves me over. I stand beside Kat.

Without looking at me, she lowers her back to the table.

Dr. Rice prepares to take the scan and places jelly on Kat's belly. A belly I now notice isn't as flat as normal. Come to think of it, her tits seem fuller. I thought it was all the good food we dine on each night. Duh.

He fiddles with the dials on the machine, then slides the wand through the jelly. Pulsating sounds fill the room.

My gaze shifts from Kat's belly to the monitor. The screen shows what I presume is the inside of her womb. A womb filled with a baby. My baby. Holy shit.

Dr. Rice clicks the machine as he peers at the screen. He shakes his head and chuckles. He shifts on the stool to face both of us.

"Your family is very fertile, Mr. Steele. I've never seen

so many children per couple in quite some time. Most lean towards one, perhaps two…"

He drones on. But I tune him out. Mesmerized by the sudden appearance of a tiny face with a clenched fist to its mouth followed by a tiny foot that's in an impossible position. The image changes and another face without a fist pops on screen.

No damn way—

"Congratulations, you're having twins!"

"Are you all right?"

My eyes open to find Dr. Rice's concerned face hovering above me. I look beyond him to Kat sitting on the edge of the exam table. Emerald eyes wide and the corner of her bottom lip tucked between her teeth. Worry etched on her face.

I sit up and winch.

"You landed pretty darn hard on your rear when you fainted," Dr. Rice says. "Do you feel anything besides discomfort?"

Fainted?

Well, damn.

I shake my head and get to my feet. Other than a sore ass—and ego—I'm fine.

Actually, more than fine. The fall must have knocked sense into me.

I let out a whoop and wrap my arms around my wife. The soon-to-be mother of my children. Twins, to be exact.

Hot damn!

My wife trembles in my arms. Her soft sobs stab my

heart. I croon words of love for her and the two gifts she's given to me. I tsk her apologies and apologize to her. She covers my mouth with her finger and tells me she understands. I respond with a kiss to her finger, and she smiles. In fact, she glows with pure happiness.

After our lovefest, Dr. Rice prints images of our twins. He gives us the option to learn about their sex in four weeks. I turn to Kat in question, and she nods eagerly. He leaves us with a reminder to book her monthly, then biweekly prenatal appointments and to call with any questions. He already greenlit sex. So I'm good. With all the pregnancies and subsequent births I've sat in hospital for, I could do his job!

Once Dr. Rice leaves, my wife calls my name softly to get my attention. I return to her side from where I walked him to the door. She fidgets with the gown. I take her hands in mine. She peeks up at me. I smile.

"Are you happy truly, Harris? I don't want you to pretend. A vow of honesty, remember?" She says as her eyes search my face for any sign of falsehood.

I bring her hands to my mouth and kiss each piece of her wedding jewelry, ending with the eternity band.

"It disappointed me when you told me," I start and hold her hands tighter when she pulls away. "But seeing you so radiant and our twins on the monitor made me realize I was a fool. How could I not be happy? A beautiful wife who loves me. And a baby—well, babies—of our own. I'm ridiculously happy. Thank you, Mrs. Steele."

She sighs in relief and sags against me.

I brush my lips against the top of her head as I slip her into my embrace and rock. I give a silent prayer of thanks for not losing my wife. Our adventure continues unfazed, just with the addition of two bundles to be.

Well, damn. Harris Steele playboy turned husband soon father. Talk about an adventure…

"Don't worry, babe. There was nothing wrong the last time. Some babies hide their stuff. Guess they're not exhibitionists, you know?"

My Hot Mama giggles at my attempt to ease her concern. We're waiting in the examination room at Dr. Rice's office for the gender reveal. The first scan we tried at eighteen weeks didn't go as planned. He assured her all was well with our Wee Twins.

Now, I rub her babies bump and kiss her soft lips. A knock on the door makes us turn. Dr. Rice enters and sets up the ultrasound as he asks My Hot Mama how she feels. She knows the drill and lies back on the examination table, gown loose, as she answers his questions.

I squeeze her hand as her anxious eyes stare at the monitor. The strong pulsating sound of their heartbeats fill the room. A leg appears on the screen, then an arm, again not in the position to belong to one baby. Out Wee Twins float about with limbs askew. Hopefully this time, they shifted for us to see a clear view.

"Here we go!" Dr. Rice says as he comes across a little tummy. He adjusts the wand on My Hot Mama's belly, then points at the screen. "There! This one is a boy!"

My heart skips a beat. A boy? A little Harris for the win!

I cup My Hot Mama's face. Tears glisten in her emerald orbs as she smiles up at me. I press my forehead to hers and thank her for my son.

"Hold on, now. We have eyes on baby number two," Dr. Rice says.

Our eyes fly to the monitor. Will it be another boy for identical twins or fraternal like Haley and me? The answer presents itself...

"A girl!" My Hot Mama exclaims as her finger points to our second twin front and center of the monitor. "Oh, Harris! Like you and Haley!"

"A Dynamic Duo 2.0!" I say with a goofy grin on my face. "Mrs. Steele, thank you for our gifts."

She shakes her head and corrects me, "Thank you, too, *Da*! Without your... ah, input... we wouldn't be here."

And *Da* it is!

After Dr. Rice leaves, I help My Hot Mama from the exam table. In anticipation of our gender reveal dinner with our family, she chose a white, one-shoulder dress ruched to cling to her curves and babies bump. White sky-high mules make her toned legs go on for miles. With her Titian hair in a high ponytail and minimal makeup, her gorgeous face glows. Did I say Hot Mama or what?

She must sense my sudden interest and winks at me over her shoulder as she saunters towards the exam room door.

"I see your bulge growing, Mr. Steele. And here I thought I was the only horny one," she says with a smirk. "Let's get going DILF. Everyone waits for us."

She leads, and I follow, happy for the view of her round ass pushed up in those fuck-me heels. If I can't get some of her lovin' now, I can at least fantasize…

"Bro, don't leave us hanging!"

"Out with it, guys!"

"Oh, honey, do tell!"

My Hot Mama stands radiant at the table beside me. Her eyes sweep the room to take in some of our family seated with us and others on the giant screen Lucien put in the private room of his restaurant for the momentous occasion.

I shift my gaze from my mesmerizing wife to the others gathered around us. The expectant faces of my parents, Baz, Lola, Malcolm, Starr, Roger, and Leonie turn to us at the table. A glance at the giant screen shows similar expressions for Lachlan, Haley, Uncle Connor, Aunt Lucie, Mum Allison, Henry, and Kat's siblings.

A tug to my hand draws my attention back to My Hot Mama. She beams up at me.

"You tell them, *Da*."

I shake my head and bring her hand to my lips. I brush mine against her eternity band.

"We tell everyone together, Mummy," I respond. "Three. Two. One. A boy and a girl!"

The room goes silent, then into an uproar as questions and cheers erupt.

We decided not to tell them about the Wee Twins, only we're pregnant. Now to spring on them twins and a boy and a girl… Well, they lose their shit.

"OMG! Just like us and Elio and Selina!" Haley exclaims as she claps her hands, bouncing on the sofa next to Lachlan, who grins. "You brought it, twin! Oh, yeah!"

"Oh, I'm sure Dr. Rice had something to say. He cracks me up!" Lola says as she hugs me. "Congratulation, brother!"

Leonie wraps her arms around My Hot Mama and says, "Well, I better get my sketch pad ready. We have nurseries to design and reconfigure! Let's start tomorrow before Roger and I return to Paris. So much fun!"

My father claps me on the back with a smile.

"Congratulations, son! You've had plenty of experience with your nieces and nephews. Now the actual work begins," he says with a chuckle.

My mother laughs and adds, "No returning them to their parents. *You* are the parents!"

After more words of wisdom, we settle at the table. The servers pour Champagne while one brings a glass of iced lemon ginger tea for the Mom-to-be. Toasts ring throughout the room from the table and the giant screen.

We don't order since Lucien had the chef prepare all My Hot Mama's favorite dishes. The others not present eat light snacks since it's after eleven in Scotland. They stay on the video conference for another thirty minutes. Before she signs off, Mum Allison tells us she'll check with her manager at STEELE Glasgow for some time off to visit us, perhaps in a month or so.

My wife's shoulders slump.

I kiss her cheek and whisper, "I got you, babe."

"Mum Allison, no need to worry about coming here. We're flying to Glasgow tomorrow. We can't only have an announcement for you and not hug your daughter in person!" I add with a grin.

They gasp, then start to talk in unison.

I hold up my hand to stop them and confirm the details of the surprise visit. I also had a realtor Lachlan suggested schedule appointments for penthouse flats. Being Glasgow is my wife's hometown, we'll need a place of our own when we travel there, especially with the Wee Twins. But I'll save that surprise for our arrival.

My wife throws her arms around my neck and kisses my face again and again. In between, she tells me she loves me and I'm the absolute best husband a lass could ever want.

Later at home, I prove I'm the only absolute best husband she'll ever have, period. Again and again.

* * *

"THIS IS a fantastic choice for your Glasgow residence. A duplex penthouse offers plenty of space for a growing family."

My Kitty Kat giggles at Uncle Connor's remarks. I shake my head with a chuckle. She hasn't even given birth before he's expanding our little family.

We flew to Glasgow yesterday morning and met with the realtor after we checked in at STEELE Glasgow. She kept this property for last, knowing it would be the one for us.

The West End duplex penthouse has six bedrooms with en suite bathrooms, lounges, an office, chef's kitchen, and more. We'll make it our own with the help of Michael. Already he makes suggestions. It would be the perfect project for him to prove himself.

"The perfect location for you! I know people who live in the area. I'll make the introductions. They'll make excellent connections," Aunt Lucie—ever the Marchioness of Huntly—says.

Mum Lucie turns from the windows overlooking a park and smiles.

"How lovely it'll be to walk through the park with the Wee Twins. It's always best for babes to have fresh air. It makes them sleep through the night," she says with a nod of her head.

My Hot Mama hugs her Mum. My wife is so excited about our new residence. She asked Leonie to fly over from Paris to review options for the nursery next week while we're still in Glasgow. She and Haley will be Kat's on-the-ground helpers once we're in New York City.

"It's good to see my sister so happy. She deserves to have the best."

I glance over at Payton—his eyes on his sisters and mother across the lounge. He continues to watch them as he goes on.

"I've been a prat to Kat for so long, I doubt she'll give me much of a chance to reconcile truly. But they say a mother is more willing to forgive. So maybe she'll forgive me. I'd like to be a part of the Wee Twins' lives."

He brings his gaze to mine.

"That is, if you will allow me the chance," he finishes.

I scan his face for any sign of deceit and find none. From what my wife tells me about her relationship with Payton and his with the rest of their family, my first inclination is a definite no. But then everyone deserves a second chance. Had I not given one to Kat, we wouldn't be married with the Wee Twins on the way.

"Kat shared with me her experiences with you and how you treated your family. I'm not impressed and find it fucked up, especially since you were the eldest after your father passed away," I respond, then flick my gaze from him to my wife.

She wants a fresh start. If she didn't want Payton in her life, she wouldn't have invited him to spend time with us. So, I'll allow him to be a part of our family. But…

"As long as you do not hurt my wife in any way, we welcome you to rekindle the familial bond," I tell him.

He holds out his hand, and I grip it in a firm shake.

"The dinner reservations start in half an hour. Let's head over to the restaurant."

Lachlan's announcement gets us out the door and to our cars for the ride to the restaurant.

"Payton asked if he could be a part of the Wee Twins' life after he expressed reconciliation with you," I tell my wife while we're alone except for our driver. "I told him he could, as long as he didn't hurt you in any way."

She gazes out the window. We pass several streets. But I give her the time she needs to process his request and my approval of it. So instead of pressing her, I wait. Eventually, she turns her head to me.

"I love my brother and wish we could have had a less strained relationship. But I do forgive him. So as long as he agrees to your terms, I'm fine with him being in our lives," she says, then thickens her Scottish accent. "Aye, the Wee Twins can't sound all American. They'll need as many authentic Scottish accents around them."

I throw my head back and laugh. My wife thinks she's got jokes as good as mine. But hers—delivered in her sultry Scottish accent—takes the win.

We arrive at the restaurant and find some of the others at the bar. My Hot Mama excuses herself and goes to the ladies' room. Haley and Charlotte go with her. Woman and going to the bathroom in groups. Go figure.

As I turn from watching them go, a small hand presses against my biceps. The smile on my face fades when I realize it's not Mum Allison.

Some random woman stares up at me. She licks her glossy bottom lip suggestively. The gold flecks in her hazel eyes sparkle.

"Hello, Harris Steele, correct? I've seen your photos online. But you're even more handsome in person. Care to have a drink… Or eat?" She says. Her husky Scottish accent deepens as she finishes with a squeeze to my arm.

I stare at her in utter disbelief.

Didn't this bird just see me talking to my wife?

Did she not notice the platinum wedding band on the hand of the arm she clings to?

Saw my photos, did she? Well…

"Miss, if you've seen my photos, then you've seen my wife. You know, the gorgeous woman I was just speaking with a second before you approached me?" I respond as I extricate my arm from her clutches. "So, no, and most definitely, no."

The woman's face flames. She opens her mouth to speak. But I hold up my hand and walk over to the real Mum Allison, who now stands beside Aunt Lucie. They flick their eyes between the woman and me. The woman huffs behind me.

"Do you know her, Harris?" Mum Allison asks. Her normally calm tone of voice is now sharp as she glares at the woman.

"No, just some random woman. You know, the kind who hang out at bars hoping to snag a husband," I answer with a shrug, then grin. "But I let her know I am not the one, not with My Hot Mama wearing my rings."

Mum Allison relaxes and pats my arm.

Another hand touches my lower back. I turn, already knowing it's my wife from the alluring scent of her perfume. My arm slips around her back, and I pull her into my side snugly. As I brush my lips over the top of her head, my gaze finds the woman on the other side of the bar glaring at us. I smirk and shake my head.

Not this bloke, miss.

KAT

"This area here would work well for the pram room and whatever other outdoor equipment you'll need for the Wee Twins—"

"Oh, Michael, you are such a guy! 'Equipment?' Really?" Leonie's laughter rings out in the entry hall for the Glasgow duplex penthouse.

The rest of us girls join her while Roger—who's used to baby stuff—grins, and Harris pats my brother on the back.

He's so enthusiastic to have the chance to work his architectural magic on the residence's remodeling. Roger agreed to assign the job to him as Project Lead with Leonie as his manager. Michael's University of Strathclyde in Glasgow dean confirmed credits will apply towards his program. I'm glad he's pursuing his passion and I get to help him achieve his dream.

"Uh… right," Michael says with a grin. "Architecture, yes. Wee ones, um, no."

We laugh along with him as he continues his recommendation.

Harris and I have been in Glasgow for the last week. It's so wonderful to spend time with my Mum and siblings. And Payton has truly stepped up. We had lunch and talked things out. It was a long time coming, but so worth it. We have a better understanding. Plus, we promise to treat each other with respect and to work things out, not let them fester. He even bought teddy bears for the Wee Twins. Uncle Payton, ready for duty!

After Michael takes us through the residence, Harris and I share our feedback. We're in sync with my brother's recommendations. Leonie beams like a proud Mum. To make it all official, we sit down and sign off on the plan. Michael looks fit to burst from excitement.

"Sweethearts, you can go through the Steele storage facility to select pieces. You may find some items to incorporate into your decor," my mother offers while my father agrees.

"And of course, you have access to the Jackson archives. Perhaps you'd like to put paintings from Iain here. It would be so appropriate. A gracious nod to our relative," Aunt Lucie adds.

Uncle Connor nods and says, "That's a great idea, *mo ghràdh*. When you return, I will take you through the facility. You will find a wide selection over centuries. A bit of family history is important to include in your home."

"And you'll love the most incredible selections from both! Lachlan and I furnished our Aberdeen penthouse flat with loads of furniture from the Jackson collection," Haley adds.

"If you want to supplement those collections, you're welcome to the Beaulieu Enterprises SAS's warehouses. My family's company travels the world for antiques, antiquities, and fabrics," Leonie says.

I clap my hands and thank them all with a promise to do so on our next trip back to Glasgow. We can spend the weekend in Paris to explore Leonie's treasure trove. All sound unbelievable and I cannot wait!

"Now tell us more about the nurseries. The rooms here you selected to combine into one are in the perfect spot from the primary bedroom," I say.

Leonie pulls out her iPad and taps on the screen. She sits next to me on the window seat. She shows me her initial design ideas for not only Glasgow and New York City. But she also includes remodels for Morgan and Shelley's New York City and Southampton Village residences and a new one for their Aberdeen flat.

Shelley's enthusiastic response makes me laugh. Then I gasp.

"What's wrong, Kat?" Harris asks, crouching before me, eyes wide in panic.

I catch my breath as I grab his hand and place it on my babies bump.

"A kick, or maybe a punch! I don't know which," I exclaim, then gasp again. "Did you feel it?"

Harris' mouth drops open. His dove gray eyes were wider than two silvery flying saucers. He jumps as though punched by Norman when another movement from our Wee Twins happens.

It's the first time they made their presences known aside from their images on the monitor and heartbeats. Well, I guess my rounder belly proves their existence!

"Babe… I—I can't believe it…" Harris' words trail off as his voice catches in his throat. His eyes glisten with unshed tears. He blinks and continues. "How does it feel to you?"

I take a moment to consider, then tell him the Wee Twins' movement makes me think of butterflies' wings brushing against my womb. He nods, absorbing my response.

"Well, butterflies would make a lovely motif for the nurseries," my Mum says with a smile as she strokes my hair. "They symbolize transformation, hope, and bravery— all excellent qualities for your Wee Twins. And remember, butterflies adorned your wedding gown and veil."

I take her hand and kiss it. My Mum is the smartest woman I know!

"Brilliant, Mum! I love it!" I respond, then turn to their father. "Harris, my love, what do you think?"

He caresses my babies bump and places two kisses on it.

"I love it, and I love all three of you," he responds before he kisses my lips softly. "And I can't wait to hold them in my arms."

The gestures and his words are so sweet. I sniff and dab the tears in my eyes, despite the yawn I try to swallow. He kisses them away, then stands.

"Well, everyone, thank you for your love and support.

But My Hot Mama needs her rest. We'll say our goodbyes now since we fly out in the morning," he says.

Our family wishes us farewell and safe travels with hugs and kisses. Promises of updates follow. We leave the duplex penthouse and take turns on the private lift to the lobby. More hugs before Harris and I slip inside of the awaiting Rolls-Royce sedan. I wave as the car joins traffic and the driver whisks us back to STEELE Glasgow.

* * *

"YOU AND THESE BLINDFOLDS, Harris Steele! I think they're your kink."

I say as he slides one off my face. It's as though he carries one around in the pocket of every bloody pair of trousers he owns—ready for any occasion.

This time, he placed it on my face before we boarded our private jet for what I thought was New York City. But based on the salty air, vibrant sun, and the sound of French accents, this can't be the City.

I shade my eyes, trying to find a clue. My breath catches.

We're standing at the top of a gated driveway. The brilliant sun shines above in a clear blue sky. Sea birds soar on the air currents. Before us, the expanse of sparking azure waters stretches out unobstructed to the horizon. My gaze follows the white-capped waves to the shore. They meet a private sandy beach between two-story stone sea walls that surround a peninsula.

The jewel above it all sits a magnificent white villa. Its five stories set atop one another like a tiered cake decreasing in size from top to bottom. Balconies overlook the panoramic view. Around it manicured lawns with mature trees lead to an infinity edge pool that juts out above the azure water. Making it impossible to tell where one ends and the other begins. Two smaller buildings occupy the secluded acres of property. It's a lavish seaside estate in its own world.

"Unimaginable..." I whisper in awe. "Wherever are we?"

Harris slips his arm around my body and leans down to place his cheek against mine. He murmurs his response, *"Bienvenue à Villa Ciel et Terre."*

Both of us are fluent in French. I translate the meaning aloud with a contented sigh.

"Welcome to Villa Heaven and Earth. How appropriate."

"We're in the South of France town of Èze off the Mediterranean Sea—also known as the Côte d'Azur for obvious reasons. Come, I'll tell you more about it on the ride down," he says as he leads me to the white-on-white convertible Aston Martin. When I hesitate to glance over my shoulder at the stunning property, he chuckles. "Oh, you'll love it even more up close. Trust me."

He helps me into the car and secures the seat belt. Even for the short ride, my protective husband wants to ensure I'm safe, especially with his babies. He hops in the driver's side.

"One day from my parents' megayacht—*Serendipity*—I saw this property and took a tender for a closer look since it didn't appear maintained or occupied. Well, I fell in love with it and bought it. Now, it's back to its original splendor and more," he tells me with pride in his voice.

I hold my hand out for him. The diamonds on my wedding jewelry sparkles in the sun beaming down on us as we pass the second gate at the bottom of the driveway. I squeeze his hand as *Villa Ciel et Terre* stands in all its glory before us.

"I love it too," I whisper. "What made you decide to surprise me with a trip here?"

Harris grins like the Cheshire Cat and slides out of the car. He opens my door and pulls me into his arms with my back to his front. His hands rest on my babies bump as he nuzzles the side of my neck.

"Welcome to our babymoon, My Hot Mama," he says huskily. "Our time before our Wee Twins arrive. Time to give me some of your good lovin'."

The warmth of his breath skitters across my skin. I tilt my head to the side to give him better access for the open-mouthed kisses he places on my neck. Heat floods my body. Immediately, my pussy softens and cream gathers. My fuller breasts grow heavy as the nipples tighten with desire. I lean back against his powerful chest and moan when he nudges his already massive erection against the crack of my ass.

Oh, bloody hell, the things this man makes me feel!

"But first a tour," he says, then chuckles wickedly when I growl in frustration. "Simmer down, naughty kitten. I know what you need... and when."

He takes me by the hand and leads me through the blue double doors. Inside, the villa's staff stand in a row to greet us. The butler steps forward and introduces them to me. The chef confirms lunch on the terrace in two hours. They take our luggage upstairs while Harris walks me through the interior of the posh villa. We end on the large balcony of the primary suite overlooking the lush greenery and colorful flowering bushes, the infinity pool, and the Mediterranean Sea.

"We have forty minutes until lunch. I guarantee I give you four orgasms before we eat."

Harris' huskily spoken words bring my attention back from the incredible view.

"Oh… Only four…" I tease.

He growls and stalks towards where I stand beside the wrought-iron railing. When he reaches me, his arm snakes around my waist to pull me as flush to his body as my babies bump allows. He bends down to rumble his displeasure at my comment in my ear.

I gasp when he spins me around. My balance rests in his firm grip. Facing the Med, Harris pulls the bow on my Diane von Furstenberg wrap dress. Like a gift, he reveals me.

"Harris! What if someone sees us?" I squeak as my eyes dart around the grounds below for any sign of the staff.

"And if they do?" He responds as his fingers unclasp the front closure of my bra. He kneads my heavy breasts and groans against my neck.

I wiggle to free myself. But he steps to the side and

gives my ass four quick spanks in succession. Through the silk of my dress, my bare cheeks sting. The black lace thong does nothing to protect my ass from my husband's ire. He continues to spank me in an erotic rhythm.

"B—but the staff," I cry out, rising to the balls of my Chanel ballet flats covered feet.

"I thought you said you trusted me, naughty kitten?" He responds, then continues when I say I do. "Well, then, why would I expose what is mine to another's eyes?"

One hand leaves my breasts to skim down the side of my belly, over my hip, and across to the apex of my thighs. Thighs pressed together to ease the ache building in my soaking core. He tugs my nipple and pinches my clit.

"Ohhh, Harris… please!" I wail, gyrating my hips.

The ripping of my thong from my body precipitates a spank to my swollen clit. I keen as the first of four orgasms hits me. My head lolls back against his shoulder. My mouth sags open on the last of my carnal cry.

"One."

The twitch of Harris' lips against my neck as he smirks makes me shiver.

Two thick digits dive into my pussy. So wet they glide in with no resistance. He curls them and strokes the sensitive tissue on the inside wall of my pussy. His thumb strokes my clit.

I grab the wrought-iron railing for support as my knees threaten to give out. My head bows forward. The red of my hair blacks out the turquoise blue of the sea.

Harris' fingers plunge in and out of my pussy as it

clenches in hopes it locks them in place to ride them to pleasure. My body craves the orgasm just on the edge. Just out of reach.

His fingers withdraw.

I screech in frustration. My head swivels to glare at him.

He chuckles and nips my shoulder.

The wrap dress slips from my body before he tosses it inside of the suite.

"Eyes forward, legs spread," Harris commands as he collects my hair and wraps it around his fist. He tugs and my head bows back. "Wider."

I hasten to spread my legs as wide as they can go. Then brace myself as my grip tightens on the railing for support.

With no warning, Harris slams his massive dick inside of my quivering pussy. I explode.

"Two."

As I revel in carnal bliss, he tugs my clit while pistoning his hips. His thick girth drags along my inner walls. A wail and shudder define my next orgasm.

"Three."

I pant as residual wave after wave of three orgasms ignite a fever pitch in my body. Legs twitch to hold my position.

Harris switches to long, slow strokes. His hands reach up to cup my breasts and to tweak the puckered nipples. When he feels the flutters of my pussy, he withdraws to his tip.

I growl and push back against him, seeking my own release.

Resounding smacks to my ass punish my attempt at self-pleasure.

"Aha, naughty kitten. I say when," Harris chastises me. "And I say it's now!"

He impales me on his rigid cock, and I wail as the orgasm takes me.

"Four."

Boneless, I can only depend upon Harris to hold me up as he chases his release. With a bellow, his hot cum coats my pussy. It triggers a fifth orgasm, and we ride our pleasure out together. I sag against Harris.

When we return from a shared state of sheer euphoria, he carries me to the shower and bathes me. He sets me on the marble bench and cleans himself. Dried and re-dressed, we settle on the terrace for a delicious lunch with the beauty of *Villa Ciel et Terre* surrounding us.

What better way to strengthen our bond before the birth of our Wee Twins?

"Harris, I think it's time!"

The mobile falls from my hand.

Haley grabs it while I stand frozen.

"Kat, honey, where are you?" Haley asks as she jabs me with her elbow. Silently she mouths, *Get it together, Har!*

"Oooh… By the lift," my thirty-six weeks pregnant wife cries.

Her distress rouses me. I snatch my mobile from Haley as I bark at Roger to call my driver for the Mercedes-Benz Sprinter. Baz says he'll call our parents. Malcolm waves for me to follow him, as Starr calls Dr. Rice. We rush from Baz's conference room at STEELE International. Behind us, I hear Lachlan call Mum Allison.

It's like déjà vu. But even more intense. Not news of Kat's pregnancy, but of her in labor.

Fuck. Me.

"Kat, babe, focus on me. I'm on my way to get you. Do

not move," I say into the phone. I remember the prenatal training Starr taught us and work with her on her breath. As always, Starr helps her sisters as their doula.

I keep my wife calm as the private elevator rises to our floor. Starr helps her to count time between contractions. She nods at me in confirmation. Our Wee Twins are on their way. Well damn!

The elevator door opens and my wife—with her hands cradling her babies bump—leans against the console. Her hospital bag sits at her feet. She raises her head and grimaces as another contraction hits. Malcolm and I carry her onto the elevator while Starr grabs the bag.

"Oooooooohhhhhh!!! *Bloody hell!*" My wife screams, then turns her head to me. "Damn you, Harris Steele!"

I swallow. Oh boy. I heard about this reaction from my brothers...

We stop at the underground parking garage and hurry to the awaiting Sprinter. Alonso barely gives us time to close the doors before he's off. During the ride, Starr does her doula magic. At least enough my wife doesn't curse me in English *and* in Scottish Gaelic. I blush, and I don't even know what the bloody hell she says.

She's got me so bollixed up I use British expressions!

"How long have you been experiencing pre-labor, Kat?" Starr asks as she braids her Titian hair down her back.

My wife groans and rubs her babies bump before she answers. The pain on her face hits me straight in the chest like a sledgehammer. A combination of pain and fear fill her emerald green eyes. I stroke her hand—to hell with holding it. So she can crush it like Leonie did to Roger? That'll be a hard pass.

"I—I thought it was just back pain sine early morning," my wife gets out before another contraction takes her breath.

Starr nods and massages her shoulders.

We make it to the hospital where Dr. Rice's in-hospital team meets us with a gurney. They bundle my wife onto it while Starr gives them her status. I rush along with the caravan to her private birthing room, leaving my siblings to find her private waiting room.

Dr. Rice enters after the nurse adjusts my wife's sheet. He greets us and sits on the stool between her spread legs. He raises the sheet to exam her.

"Mrs. Steele, however, did you manage pre-labor on your own? Your cervix is fully dilated at ten centimeters. Let's get ready to deliver your twins," he says with a warm smile. "Now to set your expectations, on average it can take up to two hours for you to birth your first twin and seventeen minutes for the second twin."

A growl fills the room.

I shudder when I realize it's directed at me. I swallow before I face my wife.

Titian hair like flames licking down her back. Emerald eyes blaze like green fire. Nostrils flare,

"Sixteen hours, Harris Steele?!?!?!" She screeches like a banshee, not my alluring Siren. "This is your fau—"

A contraction cuts off her scathing words.

I take a breath as though I'm in labor.

Despite my wife's threats, I stay at her side, cool cloth in one hand and a cup of ice chips in the other. Words of encouragement between her cries and grunts. Until at last, she gives birth to our first child. Above its cries, Dr. Rice's voice rings clear.

"Mr. and Mrs. Steele, your son."

Dr. Rice dries him off and places him in a hat and blanket on my wife's heaving chest. The skin-to-skin contact soothes both. My wife smiles through her tears as my son's cries lessen to whimpers.

I stare in awe at the start of my little family. My wife's beauty shines through all the curses, sweat, and tears. She holds our son like the most precious thing he is to both of us. I melt when she turns her radiance on me and raises her hand.

The tears shimmering in my eyes spill over when I take her hand and wrap my arm around her shoulders. She places our entwined fingers on our son's rosy cheek and strokes it together.

"Thank you, my love," I murmur.

Once again, she graces me with her smile and says, "Your son and I thank you for making this all possible, *mo ghràdh.*"

Starr tells us the pediatrician would like to check on our son. We nod and I step back to give him access but follow to watch his every move. The protective caveman rises.

Just as Dr. Rice predicted, my wife goes into labor to birth our baby girl. It's a repeat of our son's arrival in the world with Scottish Gaelic ringing out. No need to worry they won't have a Scottish accent. Their first audible words provide enough of a connection to their mother's homeland.

When Dr. Rice announces the birth of our daughter and places her on my wife's chest, my world feels complete. I catch her little fist flailing in the air while she hollers louder than her brother. However, she too settles at the contact with her Mum. I embrace them and kiss the top of my wife's damp head.

The pediatrician takes our daughter, and I follow behind closely. I watch until he places her in a bassinet beside her brother. Only when Starr comes over, I leave. I smile at her and return to my wife's side.

The nurses clean her up and help her into a lace-front nightgown—one of the Lola's Coterie maternity pieces she's collected. Refreshed she's ready to breastfeed our babies. The nurse shows her how to manage twins with my help. After they have their fill, they sleep peacefully. My wife's eyes flutter closed.

It's only then I remember to take photos. I whip out my mobile and snap away.

"Congratulations, Proud Papa! I took some photos and videotaped their births for you," Starr whispers as she approaches the bed and hugs me. "I'll let everyone know the Wee Twins and Mum are well. Take your time and let her rest before we come in."

I nod, and she massages my shoulders. I groan as the tension I didn't realize existed eases from my body.

"Thanks, sis," I say when she stops and pats my arm. She winks and leaves me with my little family.

I sit beside the bed and watch over them. After a while, my wife stirs.

"Harris? Where are you?" She asks as she turns her head to scan the suite.

I rise and kiss her forehead.

"Always here, my love. Why don't you rest some more," I respond as my knuckles brush her cheek.

She leans into the caress and smiles. But she shakes her head.

"Let's introduce our family to our Wee Twins. It's time for their debut," she says with a joyful smile.

I scan her face to be sure she's ready, and she nods, knowing my protective instincts kicked into gear.

Returning her nod, I call my father. He answers on the first ring and says they'll be right in.

The door opens immediately, and they pile into the suite. One by one they approach the bed—my mother and Mum Allison first, followed by Uncle Connor and Aunt Lucie.

Everyone exclaims how adorable they are with their ebony hair and dove gray eyes. Yup, my genes are super strong!

"So, what are their names, *Da*?" Haley asks with a grin.

I look at My Kitty Kat and her emerald green eyes twinkle. She's bursting to tell them. I take a deep breath and announce the next generation of Steeles.

"My wife and I present Felix Steele and Felicity Steele!

Felix the Cat in honor of his mother Kat, and Felicity for the Ancient Roman goddess Fortuna, symbolizing happiness, luck, and good fortune."

Everyone exclaims their love of the unique names and their meaning.

When My Kitty Kat yawns, I tell our family we'll see them in the morning. Rounds of congratulations and sweet dreams follow before they depart.

Alone with my little family, I place Felix and Felicity in their bassinets, change into a t-shirt and joggers, then settle in the bed to hold my wife. Her soft snores let me know she's knocked out. I kiss the side of her head and let my mind drift. I give thanks for their health and the love of our family before I allow my eyes to close.

THE MORNING DAWNS, and I slip from the bed so as not to awaken My Kitty Kat. I stride to the bassinets and smile at my beautiful babies. Unable to resist, I gather them in my arms and stand in front of the window. The sunrise promises a new day, a fresh start.

I may not have been ready for children. But as I hold my Wee Twins close to my heart, I know they were meant to be mine forever, just like their Mum.

***

Harris & Kat's Story Concludes For Now...

**Turn the page for the Steele and Jackson Family Trees,
Author's Note,
and Preview of The STEELE Series Book 1**
Fulfill My Desires Sebastian & Lola Part I

**Join my newsletter bit.ly/CLBooksNewsletter to learn
about the next STEELE World couples to have their
romances told.**

THE STEELE FAMILY

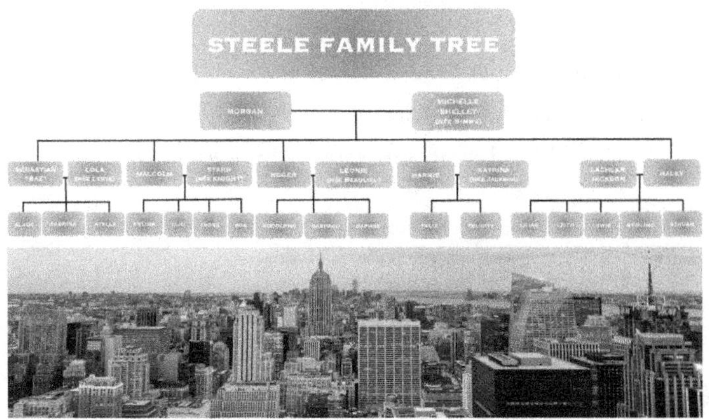

STEELE INTERNATIONAL, INC

Multigenerational, multibillion-dollar business luxury real estate development and management corporation

Headquarters & Family's Primary Residences:

The STEELE Tower, New York City

A modern, gray-tinted glass fifty-seven story mixed-use skyscraper on southwest corner of Fifty-Seventh Street and Fifth Avenue within Billionaires' Row

Global Offices:

- The United States of America (New York City, New Jersey, Chicago, California, Miami, Las Vegas)
- The Caribbean (St. Maarten, St. Barth's, St. Lucia)
- The French & Italian Rivieras (Nice, Cannes, Positano, Capri)
- Monaco (Monte Carlo)
- The United Arab Emirates (Abu Dhabi, Dubai)

STEELE FOUNDATION: A STRONG AND SUPPORTIVE HOUSE

Builds and manages attractive, affordable housing for urban, lower-income families

Available for download at **bit.ly/STEELEFamily**

THE JACKSON FAMILY

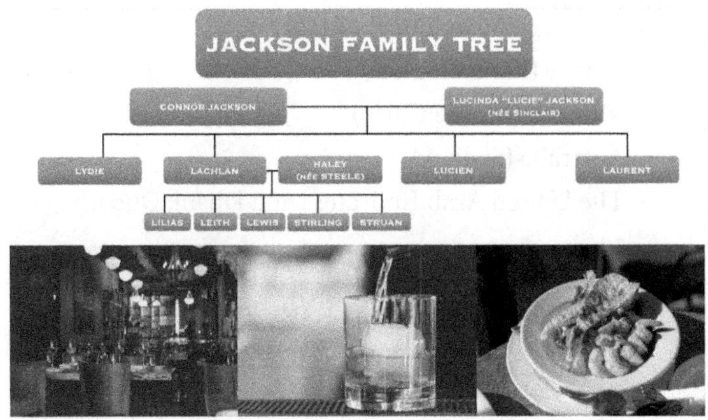

JACKSON CORPORATION

Multigenerational, multibillion-dollar business fine dining,
distilleries, and vineyards corporation

Headquarters:

Jackson Town House, Aberdeen, Scotland

A landmark property built by the founders of Aberdeen granite
on Union Street; the second largest granite building in the world.

Global Offices:

- The United Kingdom (Aberdeen, Scotland;
  London, England)
- The United States of America (New York City,
  New Orleans, Miami, Chicago, Los Angeles,
  Napa)
- The Caribbean (Puerto Rico)
- France (Paris, Cannes)
- Monaco (Monte Carlo)
- Australia (Sydney)
- The United Arab Emirates (Abu Dhabi, Dubai)

JACKSON FOUNDATION: ENJOY LIFE
RESPONSIBLY

Operates alcohol treatment centers for lower-income individuals
and support for their family members

Available for download at **bit.ly/JacksonFamilyTree**

Author's Note

Thank you for reading Part III of Harris and Kat's sexy, steamy romance! I hope you enjoyed the Happy For Now conclusion of their sizzling, The One billionaire romance. If so, I'd love to hear your thoughts, please share a review at **bit.ly/CLBooksSI-JC6Review** and tell your friends.

Wait! What's up next in the STEELE World? Follow me on social media including my CLBooks Coterie Fan Club or on your favorite channels below and subscribe to my newsletter **bit.ly/CLBooksSubscribe** for a **Free Book**.

In the meantime, did you catch on to the dynamism of Sebastian and Lola? Well, you'll have your answers! **Visit books2read.com/u/3RLy0D**

Fulfill My Desires Sebastian & Lola Part I Preview *Click Here*

At **CharmaineLouise.com** take the *Four types of lovers. Which are you?* **Quiz** to match your Sexy Fantasy: sub, Voyeur, Dominatrix, or Dominatrix sub Switch.

Fulfill Your Desires.
xoxo
Charmaine Louise

BB bookbub.com/authors/charmaine-louise-shelton
f facebook.com/CharmaineLouiseBooks
instagram.com/charmainelouisebooks
tiktok.com/@charmainelouisebooks?
g goodreads.com/charmainelouisebooks

PREVIEW STEELE SERIES BOOK 1: FULFILL MY DESIRES SEBASTIAN & LOLA PART I

Sebastian

"Good evening, Mr. Steele," one of the two stunning greeters purrs as I step into the lobby for LEVELS New York.

This is the flagship location of the global, luxury, members-only BDSM/dance clubs in Manhattan's Meatpacking District. They chose the historic location as a play on the area's name. Put a club where men pack their meat into willing women and willing men allow women to pack them with their toys. The theme for the lobby is minimal and industrial. The fixtures and furniture that appear well worn are high-end, modern replicas used to add authenticity without the grime of old pieces. The two sides have coordinating greeter stations that allow access to the separate Dine & Dance levels and the BDSM levels. The other greeter turns her head in my direction and briefly smiles at me before she returns her attention to a couple entering the BDSM side.

My cousin Lucien Jackson cooked up the idea and roped my younger brother Malcolm into it. Lucien literally cooked it up since he thought of it as he finished his hospitality and culinary training at Le Cordon Bleu in Paris.

Who the hell goes through that prestigious training to come up with a titty bar? Well, five years later his idea proves it's bigger than that and has a high profit margin with more locations in Paris and London. That's all that concerns me: will it add to STEELE International's bottom line? Yes, well, it's a go. No, then no go.

LEVELS is one of many business partnerships that STEELE has with Jackson Corporation. World-renown for their award-winning eateries, choice cigars, and distinguished liquors and wines, their products pair well within STEELE's casinos, hotels, resorts, and residential and retail properties.

On the personal side, my mother is best friends with the Jackson matriarch. They spent most of their adult lives together forming a closer bond than they have with their blood siblings and relatives. Not sharing DNA doesn't keep our families from being a close-knit group.

"Good evening," I respond as I make my way to the D&D elevator.

Once inside, I place my keycard against the panel to select the third floor for the Level 4 Restaurant. I'm a Global All Access member. I can choose from any of the seven levels: 7th Sky Lounge that offers a stunning, 360-

degree view of Manhattan and across the Hudson River to New Jersey's shoreline, a bar, restaurant by day dance club by night, a coverable pool that's open during the warmer months, and a glass-retractable roof; 6th and 5th multilevel dance club with two bars and a lounge for food and drinks; 4th Level 4 Restaurant and bar open for breakfast, lunch, and dinner; 3rd has twelve private suites for members to continue their pleasure apart from the BDSM levels; 2nd Peepshow for BDSM with seating alcoves, primary stage, mini-stages, performance rooms, and a bar that serves non-alcoholic mocktails; below ground the Cellar a BDSM dungeon with mocktails bar. The Dine/Dance members only have access to the party levels—Sky Lounge, Dance Club, and Level 4 Restaurant.

Tonight, I need to eat and fuck hard in that order. I'm bound to find a female at the restaurant or bar who's willing to be my pet for the evening. One night only, maybe two if she's not clingy or a gold digger, but two fucks is my maximum. I'm not looking for a relationship and damn sure not marriage, just enough time to satisfy my Dom needs and my physical release for the moment. A short-term encounter to balance out my business-focused life.

As president of the Retail Properties Division of STEELE, I bust my ass fourteen hours a day to make it super profitable and to prove that I deserve my future role as CEO of the entire luxury real estate development and management company when my father retires next year. It's not just my last name getting me into the head position.

I'm damn capable since I've worked my way up the ranks to learn our multigenerational, multibillion dollar business combined with my Harvard undergrad and MBA degrees.

My father, Morgan, trusts me to carry the legacy into the future and my younger brothers and sister respect me and accept my leadership. Each sibling works at STEELE: Malcolm president of the Entertainment Properties Division; Roger, president of the Residential Properties Division; Harris and Haley, fraternal twins, co-founders of the subsidiary STEELE Technology and Cyber Security. At 35, I take my role as the eldest seriously, so I don't have time for nor care to get involved in a relationship. Thanks to Lucien and Malcolm, LEVELS provides exactly what I need.

As I step off of the elevator, I take in my surroundings. The bar is bustling as usual with the crème de la crème of society. They hobnob with top-shelf drinks. Seating ranges from the leather and black metal stools at the long, reclaimed-wood covered bar to the dozen high-top tables styled to match. The bar along the right wall features a floor-to-ceiling mirrored wall of shelves of only the best spirits and wines—most are from the Jackson labels. The bartenders serve signature cocktails. Tables on the left complete the layout of the open-plan room. A path between the two areas leads to the LEVEL 4 Restaurant's maître d' station. There, the patrons eat delicious meals prepared by chefs trained by Lucien. My destination awaits.

As I stride towards the maître d', my gaze alights on

several recognizable faces enjoying nightcaps at the bar area's high-top tables. Tonight, the U.S. Attorney for the Southern District of New York, the former governor of California, and a high-powered female CFO of a Wall Street investment bank are present. The club caters to the most wealthy and influential in society. They prefer the relative safety that one can expect from the ironclad nondisclosure agreement that LEVELS requires every member and their guests to sign.

I smile and nod in greeting—every Steele is instantly recognizable—but keep it moving as I'm not here tonight for small talk. As I approach the hostess at the dining area's maître d' podium, I also notice several pairs of lust-filled eyes including those of a few men track my movement as I walk past them. Sadly for the men, I'm strictly a female to a male individual. As I approach the station, the maître d' on duty tonight looks up with an alluring smile on her pretty face.

"Good evening, Mr. Steele," says Susan, as her name tag denotes. She angles her chin down to allow her to peek up at me from beneath her long eyelashes without direct eye contact.

"Your usual table, Sir?"

I don't miss her emphasis on Sir as a sub innuendo. Susan is one of many LEVELS employees who want to have my marks on them and my dick in every one of their holes. Disappointingly for the staff though, I don't mix business with pleasure. That can only end in a messy situation and unnecessarily complicate matters—doesn't fit with my trajectory.

"Good evening, Susan. That's good, thank you," I reply.

Susan's full lips curl up into a dazzling smile as she visibly preens. Her reaction as though I petted her head for a job well done after I fucked her throat and she didn't spill a single drop of my copious amount of cum. Susan seductively sways her hips, long legs stressed by stilettos and her form-fitted, black mini dress molded to her curvy body. She leads me to my table in the center of the room with an unobstructed view of the large dining area and of the bar. A spot from which I can easily observe all the patrons to cherry-pick my companion for tonight. However, the sight before me has me second-guessing my no business/pleasure rule. Susan deliberately bends over the table to straighten the napkin, giving me a visual of her cuffed to my pommel horse and a cane in my hand. Damn if my cock didn't just twitch from looking at her plump bottom and grip-worthy hips. Fortunately, I hadn't unbuttoned my suit jacket, or my piqued dick would be on full display.

I give the heads, on my neck and at my groin, firm, shakes to clear the vision. Then, without making eye contact, I thank Susan, take my seat, and pick up the menu discouraging further attention.

With an audible sigh, Susan bids me, "Enjoy your dinner, Mr. Steele," and walks away. Then on second thought she turns and offers, "Should you need anything at all, please let me know."

Keeping my gaze on the menu, I nod, and Susan dejectedly walks away with less sway to her hips, albeit still an eye-catching vision. Sorry, sweetheart.

If I'm not entertaining business associates or attending social gatherings like charity functions, I frequently dine at Level 4. I prefer that then eating takeout at home or hiring a personal chef to cook for only one person. Both are extravagances that I can afford, but why waste resources with my mutable schedule that changes as often as I change boxers.

Dinner out at whatever time is convenient in a city with thousands of excellent restaurants suits my lifestyle. Level 4 is one of them with a menu that offers the expected fare typical of Continental cuisine of pastas, meat, and steaks with favorable sauces. Lucien complements the usual dishes with appealing specials that change daily to keep the choices fresh and habitual guests like me from getting bored.

The client care is impeccable. So, I don't flinch when the server quietly appears at my side and places a napkin-covered basket with an assortment of warm, fresh-baked breads on the table. I glance up to see a youthful man who is model-perfect and well-groomed with a clean-shaven jaw, slicked-back ebony hair, and intelligent brown eyes. His all-black uniform of a long-sleeved shirt, pants, butcher apron, and shiny Oxford shoes is spotless—the de rigueur fashion for LEVELS employees.

"Welcome to Level 4, sir. My name is Andrew and I'll be your server this evening. May I take your drink order?"

"Thank you, Andrew. I'll have a bottle of Pellegrino," I respond with a pleasant smile.

"Very good, sir. We have some lovely specials tonight. May I share them with you?"

Since I plan to play tonight, I select a light meal comprising the tossed salad to start and the grilled langoustines with white wine sauce entrée. A clear head is best for my evening plan of play.

As Andrew heads to the kitchen to submit my order, my gaze wanders around the room admiring the décor. Just as with the lobby and the bar, Lucien and Malcolm stayed true to the original use of the warehouse. Clean lines and antique pieces for the decor: floor-to-ceiling mullion windows allow natural light to filter through to the room during the day, now dimly lit for dinner; light fixtures hang from the ceiling where the dark metal duct work and copper pipes are visible; exposed brick walls; the floor poured concrete; the well-heeled patrons sit on antique leather chairs at wooden tables. The guys really did a hell of a job with their enterprise. Few can pull off and maintain a high-end, respectable establishment, especially one that's a combo BDSM/dance club with a restaurant.

Perfectly situated for visibility by those at the bar and within the dining room, sit two lovely beauties laughing and tossing their long, glossy hair over their shoulders. Their eyes roam the vicinity hoping to connect with potential partners. The duo is more focused on attracting company for the evening, then on eating the salads that they absentmindedly move around on their plates.

The blonde spots me watching them, and a grin appears on her face lighting up her baby blues. As she nods her head to show her friend she's spotted a potential hookup, her little pink tongue pokes out to dampen her glossy, lush lips.

I wonder if her pussy is as shiny and wet as that mouth.

Her friend shifts slightly in her seat to adjust her position casually. As she runs her red-manicured hand through her sable-colored, shoulder-length hair, she spies me. The green darkens with lust when I wink at her. With a smirk, I turn my attention to Andrew as he places my salad in front of me. Now that I have the attention of both women, I nod and eat. I know they're interested, so no need to rush my meal. They'll be a double order of tonight's dessert special.

I spend the next thirty-five minutes purposely ignoring them. I only allow my gaze to shift occasionally in their direction, never direct eye contact. That dominant behavior—and who I am—will keep them intrigued. As they cross and uncross their legs, the movement affords me a better view higher up their toned thighs. Green Eyes has on a clingy, silk wrap dress that showcases her ample cleavage, the red color complementing her bronze skin. The blue of Luscious' eyes, enhanced by the cobalt color of her strapless, stretch-jersey dress, make them as prominent as her pebbled nipples. Delightful.

First item on tonight's agenda is complete—dinner eaten, now it's time to fuck.

They automatically place the bill on my membership account, so no need to waste time signing the check. I stand and take my time to button my suit jacket, drawing the attention of my pets. Once our eyes lock, I walk past their table to head to one of the high-tops at the bar.

Susan gives me a wistful stare and bids me, "Good night, Mr. Steele. We look forward to seeing you again soon."

"It was a pleasure as always, Susan. Good night," I offer her in consolation.

Moments after I settle at the closest available table, I feel one hand caress my back and another hand lands on my forearm.

I glance to my left and am greeted with a sultry, "Hello." Green eyes glitter in the candlelight like vivid emeralds.

A squeeze to my forearm draws my attention to my right to see freshly glossed lips beaming, "Hello. There aren't any other tables available, would you mind it if my friend and I share with you?"

"Would your friend and you mind sharing me for a fuck?"

Without missing a beat, Green Eyes responds breathlessly, "Absolutely."

***

**Click the Link Below or Visit books2read.com/u/
3RLy0D For Your Copy**

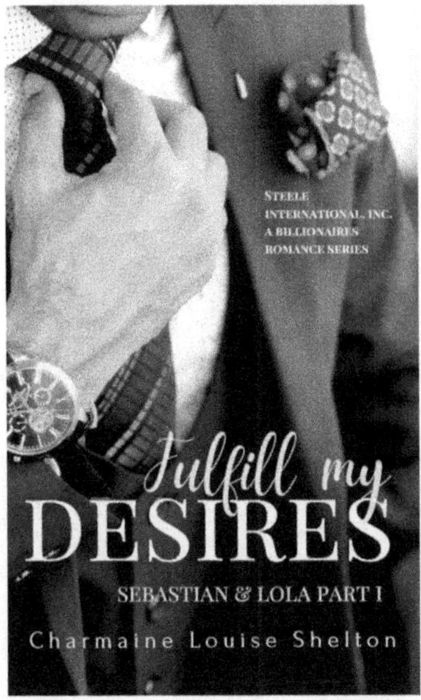

Fulfill My Desires Sebastian & Lola Part I

I dedicate this novel to those who never give up no matter the challenges they face in life and in love.

Fulfill Your Desires.

xoxo
Charmaine Louise

WELCOME TO CHARMAINELOUISE — THE SENSUAL LIFESTYLE

GLITZY. GLAMOROUS. STEAMY.

CharmaineLouise New York, Inc. invites you to indulge in *The Sensual Lifestyle* through **CharmaineLouise Books** and **CharmaineLouise Intimates**. CLBrands immerse you in *Sexy Fantasies* with CLBooks contemporary romance novels and give you *Sexy Under Things & Loungewear* with CLIntimates.

Charmaine Louise Shelton the Founder, CEO & Author of CLNY loves all things classic, elegant, feminine, and of course with an erotic edge! Favorite outfit of choice is a cashmere cardigan, leather pencil skirt, and seamed silk stockings with stiletto heels. Sexy Fantasy Type: sub with a dash of Voyeur. When not writing and designing, Charmaine Louise travels and spends time with her Maltese buddies, ZIGGY and Jynger.

CharmaineLouise — *The Sensual Lifestyle*

~ Visit online at **CharmaineLouise.com**

~ Subscribe to **CharmaineLouise Newsletter**

~ Find us on Facebook **@CharmaineLouiseNewYork**

~ Instagram **@CharLouNY**

CharmaineLouise Books *Sexy Fantasies* launched summer 2020. Sizzling, contemporary romance with your soon-to-be favorite Alpha Doms, Powerful Billionaires, and the women they lust after and love for second chances, insta-love, enemies-to-lovers, and more.

Want to chat it up and share your thoughts with other CLBooks Lovers? Read our blog, join our Charmaine-Louise Books Coterie Fan Club and follow us on my author pages and social media to be in the know about the book release dates, exclusive content, giveaways, contests, and more!

~ **Purchase your eBook and paperback novels from my Author Page by clicking here!**

~ Read and subscribe to our blog ***The World of Sex***

~ Connect on **Amazon Author Page**

~ **Goodreads Author Profile**

~ <u>**BookBub Author Profile**</u>

CharmaineLouise Intimates *Sexy Under Things &* *Loungewear* debuted in 2003. Inspired by the sensuous sirens and sylph swans of the past and present, the hand crochet cashmere and silk collections are for the sexy: hence, the line names Ginger — Bombshell; Diana — Showstopper; Jackie — Timeless; Lena — Classic. Also known as The Movie-Star from Gilligan's Island; Ms. Ross The Boss; Mrs. Kennedy Onassis; Ms. Horne.

Do you thrive on seduction and being sexy lounging at home? Read our blog and follow us on social media to receive the tips, the latest additions to the collections, private sales, and more!

~ Read and subscribe to our blog *The Art of Seduction*

~ Find us on Facebook **@CharmaineLousieIntimates**

~ Instagram **@CharmaineLouiseIntimates**

Fulfill Your Desires.

www.ingramcontent.com/pod-product-compliance
Lightning Source LLC
Chambersburg PA
CBHW071230190726
48292CB00007B/2204

9781956804096